The Tiptoe Boys

'Look Frankie,' growled Skellen, 'don't get me wrong. I don't want to see this country incinerated. If I thought all this hot air would do any good, I'd be right up there on the platform. But we've had it all before. CND. Marches. Demonstrations. A waste of bloody time. Who takes a blind bit of notice?'

'Christ, you've been well brainwashed,' said Frankie bitterly.

'No, I'm just a realist. I don't kid myself.'

'So!' she challenged him. 'What's your solution?'

'Direct action,' said Skellen quietly.

She stared at him.

'That's the only way to get results,' he went on. 'Direct action. All those dirty little wars I've fought in the SAS taught me one thing.'

'Taught you what?'

He paused. 'That bullets speak louder than words.'

James Follett trained to be a marine engineer, and also spent some time hunting for underwater treasure, filming sharks, designing powerboats, and writing technical material for the Ministry of Defence before becoming a full-time writer. He is the author of numerous radio plays and television dramas, as well as seventeen novels including *Savant*, *Churchill's Gold*, *Dominator*, *Swift* and *Trojan*. He lives in Surrey.

JAMES FOLLETT

The Tiptoe Boys

Based on an original story by
GEORGE MARKSTEIN

Mandarin

A Mandarin Paperback
THE TIPTOE BOYS

First published in Great Britain 1992
by Severn House Publishers Ltd
This edition published 1994
by Mandarin Paperbacks
an imprint of Reed Consumer Books Ltd
Michelin House, 81 Fulham Road, London SW3 6RB
and Auckland, Melbourne, Singapore and Toronto

Reprinted 1994

A CIP catalogue record for this title
is available from the British Library
ISBN 0 7493 1286 6

Printed and bound in Great Britain
by Cox & Wyman Ltd, Reading, Berks

Foreword

When the Berlin Wall came tumbling down, the dust of its welcome and overdue fall temporarily deprived a generation of thriller writers of their arch villain the Soviet Union. From Ian Fleming onwards, postwar writers had portrayed the USSR and its spymasters, the KGB, as a ruthless and efficient machine dedicated to the destruction of the West. The ruthlessness is still there – it's an attribute that doesn't require skill or efficiency, but the truth that has since emerged is that the Soviet Union was so riddled with corruption and vice that it couldn't even feed its populace. Even its much-feared conventional weaponry has turned out to be a myth. When I surveyed the gutted wreckage of Soviet tanks in Southern Iraq in the aftermath of the Gulf War, I saw at firsthand the results of shoddy welding and workmanship when pitted against the bullseye weaponry of the West.

Consequently I was a little worried when my publishers suggested reissuing this book. It was written ten years ago against the background of four-minute warnings and cruise missiles, and massive peace marches in Western capitals. Indeed, the protests about the cruise missiles based at Greenham Common are a cornerstone of the book's plot. Now that the cruise missiles have gone, hopefully forever, I wondered how readers would react to a reissue of a book that has been overtaken by events. Not only have there been profound political changes during the past ten years, but there have been huge improvements in technology, particularly communications. In *The Tiptoe Boys* police officers were hunting for phone boxes. Nowadays they're equipped with PMR radios which are a lot more advanced than the Pye PF8s that Bodie and Doyle used to yap into in *The Professionals*. Teleprinters have largely been ousted in favour of facsimile machines, and no self-respecting thug-about-town is without a cellular telephone in his pocket with the telephone number of a bent lawyer held in its memory.

(For the techies out there, I wrote *The Tiptoe Boys* using a Radio Shack Model 1 microcomputer a decade ago when word-processors were virtually unheard of. It needed a special modification to handle lower case letters, ran out of memory every ten pages, and was linked to a daisywheel printer that could shred reams of paper into thin strips while giving a passable imitation of a submachine-gun. Ten years later I'm writing this afterword on a machine that can hold several full-length novels in its memory, bully me with loud bleeps when I make a spelling error, which isn't often of course, and play chess at grand master level – all at the same time. Maybe in another ten years or so I'll be able to feed a plot into a computer and sit back and watch while it writes the story; a grisly thought but I'm nursing a suspicion that some writers are already using such a technique.)

With these thoughts in mind, I carried out a major revision of *The Tiptoe Boys* to bring it up-to-date. Motives and villains were changed. Malek the paymaster and the real nasty, changed his nationality. The hardware used by the SAS was revamped. Revising the book was like gutting and modernizing a period house so that not even the facade remained. And like such a house subjected to such treatment, the result pleased no-one, least of all my editor.

Her view was that the sweaty pace, the peace riots, the horrifying terrorist violence, and general atmosphere of the original version was something that sprang naturally from the political and social turmoil of the early 1980s; that it was a book that belonged to that period and should be read as such without changes. I reread both versions and concluded that she was right. Therefore this book *is* the original version. I've tidied it up a little because the first typescript was written in a great hurry to meet the movie tie-in deadlines. The film *Who Dares Wins* was a great success, as was this book. Unfortunately I couldn't use *Who Dares Wins* as its title, much as I would've liked to, because Tony Geraghty had already collared it for his excellent history of the SAS.

James Follett
Godalming, Surrey.
May 1992

1

The scruffily dressed young man wearing a crumpled plastic anorak crossed the road opposite the St Stephen's entrance of the House of Commons. His straggly hair needed washing, and his unshaven chin, betraying the hint of an incipient beard, added to his unkempt appearance. He was wearing blue patched denims. Pinned to his anorak were a couple of the mandatory political badges.

He was in a hurry. He dodged a couple of taxis as he crossed the road to the phone box opposite the Palace of Westminster. Inside the booth he dialled seven digits. It was a special number that provided a direct connection from wherever in the United Kingdom one dialled it. It was a number listed in no directory, which he knew by heart, and which he and those who did his kind of work never wrote down.

'Come on,' urged the young man impatiently under his breath. 'Move it.'

He didn't notice the moped rider pulling up at the kerbside, level with the phone booth. The rider's face was hidden by the crash helmet's black-tinted visor. Outwardly the rider was a 'knowledge boy': a would-be taxi-driver studying for his 'bill' by learning his way around London armed with maps attached to a clipboard mounted on his handlebars.

The number rang three times before it was answered. No coin had to be inserted by the caller. Instead, a voice said: 'Duty officer.'

The moped rider studied the clipboard under which was concealed a gun with a silencer. Seemingly casual adjustments of the position of the handlebars enabled the rider to aim the gun. Suddenly a glass pane in the kiosk shattered. A nine millimetre slug ploughed into the young man's body, smashing its way between his ribs and through his heart's main ventricle, coming to rest in his left lung.

'Duty officer,' repeated the phone voice, but the young man had already slipped to the floor of the booth, dead, and the receiver dangled from its cord.

'Duty officer,' said the voice for the third time, more urgently.

The call was already being traced because it was standing practice to track any unexplained calls to this classified exchange and number.

But before the location was identified, a woman opened the door of the kiosk. When she saw the young man in the anorak, slumped on the floor, and the blood, she screamed.

The moped rider was half way across Westminster Bridge before the first police cars arrived, sirens howling.

The rider stopped in York Road outside Waterloo Station and also entered a phone kiosk while tugging off the crash helmet and shaking out her dark hair.

She dialled a number and pushed a coin in the slot when the pips started.

2

'Hallo, Frankie? Trisha. I've stopped that order going through.'

The voice at the other end raised a query. Trisha pouted at her reflection. 'Of course I'm sure, O one of little faith.'

Frankie asked another question.

'He didn't have time to phone the order through, believe me,' replied Trisha.

They talked for another minute. Trisha left the phone box, and slung the duffel bag she was carrying casually over her shoulder. She spotted a sandwich bar. She held British Rail refreshments in contempt but decided that even a cup of their coffee would be most welcome.

As she walked past two policemen on her way to the buffet, it amused her to speculate how they would feel if they knew that in her duffel bag was the gun that had just killed a man.

2

They had both seen a lot of dead bodies. Commander David Powell, head of Scotland Yard's C13 Anti-Terrorist branch, had started as a constable in the East End, where sudden death is not uncommon, spent five years as chief of the Murder Squad, and lately had often seen the work of maniacs who use bombs and bullets to promote their politics.

Unlike him, Major Grant had also killed a few people. An Arab assassin in Oman, an Irish gunman in Co Armagh, and two Palestinian hi-jackers at Nicosia airport. But the everyday uniform of this SAS man tended to be a well-cut business suit, skillfully tailored to conceal the shoulder holster of a Webley revolver. His Jermyn Street shirt covered a long scar that was a memento of a sniper's bullet in Aden. In his breast pocket was a radio pager. It was only his tie that hinted at his identity: the colours of the Brigade of Guards. Otherwise, he could be taken for a successful stockbroker.

They stood in the cold, flaty-lit chamber of Westminster mortuary, and looked down at the body of the young man with the unshaven chin.

'I need formal confirmation, you understand,' said the commander.

Grant nodded. 'He's Lieutenant Andrew Finlay Wilcox, Special Air Service Regiment,' he said flatly.

Powell nodded.

'I know it's no consolation, major, but the pathologist doesn't think there would have been much pain. It was pretty instantaneous.'

'It's no consolation.' But Grant was a courteous man; he appreciated Powell's intention, 'Thank you, he added. He turned from the body. 'So what kind of gun was it?'

Powell looked unhappy. 'Something special. Nine mill. Ballistics are working on it. They don't think it's a commercial gun. Something high velocity. More like a machine pistol . . . a military weapon.'

'That figures.' Grant was grim-faced.

4

The commander cleared his throat. 'I know he was working undercover, and I've read the file . . .' he began.

'Yes?'

Powell faced the SAS officer. 'How deep was he really in it?'

Grant hesitated before replying. 'Not deep enough to tell us what they're planning. But deep enough for them to kill him.'

'So maybe he was trying to . . . when he made the call . . . Trying to tell you what he had found out.'

'But he didn't succeed,' cut in Grant harshly, and Powell sensed a touch of the ruthlessness the man personified. 'They got to him first.'

He looked angry. Powell wondered if it was at the waste of Wilcox's life, or the fact that he had failed. He decided to change the subject, to another equally delicate matter. 'The inquest . . .' he began. 'There will be difficulties.'

'Because he was killed on active service?'

Powell nodded.

'We're thinking on the same lines, commander. You'll be receiving detailed suggestions from the Ministry of Defence this afternoon.'

Powell smiled wryly. He knew this world. 'You mean instructions, Major Grant?'

'Suggestions,' corrected the SAS man smoothly. 'Guidance, if you like. We'll collect Lieutenant Wilcox ourselves, and leave you to arrange the burial of an empty coffin.'

Powell began to say something, and then shut his mouth. Tight.

'There will be two death certificates,' went on Major Grant. 'One for Lieutenant Wilcox – killed on active service – and that won't specify where or when. And the other you will need for an unidentified young man . . .'

'Unidentified?'

'Yes,' said Grant suavely. 'A gang shooting. In a phone booth. Nasty.'

'What happens to . . .' asked Powell very quietly, indicating the dead body.

'Lieutenant Wilcox will be buried with full military honours, and his name recorded by the regiment,' replied Grant, rather stiffly. 'But where and how certain SAS men die is never publicized. And it will not be in this case.'

They emerged into Horseferry Road, and both men breathed in deeply. It was good to get out of the atmosphere of the mortuary.

'Was Lieutenant Wilcox married?' asked Powell.

'Two years ago,' said Grant bitterly, and the commander shot him a sideways look. There was a lot he'd like to know about Major Grant.

They shook hands. Grant slid behind the wheel of his four-wheel drive Subaru saloon. It was a car which, outwardly, would not draw a lot of attention. But it had, among other features, special two-way radio equipment, and communications facilities linked directly into the army's radio network. The complex key that Grant inserted in the driver's door suggested the doors too were non-standard. Also it was a very heavy automobile because it was bullet proof.

Powell watched the major driving off through the Victoria traffic before getting into his own car. C13 had close contacts with a lot of shadowy organizations: the security services, MI5 and MI6, Special Branch, SIB, and many others. But the SAS remained the most self-enclosed. This whole business only confirmed it yet once again.

Major Grant swung down Queen Victoria Street. He was on his way to Chelsea Barracks, where the regiment's No.1 Counter Revolutionary Warfare Squadron was always on standby. Eventually news of Wilcox's death would filter through the whole regiment, but that was only the beginning of the story.

They were back to square one. They had to catch up, quickly. They were working against time, and against people who were fighting their own kind of war.

The first thing he had to do, decided Major Grant, was to make a very secret phone call on a line which was secure against the devil himself.

3

The herring gull gave a shrill cry and, without an instant's hesitation, drove its razored stiletto beak straight at Skellen's left eye.

The SAS captain nearly lost his tenuous finger hold

on the cliff face as he brought his hand up sharply to ward off the slashing beak. He swore as the bird skewered its bill across his upraised knuckles, drawing a weal of blood. Screaming raucous anger, the bird beat its wings savagely and dived away towards the sea that was raging against the rocks 300 feet below.

'For Christ's sake, Peter,' shouted Clegg, the man immediately below Skellen. 'Stop buggering about with the wildlife and keep moving.'

Clegg's complaint was unnecessary. Skellen was already moving – swinging his tough wiry body up the sandstone escarpment – the toes of his boots skillfully locating the holds in the stratified rock that his fingers had found a few seconds before. Two more gulls screamed and slashed with a demented courage at the faces of the four soldiers who were invading their nesting sanctuary. The defiance of a third one ended with a well-timed mid-air snatch by Skellen. His fingers, lacerated red by the gruelling climb, closed round the creature's throat and broke its neck.

'Hey, Peter,' Clegg called up. 'Let's grab a breather on that outcrop before my arms drop off.' Clegg was from the East End of London with a Cockney's indomitable spirit. He had stayed doggedly behind Skellen during the entire climb.

'No,' Skellen replied curtly, flattening his hard body against the sandstone edifice and reaching for a difficult finger hold. 'I want to take them before dark. No more talking.'

The three men followed Skellen up the tortuous

escarpment in stoic silence, driving themselves on, grimly trying to ignore exhaustion, torn bleeding fingernails, aching arms and legs, the dead weight of packs and rifles, and the late spring sun that squeezed sweat from them as though their bodies were sponges. They were making painfully slow progress. The summit was a dream – something that the mind-numbing fatigue had convinced their brains no longer existed.

They reached the outcrop – the first horizontal surface larger than a toehold that they had encountered during the three hour climb. But there was no respite; Skellen was already twenty feet above them, driving himself on with a determination that Clegg reckoned was suicidal.

'Christ,' Dowesett muttered, trying to wring out his sweat-band without taking it off. 'If there's a bundle at the top, we'll be too knackered to fight.'

'So catch up and tell him,' Clegg invited as they waited for Trooper Gemhal, the last member of the four-man patrol, to draw level.

'Gemhal, a Sikh with an indefatigable sense of humour, was a gifted tracker but not a proficient climber and therefore, in the cold logic of the SAS, he went last so that there was no danger of him falling on a comrade if he lost his footing. He grinned amiably through his black beard at Clegg and Dowsett.

'Pretty bloody climb, eh, lads?'

'If you're wrong about this, Gemmy,' threatened Dowsett, 'I shall personally arrange for something particularly agonizing to happen to you.'

The threat didn't worry the Sikh. 'I'm not wrong and the climb will save us eight hours. You'll see, boys.'

'Thanks for nothing,' muttered Dowsett. 'But I'd rather have the eight hour trek.' He glanced up at Skellen who was climbing steadily.

'I think our patrol commander's getting a bit mad,' Dowsett observed, heaving his pack into a new position so that the straps had some fresh skin to turn into raw meat.

'Can you blame him? The right cock-up that this is turning out to be is bound to send his reputation down the chute,' remarked Clegg disconsolately. 'Three days we been chasing that bastard. Jesus – we should've caught him yesterday, so who the hell is he for Christ's sake, because I'm bloody certain he's not one of our mob.'

'A Kraut,' said Dowsett.

'Never,' said Gemhal.

'A fiver,' said Clegg.

'Fix those pink little mitts and climb, you lazy bastards,' Skellen hissed down at them.

The three men each took swigs from their water canteens and prised some heather from a niche. They bit the roots off and proceeded to chew them and the clinging soil to a dark paste which they smeared over their faces and the backs of their hands. The efficiency of the four-man SAS patrol – the smallest fighting unit in the British Army – depended to a considerable extent on the ability of its soldiers to live off the land – to improvise even to the point of providing face blacking from the materials they found around them. The men had blacked-up with mud from a stream before starting the climb but most of it had been washed away by sweat and the constant wiping of their foreheads with the sleeves of their combat jackets. Blacking up in bright daylight was a simple precaution that made men that much harder to spot from a helicopter. In Gemhal's case, blacking-up was hardly necessary but he did it out of a spirit of comradeship.

Skellen stretched up but his fingers were a few inches short of the nearest crevice.

'Damn!' he swore.

Clegg pulled himself up beside Skellen and saw the problem immediately. In low tones he said: 'It's a bloody miracle we've got this far, Peter. So a bit of the old levitation shouldn't be beyond us.'

Skellen nodded.

Clegg stared at the captain. The four men were hopelessly inadequately equipped for the assault on the cliff. All they had were their packs and their rifles.

'How?' whispered Clegg.

'You realise,' Clegg whispered to Dowsett and Gemhal five minutes later as he tested his weight on the makeshift rope that the four soldiers had fashioned from the webbing straps of their packs, 'that this gear was made by the contractor that pitched in with the lowest tender?'

'That's what I like about you, Cleggy,' Dowsett muttered sourly. 'Always there with warm, uplifting words of encouragement.'

Skellen was already on the clifftop, leaning back against a boulder with the webbing knotted around his wrists, his legs straight to take the weight of the men, and his heels dug into the thin layer of top soil.

Clegg's head appeared. He scrambled silently over the edge and rolled behind a rock. Dowsett and Gemhal followed at one minute intervals – their expressions signalling their immense relief now that the harrowing climb was over.

The four men unknotted the straps and used their packs to muffle any unwanted noises as they checked their Sterling submachine-guns. They listened intently but the only sound was the sea surging against the distant rocks and the cries of the seagulls.

Skellen nodded to Gemhal and jerked his thumb at the maze of sheep and goat tracks leading away from the cliff's edge among the tangle of boulders and outcrops. The Sikh's permanent grin broadened. He clipped his Sterling to the carbineers on his pack and crawled along one of the tracks while holding his rifle across his forearms.

Skellen, Clegg and Dowsett waited – not moving – not talking. Ten minutes later a low whistle heralded the tracker's return. He was looking very pleased with himself.

'Same man. Two hours,' he said with his usual economy of language.

Skellen released his pack and stretched, keeping his rifle across his knees. 'Okay. We'll take fifteen and then we'll get him.'

4

Captain Robert Hagen of the United States Army Rangers flattened the adder's head with a single blow from a fist-sized rock. He knew it was the country's only species of venomous snake because the US Rangers had survival manuals for every country in the world. Hagen had even helped write the manual on Vietnam. A kilogramme of snake represented a high-calorie meal rich in proteins and carbohydrates.

Hagen cut off the snake's head and tail with his knife, slit it open down the belly and removed its elongated organs before drawing off its tough skin and slicing the meat into sections as though he was making a cucumber sandwich. Exhaustion made the simple operation take longer than usual. From a hipflask he poured a finger of brandy into a tin and lit the liquid with a match, carefully returning the spent match to its waterproof box. He dropped two pieces of snake into the invisible flames and watched them sizzle. Eventually the heat released some of the snake's fat so that it began cooking in its own juices. He added the rest of the segments. The advantage of snake fat was that it burned without smoke. It was knowing minor things like that which was the reason why he was alive and a number of Viet Cong weren't. He moved a few yards away while the snake cooked so that the soft spitting sound would not interfere with his hearing while he checked his position against a map.

Hagen counted off the kilometre squares and estimated that he had put twenty miles between himself and the position where he had concealed the homing transmitter. He had every reason to be pleased with his progress. He had been on the run for thirty-six hours. Two nights and days behind 'enemy' lines in this craggy, mountainous country and he was within ten miles, three hours in his present state, of the pick-up point where a chopper would snatch him to safety. But it was too early to be too complacent: the 56 miles he had covered since the start of the joint-service combat exercise had pushed him near to the limit of his endurance. The SAS patrol would also be exhausted but they had the psychological advantage of being in 'friendly' country. He was the outsider – the hare – and the four-man SAS patrol the hunters.

He ate the half-cooked snake and buried the remains of the meal beneath a square of turf cut out with his dagger. He tamped the grass carefully back into place and brushed the blades upright. The stone which he had used to kill the snake was lobbed into a gully. He crawled to a rise and waited for a cloud to drift across the sun before using his field glasses: light flaring on the exposed lenses was an invitation to a mortar and rocket attack as had happened once on Hill 937 near the Laos border when a fellow Ranger had been careless.

And then he spotted them: four men in combat

14

dress two miles away moving towards his position. They four men were less than an hour away.

Jesus H!

They had to be another patrol on another exercise. But Hagen knew it was wishful thinking: the four men were after him. Cursing his stupidity in assuming that not even the SAS would take the shortcut up that impossible cliff face, he rolled away from the rise so that he wouldn't provide them with a silhouette and scrambled to his feet. His exhaustion was forgotten as he drove himself up the incline and towards the pick-up zone that lay beyond the next hill.

5

Gemhal found the specks of blood on the stunted grass where the snake had been basking when Hagen had killed it.

'Could've been a hawk's kill, Gemmy.' Skellen pointed out.

The Sikh shook his head. 'A hawk would leave other traces, Peter. Feathers and bits of fur.'

'He's good,' said Dowsett, flopping on his back. 'Which means he wouldn't leave such an obvious visiting card.'

'How good, Gemmy?' asked Skellen.

The three SAS men showed no surprise when the tracker threw himself flat on his face and surveyed the area around them at eye level height. They knew what he was looking for: the footprint-size areas of bent and broken blades of grass catching the light at the wrong angle which could still be springing upright for as long as three hours after they had been trodden down. Gemhal moved a little way down the incline and produced his dagger. He prised up a square of turf and signalled to Skellen.

'Pretty good, Peter,' said Gemhal. 'But not good enough.'

The remains of the half-cooked snake flesh were slightly warm to Skellen's touch. 'How long, Gemmy?'

The Sikh pressed the piece of flesh to his cheek. 'Fifty minutes. An hour.'

Skellen exchanged grins with his three comrades and said: 'I reckon we've got the bastard. Okay – we step it up a bit.'

6

Hagen slithered off the rock and pushed his field glasses back into their lightweight case. His pursuers were not where they should be. He felt the familiar pricking sensation at the back of his neck which told him when the enemy was near. Where ever they were, his tenacious pursuers were now close enough for it to be impossible to cover his tracks from now on. He had to cross the stream in the ravine and yet to do so meant leaving a spoor through the young trees on the slope that would be as conspicuous to a skilled tracker as a trail of soot across a snowfield. He knew that the SAS trackers were good. He started down the slope, cursing the soft ground that his boots marked easily. He pulled them off, hung them round his neck by their laces and continued down. He didn't realise just how badly fatigue had affected his judgement until he mistimed a jump. The slender ash branch he grabbed to recover his balance tore away, leaving the tree's white cambium shining like a beacon. His foot slipped from under him and a small rock went crashing down, dislodging smaller rocks which fell into a stream in a series of echoing splashes.

He swore bitterly to himself when he reached the edge of the stream and glanced back along his route. He might just as well have driven down the slope in a Sherman tank. There was no point in further caution – speed was all that counted now. It took him less than two minutes to climb the slope on the far side of the stream. He ignored the contour route around the next hill and took the straightest line he could. If they caught him, at least he had given them a hard time.

Hagen had been on similar combat exercises in Wales before with the SAS but this was the longest he had been able to elude a patrol *and* he had succeeded in planting a homing transmitter that could, under real wartime conditions, be switched on from the air by a strike force, enabling choppers to home in at night on a guerilla training base. Those exercises had invariably ended riotously in a pub with his 'captors' who had proceeded to provide Hagen with the necessary training that would enable him to survive a hangover brought about by warm Welsh beer.

This time it would be different. But he had no idea just how different it was going to be.

His calf muscles were numb with pain as he drove himself on into the more difficult country. There was no time to pause to put his boots on. It didn't matter – his feet were tough. Just keep going. It was no longer an exercise – the standing of the United States Rangers was at stake. Another deep gully. Loose slate broke away under his feet. Christ! It was a disused slate quarry! He was way off course.

He stumbled across corroded, narrow-gauge railway tracks and crawled under a quarry car. It took him less than five seconds' study of the map to discover that he had crossed the stream below a fork instead of above it resulting in his misreading a hill. He had lost twenty minutes in his flight to the pick-up zone.

The beginner's map-reading error brought home to Hagen just how rusty he had become. He wormed his way out from under the quarry car. A voice suddenly rang out:

'One move, soldier, and you're dead!'

Hagen froze and lifted his eyes to the direction of the voice. There was no one. No silhouettes against the sky. Nothing. Not that he expected to see anyone.

'Flat on the ground, arms outstretched!' barked the voice.

To give emphasis to the order, a single shot from a submachine-gun smacked into the ground within a yard of Hagen, showering him with shards of slate.

Hagen obeyed. He heard four men scrambling down the quarry's crumbling slopes.

Four pairs of boots surrounded him.

'On your feet, soldier. And put your hands on your head.'

Hagen climbed to his feet and grinned amiably at the four SAS men. They looked in worse shape than him. Their leader was unshaven. Lantern-jawed, lean, hard and unsmiling. Hagen looked at his watch. 'Nearly forty hours, fellers. Pretty good, huh?' He tried to sound jocular but the expression on the leader's face told him that they did not regard the exercise as over.

'I said put your hands on your head!' snarled Skellen.

Hagen shrugged and complied. The four men studied him, taking in his green beret with its coveted Ranger badge.

'Name?'

'Robert Hagen, Captain.'

Hagen began to feel uneasy. He knew that this exercise was going to be different. But staring back at the unsmiling SAS leader gave him the uncomfortable feeling that this time the exercise was going to be very different.

'What unit are you with, soldier?'

'Name, rank and number is all you need,' Hagen growled.

Skellen's submarine-gun butt went into Hagen's solar plexus with a suddenness that didn't give the American a chance to tighten his stomach muscles. He doubled up in blinding agony and sank to his knees. His arms were yanked behind his back and his wrists were lashed tightly together with thin cord. A boot pushed him onto his side.

Skellen pulled the map out of Hagen's thigh pocket and unfolded it. He thrust it under Hagen's nose. 'Where's the transmitter?'

'Now look, fellers – ' Hagen began.

Skellen jerked the Ranger's head back by his hair and thrust his dagger against Hagen's jugular vein. 'Five seconds and you're a dead man. Yank.'

'Go fuck yourself.'

Skellen stood and gave a signal. Dowsett hauled Hagen to a kneeling position and pulled a black hood over his head, tying it tightly but not too tightly to prevent him breathing.

'The transmitter,' Skellen repeated.

Again Hagen swore and again he was knocked to the ground.

Dowsett and Clegg exchanged glances. The long chase had conditioned them into thinking of Hagen as the enemy but not to the point where they would hit him in the stomach with the butt of a Sterling. Despite their feelings, they remained staring down impassively at the American writhing on the ground. Skellen was standing over his captor, his eyes wild and red-rimmed from exhaustion and lack of sleep.

Both men knew that physical violence was an inefficient way of obtaining reliable information from hardened professional soldiers like Hagen. They sensed that worse was to come.

Skellen drew back his foot with the intention of kicking the American in the groin and changed his mind when he caught the sight of the quarry car sitting on the railway line.

'Okay,' said Skellen shortly. 'Tie him across the tracks.'

Hands closed round Hagen's ankles and he was dragged painfully on his back across the railway tracks. He swore and tried to struggle up but a cord pulled round his neck jerked his head backwards onto one of the rusting rails. His befuddled brain swam with the impact. Two more cords tightened round his ankles, doubling his legs under himself, and he realised that he was being lashed to the tracks like a heroine in a silent movie.

'For Chrissake, you crazy guys,' he moaned into the black hood. 'Just what the hell are you trying to pull!'

'We're interested in what you've pulled, Captain Hagen,' said Skellen. 'Especially in where you hid the transmitter.'

'You've flipped. You're a fucking maniac – you know that?'

A planet seemed to fall on Hagen's genitals. His body arched up and his scream of agony echoed round the derelict quarry.

Gemhal licked his lips nervously. Clegg returned his questioning look with a shrug.

'You talk, cowboy,' Skellen rasped, 'or I'll kick your balls from here to Cardiff and back.'

Hagen's moan was muffled by the black bag. The cord slicing into ankles and wrists began staining red as he struggled to free himself. Despite pain he managed to swear at Skellen.

'Okay,' said Skellen. 'If that's the way you want it, Yank . . .' He nodded to Clegg, Dowsett and Gemhal. 'Stand near him and cut him loose if he decides to talk.'

The SAS officer turned and walked along the track. He stepped over a set of points and made his way up the slight incline to the quarry car.

'Captain Hagen, sir,' said Dowsett uneasily, watching Skellen climb onto the quarry car and examine the brake crank-handle. 'It's only an exercise. Maybe it would be better if you told us.'

Hagen managed to choke back his moans of pain. He didn't want to give these sadistic bastards any more pleasure than he could help, even though the pain was triggering lights that danced before his eyes in the disorientating blackness. A fragment of his conscious brain that was still functioning logically wondered if the behaviour of his tormentors was because of a monumental official foul-up that had resulted in someone getting the wrong orders.

He heard protesting squeals of rusty metal turning against rusty metal.

'Christ – he's releasing the brake,' said one of the soldiers.

A series of tremors were transmitted through the rails to Hagen's body. The harsh grating noise of steel wheels that had not turned for a long time. A rattle of coupling. The tremors became a dull rumble.

'I don't believe it,' said another voice.

'What's the crazy sonovabitch doing!' Hagen demanded.

Skellen's voice from some way off. 'Well, soldier? You ready to talk?'

Hagen frantically began sawing the knots around his wrists against the rusting rail. The vibration through the rails from the approaching quarry car hammered brutally against the back of his neck.

'You talk, soldier or your fucking head gets cut off!'

'I don't believe it,' said a stunned voice. 'He's out of his tiny.'

Hagen could hear the bogies grate and slam across neglected joins in the time-buckled rails as the quarry car gathered speed. Then the leader's voice yelling out again. This time in desperation:

'Christ Almighty – I can't stop it! Fucking brake's jammed. Cut him loose! Move! Move!'

Boots scrabbling beside him – barely audible above the thunder of the charging quarry car. Suddenly his feet were free. He struggled to roll clear but the cord sank into his neck like a wire cheese cutter. A knife clattering on the rail by his ear. An expletive.

Hagen could hear himself screaming out. 'Cut my head free, you fucking goon!'

Then the leader's voice. This time despairingly: 'Too late! Leave him! Leave him! Get clear!'

The uproar from the unseen nightmare bearing down on him was such that Hagen didn't hear the crunch on slate as the soldier who was about to cut him free jumped clear. In those final seconds Hagen panicked. He screamed in fear and summoned up all his reserves of strength to break the cord around his neck by brute force.

At the moment of impact, when cold steel touched his neck, Hagen lost control of his bladder and fainted.

7

The SAS colonel sitting beside the Scout helicopter pilot surveyed the inhospitable terrain passing 300 feet below the machine. The pilot concentrated on flying at the dangerously low height between crags and along valleys while the senior officer studied the ground, occasionally raising a pair of binoculars to his eyes.

The deadline had passed for picking up Hagen which meant that the colonel's crack four-man patrol had found him.

For once Colonel Hadley, commanding officer of the Special Air Service, lacked confidence in Skellen's ability. All the reports on Hagen indicated that he was one of the best men the US Army Rangers had – a battle-hardened veteran of Vietnam – a survivor. The forty hours that had lapsed since the exercise had started meant that Hagen must have planted the transmitter.

Hadly spotted a movement on the ground in a derelict slate quarry. He jabbed a finger. The pilot nodded, slewed the machine round in mid-air and decreased cyclic pitch so that it lost height.

Hadley refocussed his binoculars. A man appeared to be lashed down to a railway track in the path of a moving quarry car. The car hit the points and veered down the track that ran alongside the track where the man was tied. Hadley recognised Skellen as the figure that jumped from the moving car, ran towards the captive and hit him on the side of the neck with his Sterling submachine-gun. The other three men heard the Scout's approach. They wheeled round and immediately dived for cover. Skellen was standing over the shape, ignoring the helicopter as it dropped into the quarry.

With ten feet to go before the Scout touched down, Hadley pushed his door open and leapt to the ground. A difficult jump, but he kept himself in trim by regularly placing himself at the mercy of one of his NCO instructors, who willingly obeyed orders by putting his CO 'through it'. Hadley was a tough, wiry, no-nonsense man with a stare that could, if the rumours that circulated the SAS's headquarters at Hereford were to be believed, kill a man at ten paces. There were some SAS soldiers who freely admitted that they would rather face a dozen IRA terrorists single-handed than the colonel when he was on the rampage after someone's scalp.

Taking in everything at a glance – the menacing stare of the SAS officer and the lifeless shape half-tied to the railway tracks – Hadley stormed across and confronted Skellen.

'Captain Skellen!'

'Sir,' Skellen came to attention and saluted.

'What's going on here?' Hadley demanded curtly.

'Interrogation, sir.'

Hadley frowned, knelt beside Hagen and removed the hood. He lifted an eyelid. 'This man is unconscious, captain.'

'He'll be all right, sir. He's only fainted.'

Hadley noticed the severed cords around Hagen's ankles. He picked up an army-issue knife that was lying between the rails and straightened up. 'Dowsett! Clegg! Gemhal!' he barked. 'Show yourselves!'

The three troopers emerged sheepishly from their respective hiding places. Their CO's thunderous expression told them what they had already suspected, that things had gone badly wrong.

'Whose knife is this?'

Clegg stepped forward. 'Mine, sir.'

'Finish what you were going to do, sergeant. Cut this man loose.'

Hagen was already stirring as Clegg cut the cords binding his wrists and neck and helped him to his feet. Hagen's trousers were stained dark with urine. He pushed Clegg away and stood unaided but unsteadily, blinking in the sunlight after the darkness of the hood. He gingerly massaged his neck where the cord had bruised the flesh and drawn blood.

'You all right, Captain Hagen?' asked the colonel.

It was bitter humiliation as much as pain that prevented Hagen from answering right away. He nodded and croaked: 'Kinda of . . . sore, colonel.' His eyes blazed raw hatred for an instant at Skellen after they had focussed on the points and then on the quarry car that had come to rest on the track parallel to the one he had been lashed to.

'What happened?' Hadley demanded.

'He's planted the transmitter, sir,' said the SAS captain. 'We were questioning him as to where. It could take a battalion a week to scour those hills – '

'We?' queried Hadley, glancing at the three soldiers.

'*I* was questioning him,' Skellen amended.

'I see.' There was no note of accusation. There didn't have to be – Hadley had seen exactly what had happened. 'Just questioning.'

'Robust persuasion, sir,' Skellen added expression-lessly, his cold blue eyes watching Hadley carefully. 'The usual routine.'

Hadley considered sending the three troopers out of earshot but decided against it. This was something they should hear. He took a deep breath before speaking. He had the professional soldier's distaste of dirty tricks. 'You've been warned about this before, Skellen.'

Even Hagen, who was in no state to worry about anyone but himself, was surprised by the British officer's omission of Skellen's rank.

'This is the third instance when you have used brutality – '

'Strict interrogation, sir,' Skellen interrupted.

'Using techniques that were discredited ten years ago!' Hadley snapped. He stared straight back at the

27

officer. 'You're under arrest, Captain Skellen. Sergeant Dowsett will relieve you of your arms.'

8

From the police helicopter hovering over central London, its television camera transmitting pictures back to Scotland Yard's control room, they looked like swarms of ants converging on a pot of honey.

The ants were thousands of demonstrators gathering for their big march. The pot of honey was Hyde Park's Speaker's Corner, the assembly point to which they came from far and wide. Since breakfast, long-distance coaches had been disgorging them, and train loads had brought more. They were all kinds, young and old, spike-haired punks, dignified veterans, pretty young girls in tight-fitting jeans, and middle-aged mothers, students, wearing their college scarves like battle colours, and hard, tough miners and dock workers.

And there was a rent-a-crowd, in full strength, the badge festooned, untidy, banner carrying activists who joined in any protest demonstration that was fashionably trendy. But enemies of the movement, only too ready to dismiss the march as another frolic of the radical chic, deluded themselves. Of course the anarchists, brandishing their red and black flags, hurried to tag onto the Trotskyists screaming their slogans, and the yobs hoping for a good punch up at the end of the day.

But, overwhelmingly, it was a carnival of ordinary people, united by a message of peace, disarmament, pacifism. There were grey-haired ex-servicemen, some wearing their World War II medals. One legless former RAF pilot was being pushed in his wheelchair by his wife. There were teachers, old age pensioners, nurses, men and women streaming to the meeting place, joining the long line that was forming itself into a procession. But the TV news teams weren't interested in teachers and pensioners – they didn't make for the dramatic footage that editors liked, so they pointed their cameras at the rowdy minorities.

Then the organizers took over. The marshals emerged, young men and women with armbands. Leaflets were handed out. 'Why We Are Marching.' 'Black the Bomb, Black the Bases.' 'Go Home, Uncle Sam.' 'Schools Not Missiles.' Through loudhailers, instructions were given:

'Dagenham, move to the front.' 'Essex University, line up over there.' 'Don't straggle.' 'Keep up with your friends.'

And the banners appeared. 'Women for Peace.' 'Power to the People.' 'To Hell with NATO.' They made a special point of identifying various contingents: 'Australians Against the Bomb.' 'Germans for Disarmament.' 'Pakistanis for Peace.' 'Notting Hill Says No.'

It was well organized, well planned. Fifty thousand leaflets printed, hundreds of posters stuck up, scores of banners and flags available for eager hands to

carry. Badges by the crateful. And dozens of newspaper sellers offering their publications: 'Sanity.'
'Militant.' 'Peace News.'

To the American tourists, going for a walk from
Grosvenor House, and finding themselves caught up
in a tide of demonstrators, it looked impressive. For
months afterwards, they would be telling their
friends in Topeka and Bakersville and Glendale about
the Sunday they saw the Big March.

Already, all over the West End, police were divert-
ing traffic. The white-helmetted motor-cycle cops
gathered in clusters at street junctions. Bus loads of
policemen parked in Rotten Row, waiting for the
signal to move. Park Lane, Piccadilly, Hyde Park
Corner were barred to motorists.

And overhead whirred the helicopters observing,
watching, reporting . . .

The stars of the show arrived. At their head, the
Rt. Rev. Horace Wilberforce Crick, Bishop of Camden
Town, honorary president of the People's Lobby for
Peace; platform speaker at all good causes; letter
writer to the *Times* on racism, sexism, apartheid,
colonialism, imperialism, nationalism and all other
evils and 'isms. Leading light of the nation's disarmament movement. A dedicated man.

He didn't look like the powerhouse he was. A
smallish man, mild faced, with a ready, genial smile,
an air of benevolence, and quick-moving, intelligent
eyes.

His gentleness could be misleading. He had sued a
tabloid for £10,000 libel damages because they had
called him a Communist, and he had won.

He had been arrested for throwing a tin of paint over the steps of the Ministry of Defence in Horse Guards Avenue. In court, he made a defiant speech, was bound over to keep the peace in future, and carried shoulder high through the street by his followers.

He had led an anti-cruise missile protest to Greenham Common airbase in Berkshire, and denounced American air force installations during a television broadcast as 'cess pools of murder'.

When the US Embassy declined to give him a visa so that he could speak on a platform with Jane Fonda during the Vietnam War, he wrote another of his famous letters to the *Times*, and got six friendly Members of Parliament to raise the matter in the Commons. He got his visa.

Vietnam was now a distant memory but Bishop Crick kept busy on other matters. Curiously, though, he stayed very quiet on some issues. When Solidarity was crushed in Poland, he concentrated his thunder on Chile and United States' iniquities in Latin America.

As he stepped out of his car at Marble Arch, he got a cheer. He waved. It was like a benediction.

'Am I on time, Frankie?' he anxiously asked the woman who greeted him.

She was blonde, attractive and though the overall-style trouser suit she wore concealed her curves, she clearly had a very good figure.

'Plenty of time, bishop,' she assured him. She took him by the arm. 'This way . . .'

She wore a couple of badges, a nuclear disarmament emblem, and the People's Lobby insignia, but otherwise there was little to indicate what an important person Frankie was in the movement.

She led Bishop Crick through the throng to the head of the march gathering near the Tyburn plaque. They passed a group of women carrying a large coffin imaginatively labelled 'Peace', dodged under a huge banner proclaiming 'Teachers Say No to Nukes', sidestepped 'Trade Unionists For Peace', and 'Vegetarians Against War', pushed their way through a small group of earnest looking young people holding a placard declaring the 'Young Conservatives Are For Peace'.

'You see,' beamed the Bishop, 'the whole world is with us. Even the YC.'

'Of course,' said Frankie. She gave the young Tories, bespectacled and soberly dressed, a dazzling smile.

On a truck festooned with amplifiers a rock group started playing amid cheers. Frankie and the Bishop caught the full blast, but Crick didn't mind.

'It's so good to see the people enjoy themselves,' he shouted into her ear.

Frankie pulled a slight grimace. But she nodded.

It was getting noisier all round. The crowd was waiting impatiently to move off. A huge serpent of people, twelve, fifteen abreast, was stretching back into the park as far as the bandstand in the distance. Cheer leaders began encouraging the demonstrators to bellow rhythmic slogans.

'NATO Out! Out! Out!' 'Peace Yes! Yes! Yes!' 'US Bases Out! Out! Out!'

32

'This way, Bishop,' indicated Frankie. She had brought him to the head of the assembled march where the VIP contingent was to be vanguard. There were familiar faces already on parade. The revolutionary actress; the Troops Out of Ireland MP; the Trotskyist journalist who had lauded the Red Brigade; the television commentator who had unlimited access to Yasser Arafat. And three trade union bosses who, between them, had brought one and a half million men out on strike over a man being fired for breaking his foreman's nose. But this time they were all united over one issue: the abolition of nuclear weapons.

The Bishop received an equally warm welcome from other, less controversial, members of the vanguard. Two distinguished scientists, one a Nobel Prize winner; a Jewish rabbi; the vice-chancellor of a leading provincial university; a famous violinist; a group of academics from Cambridge. There was even a retired vice-admiral.

The demonstration had indeed mobilised a formidable array of star supporters.

Frankie excused herself and shouldered her way to a tall, lanky man wearing rimless glasses. Long hair flowed from under his beret. He called it his 'Battle Beret' – he had first worn it at the Lewisham riots, then at several violent clashes finally culminating in Brixton, and Southall. When Rod wore his beret, it was time for action.

'Everything OK, Rod?' Frankie asked him. His badge of office was the loudhailer he carried.

He grinned. He had bad teeth. 'I've seen three Special Branch gooks.'

'Great,' smiled Frankie and there was contempt in her voice. 'I hope they do a nice fat report in triplicate.'

'Listen,' said Rod. 'Will you take this thing? I'm already croaking like a frog.'

He offered her the loudhailer.

She shook her head. 'You'll be alright,' she assured him.

'Oh come on, there hasn't been a peep out of you yet.'

She was already moving away, but she stopped just long enough to say: 'Don't worry. You'll hear plenty. Soon . . .'

9

The adjutant replaced his telephone and nodded to the door leading to Colonel Hadley's office.

'You can go in now, Captain Skellen.'

Skellen knocked on the colonel's door and entered, reflecting that at least he was being spared the indignity of being marched into his commanding officer's presence. He came to attention in front of Colonel Hadley's desk and noticed out of the corner of his eye that Major Grant, commanding officer of the Counter Terrorist Squadron based in London's Chelsea Barracks, was present.

Hadley nodded to a chair. 'You may sit down if you wish.'

'Thank you, sir, but I prefer to stand.'

Hadley studied the man rigidly at attention before him: lantern-jawed; incredibly blue eyes that were staring fixedly at the SAS's regimental insignia on the wall behind his desk. It was a winged dagger emblazoned with the motto: 'Who Dares Wins'. He opened the file in front of him that contained statements from Captain Hagen and the three other men in Skellen's patrol. He came straight to the point: 'I could have you court marshalled, but I've decided against it.'

Skellen remained motionless.

'Not for your sake, but for the sake of the regiment,' continued the colonel. 'I couldn't care less about you but I care a great deal about the SAS, therefore you're being returned to your unit.'

Skellen's impassiveness faltered momentarily. To be RTU'd – kicked out of the regiment – was as much as a disgrace as being found guilty by court martial.

'May I ask why, sir?'

'Don't come that with me, Skellen,' Hadley growled. 'You know damn well why.'

'I would prefer to be court-marshalled, sir.'

'Well it's not what I want. I want you out. There's no room for sadists in the SAS. These statements from Clegg, Dowsett and Gemhal leave no doubt in my mind that you enjoyed torturing Captain Hagen.'

'I used intensive interrogation on Captain Hagen, sir.'

Hadley snorted. 'I saw what you were using, Captain Skellen. It was torture.'

'The object of the exercise – '

' – wasn't sadism! You know as much about intelligence-gathering as anyone. You ought to know that torture is one of the least efficient means of obtaining reliable information from men like Captain Hagen. Your duty on that exercise was to take him prisoner and hand him over to a field interrogation unit.'

'There wasn't time, sir,' Skellen muttered. He noticed that Major Grant was making notes.

'It's not as if this is the first time,' Hadley continued. 'There was that suspect in Londonderry – '

'Later convicted,' Skellen pointed out.

'On the basis of information obtained by the RUC! Not by your methods!'

Skellen fell silent.

Hadley closed the file in front of him and tossed it into his 'out' tray. He steepled his fingers and regarded Skellen in contempt. 'You tortured Captain Hagen beyond and above any necessity using methods that were declared to be illegal over ten years ago. In view of this and the earlier incidents, I can only conclude that you enjoy inflicting pain on your fellow man.'

'I think it would be fairer if such conclusion were decided by a court-marshall, sir.'

Hadley's scalp went back but he let the jibe pass. 'You've been a good soldier, Skellen, but you've turned rotten. We've no room for sadists. That is all.'

Skellen remained at attention. 'I'm not going back

to the Parachute Regiment, sir,' he declared. 'Not after six years here. I'm SAS or I'm nothing.'

'Then you're nothing,' said Hadley flatly.

For a moment Skellen seemed unable to speak. His eyes met Hadley's gaze for the first time. 'In that case, sir, I shall resign my commission.'

Major Grant stopped making notes and regarded Skellen thoughtfully.

Colonel Hadley nodded indifferently and opened a file from his 'in' tray. 'That's your privilege, Captain Skellen,' he remarked casually.

Skellen realised that he was dismissed. The colonel's disinterest was the final blow. White-faced, he saluted smartly and left the office, managing to suppress a desire to slam the door.

The adjutant looked up questioningly from his papers as Skellen strode across the office.

'Captain Skellen. I have some forms for you to sign regarding your married quarters.'

Skellen stared at the administration officer in disbelief. 'You've what?'

'I understand you've put in an RTU request.' The adjutant looked embarrassed. 'The paras are short of accommodation but SE District have some new quarters at Aldershot – ' He stopped in mid-sentence and gaped in surprise as Skellen took the forms from his fingers and calmly tore them to shreds, allowing the pieces to flutter onto his desk.

'You understood wrong,' Skellen grated. 'I won't be qualifying for a new anything.' He gestured to the regimental insignia on the wall. 'But how about a new motto for the SAS?'

The adjutant looked bewildered. 'New motto?'

'Who fucking cares who wins?'

This time Skellen slammed the door.

Skellen walked slowly across the parade ground and stopped when he came to the memorial clock. On its base were inscribed the names of SAS men who had, in regimental parlance, failed to 'beat the clock'.

There were nearly a hundred names under the various shadowy campaigns that the SAS fought in over thirty years and was still fighting.

Skellen stood before the clock his blue eyes moving down the bleak list of names as if he was saying goodbye to old friends. Much of the ethos of the SAS was reflected in the way the names were presented – there was no rank priority. Just names in the chronological sequence in which they had failed to 'beat the clock'. They had died, often mysteriously, in many strange places; in the jungles of Malaya; in the stupefying heat of the Gulf States; in the grimy, slogan-daubed back alleys of Londonderry. The enemy had ranged from tribesmen who, when taking prisoners only took the prisoners' heads, to men in Northern Ireland who had never bothered with toy guns when they were kids because their fathers had trained them to use real ones.

Skellen stood in silence, ignoring the man approaching him from behind. Major Grant stood uncomfortably beside Skellen. It was some seconds before he spoke.

'It's not going to be easy, Peter.'

'Yeah.'

'I'm going into Hereford. If you'd like to join me for a bite at the Green Dragon . . .'

'Thank you, no.'

'We need to talk, Peter.'

'Yeah.'

Grant said gently: 'You'll get used to it. You'll adjust.'

'Think so?'

'They always do.'

10

'I've quit,' Skellen announced to his wife.

Jenny propped herself up on one elbow, allowing the bed cover to slide off her shoulders. Skellen sounded so casual about it that the words took a moment to sink in.

'I don't understand, Peter.'

'I'm through. Finished.'

'You're . . . you're being posted?'

'I've resigned. You're looking at *Mister* Peter Skellen.'

She stared at him, bewildered. 'What do you mean?'

'I've jacked it all in. The army. The SAS. Everything.'

Jenny was still trying to grasp what Skellen was telling her.

'You've left the army,' she repeated, almost as if she was spelling it out for herself.

He gave a brief, bitter laugh. 'Maybe you could say the army's left me. Anyway, yes; I've thrown in my commission.'

She closed her eyes for a moment. Then she whispered: 'Oh, Peter!'

But it wasn't distress or sadness. She sounded almost relieved.

'I'm afraid I hadn't much choice,' he went on, as if to justify himself.

Jenny suddenly threw her arms around her husband and held him close. 'Thank God,' she murmured. 'Oh, darling, thank God.'

'But Jenny . . .'

'I can't tell you how often I've prayed for this day,' she told him. 'Prayed every night. Hoping that one morning I'll wake up and you'd tell me that you're quitting whilst you're safe and sound and still in one piece.'

She kissed him.

It was Skellen's turn to be confused. 'You *wanted* me out?'

'Peter, can't you guess what I've been going through all these years? Waving you goodbye, not knowing if I'd ever see you again alive. Watching you disappear for weeks and months on end, waiting and praying for you to come back, not knowing where you were, what you were doing. Wondering in what dark alley you'll get shot in the back. Dreading every knock on the door . . .'

He put his arm around her. 'I had no idea . . .' He appeared almost baffled. 'You never said . . .'

Jenny had tears in her eyes, but they seemed to be tears of happiness.

'Of course not,' she croaked. 'Do you think I ever would have? I married a soldier, didn't I? I had no idea what the SAS was except that if there's a war you'd be first to go. But I didn't know the SAS is already at war. I thought I was marrying into a peace-time army – not an outfit which has never stopped fighting . . .' She blew her nose. 'I couldn't say anything, could I? It was your life, I know how proud you've been of belonging . . .' She smiled at him through the tears. 'I think you're very brave for quitting. It can't have been an easy decision for you. But, darling, I'm so glad . . .'

Skellen shifted uncomfortably, avoiding her eyes. 'It's going to be tough. I don't know anything else. Civvy Street's not going to be a piece of cake . . .'

'You'll make out,' she assured him, smiling.

'Well, I'll find something.' His tone was doubtful though. 'A security outfit. Something like that. They often need bodyguards.'

The way he said it made her suddenly tense.

'You're not considering becoming a mercenary, are you? Joining some crazy private war somewhere?' Jenny asked anxiously. 'You can't! Anyway, you're not allowed to, are you? you signed an agreement, didn't you? It's the same for everybody in the SAS isn't it?'

Skellen's violent reaction took him back. 'You think I have to stick to agreements with those bastards?' he

41

spat savagely. 'You know what they can do with their fucking pieces of paper? The whole bloody Ministry of Defence, the Army Council, the lot of them. You think I owe them anything?'

'Ssh. Not so loud. You'll wake Samantha.'

'Sorry.'

They were quiet for a moment but there was no sound from their eighteen-month old daughter.

'What's the matter, Peter?' Jenny eventually asked, regarding him gravely. 'What really happened?'

'Forget it,' he snapped. Then he flashed her a sheepish grin. 'Sorry, Jen . . . It's not easy to adjust.'

In his mind he was thihnking of Major Grant's words.

'Don't you, worry,' said Jenny reassuringly, 'the three of us make a good team. We'll do fine.'

They held each other tightly. Their love-making was fervently passionate. It was the way they made love when he returned after a long absence, their bodies rejoicing in a mutual reunion and the fulfillment of a great need.

As they lay beside each other, Skellen forgot about the lies and deceptions, the violence and ruthlessness, the danger and the risks that had become the fabric of his life. For a short while he had other thoughts, knew other sensations.

Then relaxing later, he was brought back to earth.

'Darling,' began Jenny, gently. 'Where will we live? We won't be able to stay here.'

The officers married quarters of the Hereford barracks had been their home for so long it was difficult to imagine living anywhere else.

'We've got twenty-eight days to find ourselves alternative accommodation. Technically.'

'What do you mean, technically?'

'They'd like me out sooner,' answered Skellen grimly. 'Like yesterday.'

'How bloody unfair,' said Jenny indignantly. 'After six years in the regiment.'

'That's the SAS for you,' he shrugged. 'Anyway, it'll be nice for you to be back in London.'

'London?'

'Of course. That's where it all happens.'

'How about money?'

'Don't worry,' replied Skellen evenly. 'We'll be all right.'

At that moment money was the least of his problems.

11

The British Airways Boeing from Rome touched down on Heathrow's Runway 28 Right. Twenty minutes later a dark, good-looking Libyan in his early thirties presented a Maltese passport to the woman immigration officer behind the desk. She flipped through the pages without appearing to read them. The expensive suit, silk shirt, and gold Rolex Oyster wristwatch, plus the air of a man accustomed to wearing such trappings, told her a good deal about the new arrival. The manicured nails and the aroma of perfume spoke of other things.

'What is the purpose of your visit to the United Kingdom, Mr Malek?' she inquired politely.

'Business,' beamed Malek, showing spotless symmetrical teeth. 'And just a little pleasure.' He spoke good English, some of it acquired at the American University in Beirut. He had also polished it at the London School of Economics.

The immigration officer opened her black book with its lists of suspect foreigners.

'I have a letter of credit from one of my banks,' purred Malek.

She read the document from the Bank of Credit and Commerce International and was impressed.

'How long will you be staying, Mr Malek?'

He shrugged. 'Not long. A couple of weeks, perhaps.'

She glanced at his landing card, and was also impressed by the London address he gave.

'You'll be staying in Knightsbridge?'

'I find it convenient for Harrods,' smiled Malek.

It was just the right thing to say. She stamped his passport. 'A month, Mr Malek.'

Malek was pleased. A month was plenty of time . . .

He made his way into the customs hall, and did not notice the immigration offier talking to a Special Branch man. Mr Malek was a person of some interest at most airports.

Outside the arrival building, the chauffeur greeted him.

'Mr Malek?'

'Yes.'

'I'm Curtis. I have your car, sir.'

As the Mercedes drove him into London, Malek sat back and contemplated yet once again how well things were organized. Money could open every door.

'Curtis.'

The chauffeur turned his head slightly. 'Sir?'

'Sometime I might like to visit a casino.'

'No problem, sir. I can arrange it.'

'Is it true the Playboy Club has had some trouble?'

The chauffeur shook his head. 'Don't worry about that, sir. It won't be any problem.'

'Good.'

His masters might not approve of him gambling, but Malek felt that if his duties took him to the fleshpots of Europe, he owed it to himself to indulge a little. Also such behaviour helped with his cover. In any case, he would not touch a drop of alcohol. Colonel Gadaffi would be pleased that his messenger only drank orange juice in London.

It was a beautiful flat. Malek had no complaints. He adored the sunken bath under a circular canopy of blue tinted double-glazed glass. He liked the exotic plants that flourished in the warmth and light, crowded against the curved walls. He was impressed by the sumptuous master bedroom that was dominated by a vast circular bed. There was even a Telex terminal in a corner of the spacious living-room.

Malek was a man of discretion, but it did strike

45

him that the bed would be a delightful playground for the right partner. Again it was something Tripoli need never know about.

Above all, Malek was impressed by the butler. Arnold came with the apartment. He had butled there for Hollywood film stars, Texas oil executives, and even gentlemen like Mr Malek. In every case, satisfaction was guaranteed.

'While I am in London, I will lead a very quiet life,' Malek briefed him.

'Yes, sir.'

'But I may invite over a few people. Important people. Just for the odd little get together.'

'I understand. I can always lay on extra staff.'

'Good.' Malek nodded approvingly. In a way, he was a sort of ambassador. He had to have a good presence.

Malek padded round the flat, followed by Arnold.

'Excellent,' he commented, inspecting the place. 'I shall like it here.'

Arnold said nothing.

Malek sat down behind the big ornate rosewood desk with an inlaid pattern.

'Yes, I shall be very comfortable here,' he announced.

'I am delighted, sir.'

'Now I want to call some friends.' Malek took out a little snake skin-covered notebook and turned the pages. 'I think I'll start with the Bishop. I haven't seen him since Geneva.'

Arnold was too polite to ask, but clearly he was slightly puzzled.

'Bishop Crick,' explained Malek. 'The Bishop of Camden Town. A most progressive man. And a very good friend.' Malek smiled to himself. The good cleric was worth every cent his patrons gave him for his causes.

12

Bishop Crick believed in field work. He was not one of those clerics who regarded the pulpit as their main platform, or considered ministering to the faithful as his chief task.

He preached on more political platforms than churches. His texts were more often taken from newspaper headlines than the good book. He was a familiar figure at Tower Hill and Speaker's Corner, in Conway House and at Friends House. He marched in demonstrations for all the good causes, and against all the bad ones.

'I am proud of being a radical,' he once told *The Guardian*, 'Jesus Christ was a radical. I am against the establishment. Was not Pontius Pilate the establishment?'

Nor did he just speak from theory. He saw with his own eyes. He had travelled widely: Mozambique, to Hanoi, to Havana. He was a welcome guest, all expenses paid. He had been an outstanding member of the Copenhagen Tribunal to Investigate American

War Crimes, and the Palestinian Committee Against Israeli Repression.

'I do not believe in simply espousing popular causes,' he declared. 'I do not seek popular acclaim. I do not believe in being fashionable. I seek the truth.'

Which is why, perhaps, he had little to say about the invasion of Afghanistan, avoided the subject of Poland, and had been on holiday during the events in Hungary and Czechoslovakia.

'I know I will never be Archbishop of Canterbury, and that makes me very proud,' he said on one occasion. 'That is a political appointment. Your face has to fit. If my face doesn't fit, it means that I am a man of God.'

The year he won the Stalin Peace Prize, he split the money between the People's Lobby, the PLO, and the Pan American Freedom Fighters Association. He kept just enough to finance a trip to San Salvador.

In a famous declaration, Bishop Crick stated at the Albert Hall: 'My parish is the street. I believe the place of the church is on the barricades. We must feed the fires of anger. Onwards, into battle.'

His rhetoric was magnificent, and his faith shone in his eyes. He had made his plain black cassock, and the simple cross which hung round his neck on a thin chain, a uniform familiar to millions.

He gave his time unstintingly. He was honorary chaplain on the London Squatters Commune, and joyfully allowed himself to be arrested for obstruction when he barred access to a house the group had seized.

48

And if in Bishop Crick the stage had lost a great actor, Madison Avenue had equally lost a genius for publicity and self advertising.

He made a point, for example, of being photographed either walking, or riding a bicycle. His chauffeur-driven car was reserved for journeys which would not, hopefully, be in the popular eye. He had also acquired a liking for Havana cigars. But that was bad for the image, so he reserved the pleasure for the privacy of his study. Instead, he made a point of publicizing frequent fasts in front of embassies whose regimes he disliked. The fast, carefully notified to the media in time to secure adequate coverage, was usually called off after the cameras had left.

There was, after all, no point in weakening himself. He needed all the strength the Lord granted him to fight the good fight.

And to write the letters to the *Times* and *The Guardian* which trumpeted the Word like a clarion call. The word of Crick.

13

At 3am the latrines of Cunningham Barracks, the depot of the Downshire Regiment's 2nd Battalion, were a lonely place, and the two sentries lay there, bound and gagged, for three hours before they were discovered.

It was only then that the duty officer got the really bad news: somebody had broken into the armoury, and removed a mini arsenal. The final tally of stolen weapons amounted to six 7.62 high-velocity rifles with sniper sights, ten Sterling submachine-guns, and forty 9mm self-loading pistols.

What interested the men from the Army's Special Investigation Branch almost as much was that the intruders had also taken thirty-six Schermuly CS grenades which, once the ring is pulled, explode within one and a half seconds, and will put anyone within a hundred feet of the fumes out of action.

'You mean you didn't even get a glimpse of them?' the SIB major asked the two sentries incredulously.

'All I know is somebody hit me from behind,' said the lance-corporal ruefully. He was still rubbing his wrists. The ropes had cut into them savagely.

'And you?' the major asked the other sentry.

'I thought I heard a noise, but before I could turn around, I got knocked out, sir. I never saw them.'

Seven weeks previously, the 2nd Battalion had returned from its tour in Ulster, so by the time Commander Powell and the men from the Anti-Terrorist branch arrived at the barracks, the SIB major presented them with a pretty clear picture.

'I think it's the IRA,' he said.

'Oh yes?' Powell tended to be sceptical about most things, especially the obvious.

'Somebody got some inside knowledge,' went on the major. 'Found out where the armoury is, the layout of the barracks, how to get over the wall . . .'

'Just like that?'

'It's a professional job,' insisted the major.

'That I agree,' nodded Powell. 'I'm not so sure about the IRA though . . .'

The SIB major bristled slightly. Two spells of duty in Londonderry and Belfast had made him an expert on the IRA. He felt he had seen more terrorism than Scotland Yard would even sniff.

'Really, sir? What makes you say that?'

'My guess is that if they'd got inside this place, they'd have blown it up. They're after spectacular coups. The regiment's just back from Ireland. What could be more spectacular than to strike at them over here?'

The major sniffed. 'So who's your guess then?'

Powell slowly sipped the mug of sweet NAAFI tea the canteen had provided. 'Don't know,' he said slowly. 'Just a gut feeling. Somebody who wants weapons. Somebody who's planning something . . .' He frowned into his mug. 'And somebody who's bloody professional. A load like that would need some carting away. They must have had a truck. And enough bodies to manhandle the goods.'

He was almost talking to himself, and seemed to have reached a decision.

'You carry on, major. Special Branch will work with you on the IRA angle. Maybe you're right. I'll follow a couple of other lines . . .'

A young fair-haired SIB lieutenant came in. He was in plain clothes, but his bearing was so military, his hair cut so neatly, his tie so crisp that he proclaimed his identity. He waited.

51

'Yes, Harris?' said the major.

'We've completed the inventory, sir.'

'And?'

'I'm afraid they also got away with twenty thousand rounds of ammo.'

'Christ!' gasped the major. 'How the hell did they manage all that?'

Powell couldn't resist it. 'I thought you had guards on duty?'

'Most of the men were away on weekend leave,' muttered the SIB major. 'This lot knew what they were doing.'

'I think that's a safe bet,' agreed Powell drily.

He drove back to London. Before he reached his office the decision had already been made in Whitehall to keep the news of the arms theft secret.

14

The silence annoyed Rod greatly. He had expected news flashes, and banner headlines. He had looked forward to gloating over the sensation his handiwork had caused.

Rod had been in charge and as the others agreed, the Red Brigade couldn't have done any better. Everything went like clockwork. A copybook caper.

Nobody had spotted them, they drove off as quietly as they came in, the trip in the van along the

M4 was uneventful and they didn't even see a police car. By the time the robbery was discovered they were already back in town, and arms and ammunition were safely secreted.

As Frankie said, Rod had many hidden talents.

15

The existence of the Twilight Committee was itself a state secret. Few minutes were kept of its proceedings, and only the committee saw the agenda.

They sat round a green baize-covered table, presided over by the Home Secretary.

Commander Powell, head of the anti-terrorist squad, had brought a file with him. Wallace, deputy director of the security service, sat near the window, staring across the courtyard. Colonel Hadley, commander of the SAS, was out of uniform, sporting a MCC tie. By his side Major Grant.

'I want to keep this short, gentlemen,' said the Home Secretary. He had a cabinet meeting to attend in an hour, and one of his under secretaries wanted to see him before then. So he was pressed for time. He looked across at Wallace. 'I have seen the security service's report. Do you have anything to add?'

The man from MI5 hesitated. 'Only to restate our fear that the peace movement, the nuclear dis armers and the rest of them, are being increasingly infiltrated by elements who are using them for their own purposes . . .'

'Yes,' growled the Home Secretary impatiently. 'That's obvious to a blind man. But facts . . . have you any evidence, any facts, anything we can proceed on?' He glanced round the table. 'Well?'

Powell tapped the slim navy blue folder in front of him.

'This arms theft at the barracks indicates, to me at least, that some group is planning a . . . Well, there's something nasty in store.'

'What group?' demanded the Home Secretary. Being a politician, he lived in dread of the arms theft becoming public. He didn't look forward to the baying of Fleet Street hounds.

Powell shrugged. 'We're working on it.'

'And what are they planning?' pressed the Home Secretary. 'An assassination? A hijack? A kidnapping? Would anything like that require such an arms haul?'

He looked at Colonel Hadley.

'Your man was on to something, wasn't he? What was his name . . .'

'Wilcox,' said Major Grant quietly. 'Lieutenant Wilcox. Yes, he had penetrated deep enough to give us the tip. But not what they had in mind. He didn't get that far . . .'

'They? Who's they?'

'The People's Lobby.'

'Some of them,' interrupted Powell. They turned to him, surprised. Powell saw their reaction, but went on: 'I think this needs to be said, gentlemen.

We're not talking about nuclear disarmers, or pacifists. They are honest, sincere people. Misguided maybe, but by God, decent folk with their heart in the right place. My own daughter is in CND, and proud of it.'

He stopped, and they stared at him.

'The people we're after aren't the anti-war movement, but the extremists who batten on them, who use their enthusiasm and their desire for peace for their own purposes. Who join in the demonstration and latch on to the meetings, and wear the badges and preach something quite different . . .'

'Go on,' said the Home Secretary.

'No, that's all. But it's so easy to tar everybody with the same brush. We're fighting fanatics, loony militants, hard-bitten anarchists, and the one thing we mustn't do is get them mixed up with real pacifists.'

There was a moment's silence. Then the MI5 man said: 'That still doesn't get us back the stolen arms. Or find Wilcox's killers.'

'I'm well aware of it,' muttered Powell.

'On the credit side, Special Branch is putting on a maximum effort, correct?' said the Home Secretary.

Powell nodded.

'And the SAS is on two hours' alert, in Hereford, and in London, with counter-insurgency teams on full standby for instant action?'

'Yes, Home Secretary,' confirmed Colonel Hadley.

'The security service is carrying out a major surveillance on classified "A" suspects?'

'That is correct, sir,' acknowledged Wallace.

The Home Secretary looked mollified but not much. 'On the debit side, the undercover man is dead and we have lost our eyes and ears inside the organization. The sketchy information he was able to get to us – but nothing else, We are groping in the dark, to a large extent.' He saw Hadley's head turn and exchange a look with Major Grant. 'Is there something I should know?'

Colonel Hadley cleared his throat.

'If you'll forgive me, Home Secretary, all I'll say is that if we're lucky, we may be lighting a little candle . . .' Grant was abstractedly studying an oil painting on the wall. 'If we're successful, you may get some light in the darkness.'

The Home Secretary's eyes were cold. He was well known for his tart rejoinders. But all he said was: 'I don't like riddles, Colonel Hadley, but I'm sure the SAS has its reasons for being mysterious.' The politician addressed all of them. 'You know what depends on you all. I don't want Baader-Meinhof gangs, Red Brigades, ETA's, Black Septembers or whatever they call themselves. We've got our hands full with the Irish, and all the other crazies, and we don't need any more. I don't want ministers found shot in cars, airliners at Heathrow blown up, and all the rest of it. We've got enough of our own troubles already. Make sure this thing is crushed.' He looked at his watch. 'If you have nothing else, I'll adjourn the meeting.'

In the corridor outside, Grant whispered to the Colonel wryly: 'I like the way he puts it. "Make sure this thing is crushed." Just like that. Sounds easy.'

'He's a politician,' remarked the Colonel.

Commander Powell heard him as he hurried past. But he made no comment. There were some things one left unsaid.

16

Frankie's rendezvous with her father were usually more in the nature of summit meetings than family reunions. They took place only rarely and were then handled with extreme tact.

Sir Geoffrey Leith adored his daughter, even if she did frequently come near driving him to distraction. He had grown to accept that she led her own life, lived in a trendy apartment, and kept little contact with home. He still found it hard to accept her outlook.

Twice married, Sir Geoffrey had never attempted to explain Frankie to his second wife and the two women had only met twice. His first wife, Frankie's mother, hadn't understood Frankie anyway.

But whenever he met her, Sir Geoffrey's misgivings about his daughter vanished, and he was filled with delight. She was a most attractive girl, he kept thinking, and he noticed with pleasure how, as she walked through the grill room at the Dorchester, a lot of men stared at her admiringly and kept staring.

Frankie always made a point of not letting her father down. She took care to look her best, dressed smartly, and made up beautifully. No radical badges.

No battle outfit or denims and T-shirt with anti-Reagan slogans.

'How are you, Darling?' Sir Geoffrey greeted her fondly.

'Fine, Daddy.'

'Daddy' sounded strange coming from Frankie's mouth. Too genteel. Too juvenile. But he loved to hear it.

She sat down, and the waiter brought her an aperitif.

'How about a nice Dover sole?' suggested Sir Geoffrey.

'I want a steak,' said Frankie. 'A nice big one. Red and bloody.'

She said it to shock him. It was quite childish for a woman of twenty-six, as if his presence gave her an urge to misbehave.

But he had learnt to cope. 'All right then, a rare fillet.'

They were into the meal, when he asked: 'Well, what have you been doing with yourself?'

Frankie's eyes sparkled mockingly. 'Blowing up people, if that's what you mean.'

'Any idea of a job yet?'

She drank the Mouton-Cadet with enjoyment. 'Daddy, you have no idea how busy I am.'

'Doing what?'

'My thing,' she replied, and her voice was hard.

He sighed. He didn't mind the fact that she was living on his allowance, that he was paying her rent. But he believed in work. She was intelligent. She was well educated. Dammit, she should work.

'Look here, Frankie – ' he began, but she cut him short.

'How many millions have you made since we last met?' she asked. It was both a sneer and a challenge.

Her tone angered him. 'You don't know how stupid that is,' he said.

'Well it's true, isn't it? You make millions. Thanks to your mines in South Africa and all the under paid workers your firm exploits . . .'

'Frankie,' he said warningly.

'You know this meal we're having? You know that would feed a family in San Salvador for six months?'

She sat back smugly, like a debater who has scored an unassailable point.

'Let's drop it,' muttered her father.

'That's what Harry Truman said when his scientists told him about the atomic bomb.' She flashed her father a smile of triumph.

The joke annoyed Sir Geoffrey. 'I'll tell you something, Frankie. I was thirteen when the Americans dropped those bombs on Japan. I was earning eight shillings a week. I never went on holiday abroad until I was in my late twenties. Everything I've got, everything you've got, I've worked for. Nobody gave me anything. So give it a rest, please.'

'You'll never understand,' sighed Frankie, and helped herself to a truffle.

After that, they indulged in small talk. He told her he was going to spend a few weeks in Miami, and why didn't she come with him. She said she had too many things on. He asked her to come down to the

country to the estate in Berkshire. She said she'd
think about it. '

As he paid the bill, he inquired casually: 'Are you
still marching on all those demos, getting involved in
all those meetings?'

'Daddy,' she began reproachfully. 'I'm an activist.
I believe. I care. Somebody has to in our family.'

He smiled wistfully. 'Let's have lunch again soon,'
he said.

'I've got a few things on,' Frankie replied. 'But
after that, yes, let's . . .'

If only he knew, she thought, what was going to
happen before they met again for one of their ritualistic get-togethers . . .

Outside the hotel, the Rolls was waiting.

'Can I give you a lift somewhere?' offered her father.

'No, thanks,' said Frankie, 'I prefer to walk.'

17

They had pitched their tents in the field across the
highway from the gates of the big American air base.
A huge banner had been strung between two poles
with the anti-nuclear emblem, and the words 'Peace
Picket'.

The camp, they announced to a television news
crew, would be there for as long as the American air
base remained in business.

'We are reclaiming the land,' said the leader. 'We want to shame those Yanks into departing. We don't want to see this pleasant countryside turned into a nuclear target.'

On the first day of the camp, three policemen arrived and stood around, rather disconsolately, wondering who, if anybody, was trespassing on whose land.

After two hours they drove off deciding that it was a matter for the chief constable. Let him sort out the tangle.

Most of the three thousand US servicemen on the base ignored the campers. To those who passed through the gates of the base, they looked like a group of gipsies.

To the commander of the tactical wing, which was in a state of constant readiness to strike at key Soviet military targets and communication centres, the group was an eyesore.

'Fucking Communists,' he called them at the morning staff meeting. 'Can't you get somebody to run them out of town?'

'They're not Communists,' protested the RAF liaison officer at the Staff Meeting. 'Anyway, they're within their rights,' he added gently.

Basically the protest made little news and the demonstrators were left to shiver with their convictions.

But they came into the political limelight when, unannounced, at eleven o'clock in the morning, Bishop Crick arrived. He had driven down the M4 unexpectedly from London to lend the Peace Picket his spiritual support.

61

Smiling benignly, he walked among the tents, shook hands, spoke a few words of Swedish with some Scandinavian students, stroked a stray cat, and gave a mass blessing to the campers.

'You are claiming back the land for the purpose for which it was intended,' he told them. 'On these fields, cattle should graze and crops grow. That monstrosity over there,' and he pointed an indignant ecclesiastical finger at the air base on the other side, 'is an abomination against the Lord.'

At that moment three jets took off from the base on a training flight, and Bishop Crick, never one to miss a sign from heaven, looked up at them and shouted: 'There go the angels of death.'

It was fortuitous that both television and press were there, thanks to a timely call by the Bishop's secretary, informing them of his unannounced, spontaneous visit.

Later in the afternoon, Frankie and Rod Walker appeared. They too had come from London, and they strolled around the camp. 'Sussing it out' in Rod's words.

They were disappointed.

'Bunch of fucking pacifists,' grumbled Rod. 'Wet behind the ears.'

'Their hearts are in the right place,' said Frankie.

'Fuck their hearts,' sneered Rod. 'We need some activists here. Some commitment. We need political action. I want these Yanks to shit themselves in their pants with fear.'

They distributed a plentiful supply of leaflets,

posters and banners. Rather more radical ones than the camp had displayed so far.

'Down with Reagan', 'No to NATO', 'No Tory Warmongers', 'No Red Scares', 'To Hell With Nukes' now began to appear opposite the air base.

It hadn't been a wasted trip. Under cover of visiting the Peace Picket, Frankie had managed to take some quite good pictures of the air base and the installations . . .

Twenty-four hours later, the nature of the Peace Camp changed. In vans and buses, six hundred demonstrators descended on the field, shouting slogans, waving banners, shaking fists. Rod had mobilised what he liked to call the task force.

The People's Lobby did its work well.

So well that some of the more non-violent pickets decided to leave. The rabble-rousers were too much for them. And far too militant. It was almost as if they were spoiling for a good punch-up.

18

'It's very simple,' the manager of Executive Appointments told Skellen. 'We place you and we charge your new employer a fee which is geared to your salary. But it doesn't cost you a penny. Naturally our executives require special abilities in order to interest potential clients.'

He paused as he studied the form that Skellen had completed. The hard stare from the ex-soldier's piercing blue eyes made him feel uncomfortable. The man generated an air of tension that made it difficult to concentrate. It was like having a panther sitting on the other side of the desk.

'What are your special abilities, Captain Skellen?'

'Executing,' Skellen replied. 'Isn't that what executives do?'

The manager raised his eyes and studied the hard, unsmiling face. 'That's hardly a special ability.'

'I can kill a man twice my weight and strength in thirty seconds without him making a sound. That's about as special as you can get.'

'And that's what you want to do?'

Skellen sighed. 'Look. I need a job and you're one of the largest agencies in London. Some of your legitimate clients may have a use for me. After all, six years in the SAS must mean I could be of some use to someone. All I need is a phone number. If I get fixed up, I'll give you a set of post-dated cheques. Made out to you personally, if you wish, so that your firm's pristine books don't have to be sullied with my name.'

The manager chose his words carefully. 'Do you mean a continuing involvement in your profession?'

'Perhaps.'

'But not for the Queen?'

'Right now, the Queen's not paying my wife and kid's upkeep. I'll consider anything if the pay's right.'

'You mean something – er – unorthodox?'

'Your words – not mine.'

'Take my advice, Captain Skellen. Stay unemployed. Right now being unemployed is more secure than anything. But if you're serious, give me a call tomorrow morning and I might have something for you.'

As soon as he was alone, the manager hunted through his desk drawers and found the card that the plainclothes policeman had given him six months previously. He dialled the number on the card. No extension number was shown – the manager guessed that it was a direct line. The call was answered immediately before the ringing tone sounded.

'Yes?'

'Detective Inspector Lawson, please.'

'Just a moment.'

A pause. Typewriters clattering faintly in the background. Phones ringing. Then:

'Lawson speaking.'

'Mr Lawson? This is Buller at Executive Appointments Ltd. You came to see me a few months ago.'

'What can I do for you, Mr Buller?'

The manager began outlining the gist of his conversation with Skellen but the voice at the other end cut him short:

'Do you have full details on the man?'

The manager glanced at the form that Skellen had completed. 'Yes – everything. Name. A Tooting address that he's just moved to. Even his service number.'

'Many thanks for calling us so promptly, Mr Buller. A Detective Sergeant Pope will be with you in thirty minutes. Please don't discuss this with anyone for the time being.'

19

Skellen took the cup of coffee from Jenny and sipped appreciatively. 'Thanks, love.'

Jenny turned up the lethal-looking gasfire and sat beside Skellen on the ancient sofa. She put her arms round her husband. He grinned at her. 'I reckon that's thirty percent affection and seventy percent because you're cold.'

'Forty percent because I'm cold,' Jenny corrected. 'But a hundred and sixty percent affection.'

The house they had rented was a small two-up, two-down, end-of-terrace semi which, like its South London neighbourhood, had fallen on hard times. What grace it once possessed had been destroyed by a previous owner who had reskinned the panelled doors with sheets of hardboard and had torn out most of the sash windows, replacing them with single panes glass that could not be opened. Damp had stained its way up the wallpaper to waist height on an outer wall. It was a house that had been built when Queen Victoria was a girl and should have been demolished by the time she was a grandmother. 'I'm sorry, love,' he said awkwardly, then angrily:

'Christ – for what they're charging for this dump, they can put some decent heating in. I'll go and see the agents tomorrow.'

'Your job is to concentrate on finding some work so that you can restore my decadent life-style as soon as possible.'

He tried to sound reassuring. 'Don't worry, I'll find something. Either that, or something will find me.'

'Oh yes? And how many people have you seen today?'

'Oh – about six,' he said airily. 'But I was only testing the water. Tomorrow I start making some useful contacts.'

They watched the late-night news on television. The winding-up story was from New York which included a video tape showing a bungled bank robbery by a gang who were unaware that they were being recorded by concealed cameras.

'They did everything wrong that they could do wrong,' Skellen grunted.

Jenny took the empty cup from Skellen and set it down on the glass coffee table – a wedding present from her parents and the only decent piece of furniture in the room. 'How do you know?' she asked.

'Because my training included a three-week course on robbing a bank.'

'You've never mentioned that before.'

'If you're fighting a guerilla war behind enemy lines, you occasionally need funds.'

Jenny smiled. 'I can just see you turning to a life of crime.'

'I can't. A life of crime is for cretins . . . But one crime . . . one big one . . . That's something else.'

Detective-Sergeant Pope of the Special Branch eventually found a phone box that had not been vandalised in Tooting Broadway. He reported that Skellen had settled down for the night and in return received instruction that he was to resume the surveillance from 0700 the following morning.

20

One of the qualities that had made Peter Skellen such a superb SAS soldier was a rare, indefinable sixth sense that could subconsciously read the most inconsequential of signals and correctly interpret the danger. Had Skellen been called upon to explain why he sensed that he was being followed as he strolled casually along Fleet Street, he would not have been able to give a rational explanation: he had an unquestioning faith in his sixth sense which told him he was being followed and that was that.

He turned into Doctor Johnson's Passage – a dark, winding lane that linked Fleet Street with Gough Square. Five minutes later he was sitting before one of the commercial radio station's sales girls, disbelievingly studying the rate card she had given him.

'You mean that one broadcast of twenty-second commercial is going to cost that?'

'Plus Value Added Tax,' said the girl brightly.

'Christ!'

'It's rare to get people advertising themselves on radio as needing a job,' said the girl. 'It shows initiative, so you're bound to get a lot of inquiries. May I have your copy please?'

'Copy of what?'

'The advertisement you want broadcast.'

Skellen unfolded the sheet of paper and gave it to the girl. 'You can shorten it to make it fit.'

The girl read the sheet and shook her head. 'I'm sorry, Mr Skellen, but we'd have to do more than shorten it. It'll have to be completely rewritten. We can't possibly broadcast this.'

'Why the hell not?'

'Well, really – you can't say "prepared to engage in unorthodox operations for the right money and prepared to kill legally".'

'Why not? It's the truth. Legal, decent and honest, and all that crap.'

'Yes, but the "prepared to kill" bit.'

'So? Ratcatchers kill legally don't they? Maybe I'll be offered a job as a ratcatcher.'

She was intrigued by the former army officer and found him attractive. 'Would you take it?' she asked.

'No way.'

'Mr Skellen. All advertising copy has to be approved by the Independent Broadcasting Authority's clearance staff. But this won't get that far because we would never dream of submitting it to them. How about starting off with "Peter Skellen is an ex-army officer, trained to use his initiative, and looking for a job that offers excitement – "' She broke off as Skellen snatched the paper back and stormed out.

Muttering underneath his breath about bureaucracy, he pushed past the security men at the radio station's front entrance and went into the street. Gough Street was quiet. The few people about were not interested in him.

He entered Doctor Johnson's Passage, walking slowly hands thrust into his jacket pockets as if deep in thought. The gloomy passage way was deserted. He walked past a recessed fire exit set into the blank side of a building.

The transformation from a seemingly aimless saunter to a cat-like silent dive for cover on the balls of his feet was instantaneous. Skellen coiled himself like a spring into the recess and waited, all his senses alert – ears straining for the faintest sound that didn't equate with the roar of traffic from nearby Fleet Street. He heard footsteps approaching. They quickened and passed his hiding place.

The training the Special Branch had given Detective Sergeant Pope was no match for Skellen's deadly skills; the young policeman never knew what hit him except that it felt like an express train and that it was on the side of his neck. He was unconscious before he hit the ground, not knowing or caring that he would have been dead had the scientifically-delivered blow been applied with even a fraction more force than it was.

Skellen dragged the unconscious plainclothes man

behind a refuse skip and went quickly through his pockets. The warrant card caused Skellen puzzlement rather than concern. The police had got onto him quickly, but he reasoned that he had little to worry about if they were all as inept as Detective Sergeant Pope.

Skellen dialled 999 from a Fleet Street phone box and told a policewoman in Scotland Yard's Information Room where she could find one of her colleagues.

He was drinking a glass of wine in El Vino's, listening to the lunchtime chatter of journalists and lawyers when the ambulance – lights flashing and siren blaring howled past from the direction of the Strand. Skellen reflected that events were moving faster then he had anticipated. Maybe it was time to make contact with the name that Major Grant had given him a million years ago outside the Bradford Line barracks at Hereford.

A man named Ryan.

21

While Skellen was drinking his lunch Malek was less than a mile away admiring the view of St Paul's Cathedral from the luxurious tenth floor office of the London director of the Tripoli Bank of Commerce and Credit. A teletext visual display unit, angled discreetly into the director's desktop, was scrolling silently through the morning's movements on the London Stock Exchange. Business had been brisk; the Financial Times Index was already up several points on the precious day's trading. Even the Cinderella War Loan was showing some life.

Although the sound of traffic from the street below barely penetrated the double-glazed windows, the frenetic tempo of London's commercial life reached into the carpeted office like a living creature, stirring the adrenalin, quickening the pulse. London was Malek's favourite European city. Vibrant. Alive. The high interest-rate money glut was straining its venerable seams to bursting point. With the abolition of exchange control regulations coupled with favourable corporation taxes, London had taken over from Beirut as the place where Jews and Arabs could do amicable business together.

'It is nice to see you again, Mr Malek,' said the director. He decided that enough time had been allocated to the customary opening pleasantries and asked: 'You have some business to transact in London?'

Malek smiled. 'It amounts to two million pounds, Sterling,' he said blandly.

He opened his briefcase and handed the director an envelope. The director inspected the seal before breaking it and removed a computer floppy disc. He swivelled his chair around and slid back a wall panel beneath a framed photograph of Colonel Gadaffi to reveal a computer terminal. It took him less than a minute to load the disc's information onto the terminal's screen. The required credit transfers appeared as neat columns of glowing characters. They included £100,000 to the International Group for Workers' Control; £250,000 to the Socialist-Islamic Study Centre; £50,000 to the Marxist Institute, and a number of similar sums to half a dozen organizations whose names suggested that they had little in common with the two expensively-dressed, gold-ringed men in the palatial office high above the City of London.

'You will find that they are the usual charitable contributions to worthy causes,' purred Malek while the director checked the sums on the screen.

'Of course,' agreed the director. What the bank's masters did with their oil billions was no concern of his. The director frowned at the list. He pointed to the screen. 'The last entry is for one million pounds, Mr Malek – but there's no special account number given.'

'You will have to allocate one,' said Malek smoothly. He scribbled deftly on a pad with a gold fountain pen and gave the pad to the director. 'That is the full name and address of the People's Lobby, and the name of their bankers. You will see that the money is made available to them in the normal way.'

'The People's Lobby, Mr Malek? A million pounds? Such a Large sum – surely there is a mistake – ?'

'No mistake,' Malek assured the director, showing a trace of irritation. He disliked having his instructions queried. 'They are a new institution that our principals wish to assist. You will see to all the arrangements.'

The director touched one of the computer terminal's keys. 'The sums have now been transferred, Mr Malek. That is with the exception of the last entry, and that I will attend to immediately.'

Malek chuckled. 'I cannot get used to the idea of money flying about as electrons in a computer.'

The director resisted an impulse to say that a million pounds was a lot of electrons for the People's Lobby, whoever they were, but decided against it. After all, not only was Malek known as the Paymaster in certain international circles, but he was also rumoured to be a close confidant of none other than the Colonel himself. He also had a reputation for arranging the meting out of savage punishment for those who incurred his displeasure.

Altogether, a depositor to be treated with the utmost respect.

22

Detective Sergeant Clover was one of the Special Branch's most experienced men at keeping people under surveillance and more successful than Pope in staying with Skellen because he had a certain intuitive instinct that was very nearly equal to his quarry's sixth sense. But nearly wasn't enough; Clover was forced to deliberately lose contact when Skellen pushed his way into the melee of the Portobello Road street market. Several coaches had shed hordes of tourists therefore the market was unusually crowded with a melting pot of nationalities haggling with foghorn-voiced traders over just about every antique small enough and light enough not to louse up airline baggage allowances. The policeman decided that maintaining a sight line on Skellen was too risky – it would mean having to move dangerously close to him through the crowds milling around the bric-a-brac laden market stalls. It would be better to wait and see if Skellen retraced his route. A fifty-fifty chance of renewing a safe distance contact was better than the definite chance of being spotted if he got too close.

Skellen pushed his way through the throng, stopping occasionally and pretending to examine horse-brasses and gloomy Victorian paintings. He was more interested in the traders.

He came to a short, thickset man with red hair who was bellowing the prices of his imitation jewellery in a vowel-mangling Irish accent. His stall consisted of a gaping case festooned with bangles and necklaces which was mounted on a sturdy photographic tripod, It was a stall that could be packed in seconds by its owner.

The trader beamed at Skellen. 'Now you're man of the world, sir. I would recognise them anywhere. How about a tiger's eye pendant for the missus? Only five quid.'

'I'm looking for something rather more exciting, and cheap at the price,' said Skellen.

'I might have something to suit you,' replied Ryan,

just as formally. Then he relaxed. 'Welcome aboard.'
He waited until an American couple, who had started
to browse at his stall, moved on. 'You know where
to contact me when I'm not here?'

Skellen nodded. 'Got anything for me?'

Ryan's voice was low. 'They've got an office in
Greek Street, above the Christian Youth Travel Association. The girl's the live wire.'

'Frankie Leith?'

'Right. Her side-kick's this bloke, Rod Walker. She
seems to run the show.'

'I read the file,' said Skellen tersely.

'They've wormed their way in and now the tail's
wagging the dog.'

Two women came up, and Ryan stopped. 'I'll be
able to get the bracelet in time for your wife's
birthday,' he declared loudly. 'No problem.'

The women went away, and Ryan said softly:
'Keep in touch.'

'I'll be needing your address,' he continued. 'Don't
like unhappy customers. You'll be wanting a
receipt . . .'

He scribbled down the address Skellen gave in a
whisper. 'Good luck.'

A bystander might have noticed that the two
shared one similarity. All the time, their eyes
roamed, as if they were on the look out for over-
curious observers. But it was unlikely that even a
curious bystander would have noticed the envelope
that the trader slipped to his customer. Skellen neatly
palmed the envelope into his pocket.

'I'll tell the boss you've called,' added Ryan.

'Do that,' said Skellen. He paused just as he was turning away. 'Can I make a suggestion, Mike?'

'Always pleased to hear customers' suggestions, sir.'

'Do something about the accent.'

Despite two changes of train, Clover stayed with Skellen on the underground by the simple expedient of keeping him under discreet observation through the windows in the emergency doors that separated the train's cars. To travel in the same compartment would be inviting trouble. Clover wondered why Skellen had visited the Portobello Road market and concluded that it had been to buy his wife a gift.

Following the former SAS officer out onto the street at Tottenham Court Road presented no problems.

He saw Skellen enter the People's Bookshop off Charing Cross Road and decided that the surveillance was at last beginning to pay off. The bookshop was well known to Clover because it was more than an outlet for extremist publications. Although the shop itself was lined with shelves displaying the words of Marx and Engels, the lives of Lenin and Mao Tse Tung, the essays and outpourings of left-wing gurus and far out theorists, it was the alcove at the back which was what the place was all about.

The alcove was a room separated from the main body of the shop by a plastic strip curtain. On its shelves were displayed the periodicals and bulletins that preached the glory of the coming revolution. Here it was all made available to the faithful: the lithographed pamphlets advocating direct action with

77

titles such as *Militancy* and *Resistance*. Among them the lurid magazines with cover pictures of black revolutionaries brandishing Soviet-made rifles; wide-eyed liberated ladies apparently tossing hand grenades; inoffensive petrol-bomb throwers being dragged into police wagons by their hair.

The back room was the gathering place of the followers who wished to re-charge their revolutionary spirit when it became too oppressed by regular meals, reasonable housing and a society that permitted such bookshops to exist. It was also a clearing-house for word of mouth information where those interested could pick up details of where and when the action was due, whether it was protest march, egg-throwing at politicians, or just a gathering of the faithful at a pub.

Clover entered the bookshop when Skellen had been browsing in the backroom for five minutes. He moved slowly along the shelves, pausing to thumb through the verbiage of numerous Trotskyist groups.

Skellen purchased nearly ten pounds worth of assorted publication and left. Clover made no attempt to follow the ex-SAS soldier but continued with his reading. Not because he found the contents of the various journals fascinating but because he considered he had gathered enough material for the day to write an even more interesting report on Skellen's activities.

23

There was no mention of the People's Lobby in any of the magazines. Skellen tore the cover off the last one and fashioned it into a paper hat. Samantha laughed delightedly when he put it on her head. She tugged it off and threw it on the floor.

'Nother!' she demanded.

Skellen made her a replacement which ended up on the floor beside the first one. Samantha considered it a great game. 'Nother!'

'You can't have another.'

Samantha screamed. 'Want mummy!'

'Mummy's shopping.'

The news did not go down too well and led to renewed howling.

'Daddy'll make you another hat.'

Samantha quietened down. Just eighteen months old and already she knew how to handle men. She watched, intrigued, as her dexterous father made her another hat.

An exposed page in the mutilated magazine caught Skellen's eye. He stopped work on the hat and studied it. The Christian Youth Travel Association were proclaiming the low price virtues of their cheap jeep all-in tours of North Africa. Mike Ryan had mentioned that morning that the offices of the People's Lobby were above the Christian Youth Travel Association. What surprised Skellen was that such a respectable sounding organization should advertise in a radical magazine. He leafed through the pages once more. It wasn't such a radical magazine after all – the theme of the articles were rational arguments in favour of nuclear disarmament. The editorial was moderate in tone and was written by a Bishop Crick. He hurriedly dropped the magazine when Samantha, realising that completion of her third hat was being delayed, let rip at maximum volume.

24

It was a minor collision but enough to bring the traffic to a standstill in the narrow confines of the Soho street.

Frankie leapt out of her Porsche, a present from her father, and took an enraged look at the smashed rear-light cluster and dented bumper of her beloved car. She dragged open the driver's door of the following car.

'You fucking careless bastard!' she rallied at Skellen. 'Look what you've done to my car!'

'I'm very sorry, miss,' began Skellen, 'but . . .'

'Sorry!' snapped Frankie. 'You're going to be more than sorry you ignorant, cack-handed burk! You're going to be broke. You know what repairs to a Porsche are going to set you back?'

Skellen wasn't given a chance to reply. He listened with a dutifully apologetic expression whilst admiring the attractive blonde tirading him with the ferocity of a Highland wildcat. A man uncoiled his lanky frame from the Porsche's passenger seat and put a hand on Frankie's arm in a futile attempt to calm her.

'Frankie . . .'

'Now look, miss,' said Skellen quickly during the break in her vitriolic attack. 'Let's swop names and addresses and let our insurance companies do the brawling.'

'For Christ's sake, Frankie,' said the lanky man nervously as carhorns started blaring and a small crowd gathered. 'Let's get out of here.'

'Not until I've dealt with this stupid cunt, Rod!'

'Let's trade names and addresses instead of insults,' suggested Skellen.

'That seems a sensible suggestion, miss' said the older of a pair of uniformed police constables who had appeared from nowhere. Clearly he didn't want to get involved in a lot of report writing.

'Look what the silly bugger's done to my car.'

'You'll be the one who's done, miss,' said the policeman, beginning to lose the patience that nowadays was in increasingly short supply in the Metropolitan Police force. 'You could be done for insulting behaviour. Now take each other's name and address, and the name of each other's insurers and get these cars moving. Please.'

Frankie refused to be calmed down so Rod was obliged to guide her firmly back into the sports car's

81

driving seat. Rod and Skellen exchanged scribbled notes and the traffic began moving again.

'Skellen smiled to himself when he reached the end of the street. In her fury, Frankie had caused a minor injury to a taxi owned by a grieving gentleman whose varicose-veined broken nose precluded him from matching his beauty with her's but whose command of expressive English surpassed even her remarkable ability.

'Fucking peasant,' she swore back at him.

It was very lacking in brotherly love for the proletariat.

25

Chief Inspector Lawson and Detective Sergeant Pope of the Special Branch arrived punctually at the Bradford Line barracks. They identified themselves to the satisfaction of the adjutant and were shown into Colonel Hadley's office.

The SAS commanding officer introduced the two policemen to Major Grant who had also travelled up from London. The dapper major shook hands and sat in a chair in the corner of the office, pencil poised above a slim notebook.

Lawson spotted this and asked: 'Do you mind if Mr Pope takes minutes as well, sir?'

'Not at all. Not at all,' said Hadley briskly, waving his guests to seats. 'Coffee will be here in a minute.' He leaned forward hands clasped together on his desk. 'I had a call from MOD to say that you were coming, so what's this all about?'

'It's about one of your former officers, sir' said Lawson.

'Oh yes? Has one of them taken up with a security risk?'

'Captain Peter Skellen,' replied Lawson, opening his briefcase and taking out some notes. 'I understand he recently left this regiment and resigned his commission?'

'Correct,' confirmed Hadley carefully.

'May I ask why?'

'If you wish.'

There was a pause.

'Why, sir?' Lawson asked, feeling that the army officer was being slightly obstructive.

'Personal reasons,' answered Hadley curtly. 'That is reasons that are personal between Skellen and this regiment. I do hope you're not going to press me on this, inspector. I have no wish to be considered churlish by refusing to give you direct answers to your question.'

Lawson thought that Hadley was being exactly that but he wasn't going to be put off that easily. 'This need not go beyond us and those who have a need to know,' he said. 'Our information is that Captain Skellen had been with your regiment for six years, with a distinguished record – '

'A satisfactory record,' Hadley interjected.

'Okay, sir – satisfactory record. Why should an officer like that suddenly up and quit?'

'Why don't you ask him?' Hadley suggested.

Lawson sighed. He felt that he was getting nowhere. 'I would appreciate your co-operation, sir.'

Major Grant stopped making notes and asked: 'What makes this man of interest to the Special Branch, Inspector Lawson?'

'Don't you take an interest in the activities of your former colleagues?' Lawson shot back. 'After all, they're carrying a lot of information around with them. Intelligence gathering techniques; training techniques; new equipment. If you don't take an interest in their activities, colonel, then we most certainly do.'

'What activities?' Hadley enquired.

'Captain Skellen has been frequenting some undesirable places.'

'Really?'

'I'm not talking about saunas and sex shops,' continued Lawson tersely, working hard to keep his shortening temper in check. 'I'm talking about places such as the "Alligator" and the "Red Queen". He saw Hadley's puzzled expression. Grant had obviously heard of the places. 'Pubs, gentlemen. Frequented by subversives. The watering holes of anarchists and revolutionaries.' He couldn't resist adding, 'I'm surprised the SAS hasn't heard of them.'

'Oh, we try to avoid places that the police have heard of,' remarked Grant. 'We've found that they tend to be full of plainclothes men and women pretending to be anarchists and revoluntionaries.'

Colonel Hadley quickly banished the grin that would have undermined his composure.

'There's more,' said Lawson. 'Skellen had been showing an uncommon interest in extremists. He's been buying revolutionary literature. Browsing in that kind of bookshop. *And* he's been trying to advertise himself as willing to take part in unorthodox operations.'

'Has he actually broken the law?' enquired Grant.

'Not as such. But his activities are causing us considerable anxiety. I'm sure I don't have to tell you just how useful his knowledge and talents would be to the more militant element of our society. So what's he doing mingling with these people? Does he bear a grudge? Is his loyalty in doubt?'

'After six years in the SAS?' Hadley queried.

'I don't know the circumstances he left under,' Lawson replied tartly. 'He hasn't got a job. He's got a wife and child to support. Rent. His money won't last for ever. The man's a walking time bomb and ought to be defused.'

Hadley was silent for a moment. 'I owe you an apology, inspector. It was good of you to take this trouble. I'm only sorry that I can't fill you in on the reasons for Skellen's resignation.'

Lawson wasn't satisfied. 'Okay. So what are we going to do about him?'

'We'll deal with him, you have my word on that,' promised Hadley.

'How?'

'I'm sorry, inspector, but that is an SAS matter. Once again – many thanks indeed for drawing the affair to our attention. I'm most grateful.'

Lawson and Pope rose and said their goodbyes.

'By the way,' said Hadley as the two policemen were about to be shown through the outer office. 'What put you on to Skellen? You don't watch every SAS man in civvy street, do you?'

'I'm sorry, colonel,' apologised Lawson, barely disguising his gleeful malice. 'But that is a Special Branch matter.'

'Cocky little bugger,' Hadley growled when the two policemen left. 'Bloody Special Branch.'

'Licenced to tread on toes,' remarked Grant.

'It's a damned nuisance. The whole thing. What are we going to do?'

'Skellen. A detuning operation.'

'Yes – but who?' demanded Hadley testily. 'It's got to be an outside job. Someone we can trust. The scent mustn't lead back to the regiment or we'll have hordes more London wooden tops like those two tramping all over us.'

The two men were silent for a while until Grant came up with a suggestion that Colonel Hadley considered was nothing short of brilliant.

26

The nights were in sharp contrast to the days. At night the clear skies over the Libyan Desert allowed the warmth that the sun had poured into the harsh terrain during the day to be sucked into space. The proximity of the sea was a help in preserving some warmth so that air temperature was −5 centigrade instead of −10 centigrade to be found a few miles inland.

The young Englishman leaning out of the upper floor window of the derelict building was well-wrapped against the cold because he was wearing the uniform of a US Marine Corps bandsman. A few hours earlier he had been playing handball on the beach with his fellow revolutionary students wearing only shorts.

He shone a torch on the closed circuit television camera that was mounted on a screw clamp attached to the window frame. The camera's lens was tilted down. The young man completed his inspection of the camera's cable and scrambled back into the room. The large Nordic-looking woman was standing before a stack of ten television monitors – all bearing flickering, unstable images of the night scenery around the building as seen from ten different view points. The televisions were powered through a tangle of electric cables that snaked across the floor of the large, once elegant room.

'Well?' demanded the Nordic-looking woman.

'Just the same, Verna. The infra-red tubes in the cameras are very sensitive to low temperatures. They won't work properly when it's below freezing.'

'The nights in England are below freezing next month?' she snapped, obviously concerned about a detail that many have been overlooked.

'No,' replied the student.

Verna nodded. 'That is good. Therefore we will continue the training without the television cameras. Call the others. There is a long schedule tonight.'

27

Colonel Hadley brought the US Ranger and Major Grant another whisky each and a lager for himself. The officers' mess was crowded but the three men were at a corner table where they could not be overheard.

Captain Robert Hagen finished reading the file on Peter Skellen. He handed it back to Grant who returned it to his briefcase.

'An intriguing read, gentlemen,' Hagen observed. 'It answers a lot of questions. Not least why you want him "discouraged".'

'I don't want to know how you do it,' said Hadley. 'Officially, we know nothing about it.'

Captain Robert Hagen was no stranger to sub rosa operations, and this one had particular appeal. Hagen had a score to settle with Peter Skellen. He still had the marks around his neck from when he had tried to tear himself from the rail tracks in the Welsh quarry, and there were occasions in his dreams when he heard again the quarry cart thundering toward him.

Hagen raised his glass in salute to the two SAS men. He grinned 'I'll "discourage" him for you. Leave everything to me.'

'Without doing anything too drastic,' Grant stressed. 'Not too much, and certainly not too little. That could be disastrous. But enough to make it clear that we don't like the people he's mixing with.'

'Will you handle him alone?' asked Hadley curiously.

Hagen nodded. 'This time it's gonna be one to one, colonel. The American way. My way.'

Hadley shrugged. 'Suit yourself, but Skellen is useful.'

'So am I, colonel.'

Grant wrote on a card and gave it to the American. 'We've managed to find out where Skellen is living.'

Hagen pocketed the card and said: 'The report said something about your Special Branch had been onto him. Are you sure they've been called off? If they're following him . . . Well we don't want witnesses . . .'

'We don't want the wrong witnesses,' Hadley

corrected carefully. 'Yes – they've been called off, captain.'

The US Ranger raised his glass again. 'Gentlemen. It's a pleasure doing business with you.'

28

When Skellen told Jenny he broke the news very suddenly.

'I'm going away for a bit.'

That was all.

'How long for, Peter?'

'I don't know. A few days. There's enough money in the bank to cover all expenses. The rent and rates are all up to date.'

'What sort of job?'

'I don't know.'

Jenny looked irritated. 'You're not in the SAS now, Peter. Surely you can tell me?'

'It's all being arranged by a management selection firm. I don't know who my new employers will be. All I know is that they're an international firm. I'm sorry, love – but I'll be back as soon as poss, I promise.'

Jenny decided not to press the matter – she knew it would be useless. Skellen was adept at shutting himself off.

'When?' she asked.

'This evening.'

Jenny nodded and managed a lukewarm smile. 'I'll help you pack a few things.'

'Later.'

Already his mind was elsewhere.

29

Alone in the bedroom, Skellen checked through the £1000 that Mike Ryan had given him in Portobello Road. He counted out £300 in six £50 banknotes and slipped them into an envelope. He wrote 'Frankie' on the outside of the envelope and put it in his jacket pocket.

He moved to the bedroom's bay window and peered down the street without disturbing the new lace curtains that Jenny had hung. The beige Ford Granada was still in position. It was a top-of-the-range Ghia estate with a current registration. Few people who lived in the street's crumbling terraces could afford such a car – especially a new one. Someone was being either very arrogant or very stupid.

30

Skellen parked his car beside Frankie's Porsche in the Princess Anne's car park. He noticed that the damage to the rear end as a result of his deliberate shunt had been expertly repaired.

There was no sign of the Granada Ghia. Skellen smiled to himself at the bizarre comedy that the whole business was turning into: he had followed Frankie and the Granada had followed him.

Skellen entered the pub just as the lights were being dimmed for the act that was advertised alongside notices boasting that the 'Princess Anne' was a pub that served real ale from the wood and not aluminium-kegged Euro-fizz. The synthesized heavy metal pounding out of the shuddering Wems was like a science-fiction force wall and the flashing strobes gave Skellen the sensation of living in a movie being shown on a slow-running projector. He had a non-smokers aversion to such places – the fumes from poisonous but chic French cigarettes pricked his throat and stung his eyes. But the real irritation was the clientele who were moving to seats as he pushed his way to the bar and ordered a pint of draught bitter. They looked alike and sounded alike. Braying laughter; nerve-grating nasal accents trained to talk loudly in restaurants. Media people, a few bright young actresses and a lot of dim ones – some wearing see-through dresses and see-through personalities. Well-heeled advertising copywriters who wanted to be authors, and broke authors who wanted to be well-heeled copywriters. Medallioned fashion photographers with open shirts and single gold ear-rings to proclaim their sexual inclination – presumably because they were too ashamed to talk about them. Intense students and a sprinkling of bearded representatives from Greater London's huge army of social workers. A few impeccably-dressed West Indians. People who would have been outraged to be branded middleclass and yet that was exactly what they were. Skellen was the outsider. The loner who didn't fit. He didn't care. He squeezed himself into a corner and sipped his beer. At least it was decent stuff he thought, and bloody well ought to be considering the outrageous amount they were charging for it.

The music faded and the audience quietened, apart from the scraping of chairs being turned to face the small, raised platform at one end of the saloon. One of the 'Princess Anne's' little shows, staged by the Red Curtain troupe, had a reputation for what aficionados called 'commitment'. Tonight was no exception. Two men took up crouching positions on each side of the platform. They were holding portable spotlights. Despite the gloom, Skellen recognised one of them as the lanky man whom Frankie had called Rod. Two girls stood beside the men, holding aloft a large banner-like red curtain suspended between two long bamboo canes so that the platform was hidden.

The sound oaf Gustav Holst's 'Mars – the God of

War' was faded up over the speakers. The red curtain dropped and the two spotlights snapped on to reveal Frankie lying horizontally on her stomach across two low stools. Her arms were outstretched in an imitation of an aircraft. Her blonde hair was gathered into a ponytail. She was wearing a body stocking with the letters USAF painted on her thighs.

A man, grinning inanely and wearing an Uncle Sam top hat, appeared on the platform. A Stars and Stripes was printed on his T-shirt. He ran his white-gloved hands lovingly and sensually along Frankie's spine. His fingers following the curve of her buttocks. His grin seemed to get broader as his hands slid underneath Frankie and glided along her breasts.

The music swelled. An electronic alarm started blaring. The man playing Uncle Sam looked worried at first – and then the grin was back – broader – more villainous than before. The mounting roar of powerful jet engines was mixed in with the music. Uncle Sam reached under the stools, seized two wooden chocks and stepped back while holding them aloft in triumph.

The thunder of the jet engines increased.

Maintaining her horizontal, arms outstretched pose, Frankie was lifted gracefully from the two stools until she was high above the platform.

The audience clapped, cheered and whistled.

At first Skellen thought that she was suspended from a cable and then he realized that she was being supported on the outstretched arms of a man wearing a black catsuit.

Uncle Sam exaggerated Frankie's upward movements by sinking to his knees, waving up at her and blowing kisses. He shuffled sideways and moved off the platform.

The audience enthusiastically applauded his performance.

Another girl was brought on. She was in the same horizontal flying position as Frankie but she was supported by a taller black-suited man so that she was above Frankie.

The volume of the insidiously primitive music swelled and the noise of the thundering jet engines increased.

The second girl was carefully manoeuvred into position so that Frankie was able to strain her head up in order to plant a long kiss on the girl's pelvis. It was a ghastly, highly erotic parody of the in-flight refuelling of a B52 bomber, with Frankie as the bomber.

The two girls, seemingly locked together, moved slowly through the air. The red curtain went up and the spotlights clicked out.

The audience went wild – clapping, stamping and cheering, falling silent immediately the curtain dropped and the spotlights came on. Uncle Sam was standing in the middle of the platform. A man dressed as a technician rushed on. He was clutching a piece of electronic equipment with wires hanging from it. He grabbed Uncle Sam by the arm and gestured frantically at the piece of electronic equipment – indicating that it was useless. But Uncle Sam wasn't interested and pushed the technician away. A girl dressed as Britannia in a flowing white dress with a Union Jack on her shield came on and tried to remonstrate with Uncle Sam. She was grabbed and forced to wear a sword in the shape of a guided weapon. Britannia tried to take the rocket-shaped sword off but Uncle Sam responded by becoming threatening. Britannia submitted and Uncle Sam gleefully thrust cardboard rockets bearing Stars and Stripes flags into her arms and down the front of her dress.

The scene changed to Frankie again – held high above the platform. The jets roaring from the speakers. The audience was silent – fully accepting that Frankie's lithe body was a B52 bomber. The three girls were crouching beneath her – raising their arms imploringly. Suddenly there was a blinding white flash as if someone had fired a hundred flashbulbs, simultaneously accompanied by a deafening explosion from the speakers. A smoke bomb burst on the platform and the girls screamed and writhed. Among them was Britannia. Smoke started billowing from the rockets she was wearing. She joined in the screaming, trying to pluck the burning rockets from herself as though they were leeches.

The sounds died away and the curtain was slowly raised. This time the spellbound audience remained silent – sensing that applause would be out of place and that the story was not yet over.

Skellen's eyes roamed around the audience. Then he watched the stage again.

The red curtain was lowered. There were no sound effects. No music. Uncle Sam was haggard. His face blackened and his top hat awry. He was stunned.

His expression glazed and unseeing. Britannia was sobbing – her once flowing white dress a mass of burnt remnants that she clutched pathetically around herself. The girls wandered listlessly about. Not caring when they bumped into each other. One of them was Frankie – no longer the bomber but one of its victims. Her tattered dress was bulging at the front to simulate an advanced state of pregnancy. She was crying and clutching her stomach in pain. She appealed to Britannia who turned away from her in shame. Still clutching her stomach, Frankie reached out an imploring hand to Uncle Sam who shrank away from her touch. The first girl, a striking brunette, took pity on Frankie and gestured to the other girls to help. They all gathered around so that Frankie was partly hidden from the silent spectators. They lowered her gently to the floor and spread her legs apart. Frankie gave a cry and arched her back off the platform. The girls soothed her – trying to stroke her brow as she twisted her head from side to side. Frankie cried out again. There was a movement and the first girl rose to her feet holding a wrapped bundle. Frankie lost consciousness. Two of the girls eased her into a sitting position. The first girl rose to her feet holding a wrapped bundle and showed it to the other girls so that they and not the audience could see what was beneath the cover. The girl's faces mirrored their horror at what they saw.

The sound of a baby crying was heard over the speakers. The girls were uncertain – not knowing what to do. Then the first girl bared one of Frankie's breasts and held the bundle in place. The cries of the baby became louder.

Then the infant's crying rose to a sustained, insistent scream. Frankie opened her eyes and reached out her arms. The first girl looked frightened. She hurriedly covered the bundle and moved away. Frankie climbed shakily to her feet and stretched out her hands in a gesture that begged the girl to give her the baby. But the girl turned away, clutching the bundle awkwardly to suggest that she was not keeping it from Frankie because she wanted it for herself, but because she was terrified of the consequences if Frankie saw it.

Frankie suddenly lunged forward and grabbed at the bundle. There was a brief tussle between the two of them. The bundle's wrappings were ripped away revealing a doll with two heads.

Frankie gave one long scream of despair. The spotlights went out and the red curtain was whipped up.

There was total silence for a few seconds and then the applause erupted like a bursting dam. The main lights came on and the audience rose to its feet, stamping whistling and cheering. A girl nearly knocked Skellen's drink flying in her wild enthusiasm. Bar service was restored and the hubbub resumed.

A few minutes later, Frankie emerged in a caftan robe and perched on a barstool next to Rod while two members of the Red Curtain company packed the props into a tea-chest.

Skellen waited. It was only a matter of time before

Rod or Frankie spotted him. It was Rod. He scowled, said something to Frankie and sauntered his lanky frame across the saloon to where Skellen was sitting.

'You. On your feet. We want to talk to you.'

Skellen decided that it was the Rod Walkers of this world that made nuclear holocausts socially useful events. 'Who's we?' he asked pleasantly.

'Me and Frankie Leith. You gave me a phoney name and address when you shunted her car.'

Skellen nodded to an empty chair. 'If Miss Leith cares to join me, I'll be happy to discuss the matter with her.'

Rod grabbed Skellen by the lapels and pulled him to his feet. 'Listen. Her car cost two-hundred and fifty quid to straighten out – '

'Straightening out your face if you don't let go of my jacket is going to cost a helluva lot more than that,' warned Skellen, keeping his voice mild.

Drinkers at nearby tables, sensing trouble, began moving away while warily eyeing the two men. Frankie slid off her stool and crossed the saloon.

'Don't go making trouble over this cunt, Rod,' she said.

'Hello, Frankie,' Skellen greeted her cheerfully. 'Why don't you tell your skinny friend to piss off so we can talk?'

Frankie was about to say something but the expression in Skellen's eyes appeared to change her mind. 'Okay, you can leave it to me, Rod,' she said shortly.

'But – '

'Just go.' Rod released Skellen in bad grace and returned to the bar. Frankie sat down.

'Well,' said Skellen, also sitting. 'You've given me a problem.'

'Which is?'

'How to open our conversation. I could say "what's a girl like you doing in a nice place like this?" but I don't suppose that'll go down too well. I could also say that I enjoyed the show – especially the bit where we got to see your left tit and what a pity we didn't see both of them.'

Frankie's eyes narrowed. 'Or you could tell me why you gave me a fake name and address and continue by explaining when you're going to repay the two-fifty it cost to have my car repaired.'

Skellen laughed. 'It's a deal, Frankie. Firstly only the address was false because the law were crowding us at the time.'

Frankie watched Skellen carefully. 'You don't like policemen, Mr Skellen?'

'I didn't want them knowing where I live, to begin with. The other problem is that I'm not insured, which makes the repairs to your car a problem, and the reason why I'm here,' Skellen dropped the envelope on the table. 'You see? It's even got your name on it. There's enough over to pay for your time and trouble, and to buy me another pint.' He slid his glass towards her and grinned at her surprised expression when she had examined the envelope's contents. 'A bitter please, my angel.'

'I only hope for your sake that those fifties aren't

going to attract interest. I'm known here,' Frankie warned.

'I can guarantee their source,' said Skellen solemnly. 'You don't know how lucky you are, Frankie.'

Frankie raised a quizzical eyebrow. 'Drinking with you, Mr Skellen?'

'Because I think you feel as I do.'

'And how's that?'

'Let's not waste time talking about it. Let's just say we're both people who believe in taking direct action.'

Frankie drained her glass. 'I think,' she said slowly, 'that this is the most blatant pick-up I've ever experienced.' She stood up. 'All right,' she said, edging her way round the table. 'Let's put your monumental conceit and arrogance to the test, shall we?' Rod was waiting for them in the pub's car park.

'What's going on?' he demanded as Frankie unlocked the passenger door of her Porsche.

'None of your business,' she replied, opening the car door.

'Who is this cunt, anyway?'

'Don't be a bore, Rod,' she sighed.

Rod gripped her arm. 'For Christ's sake, Frankie. We don't know who the hell he is or anything about him.'

Frankie's anger flashed. 'Look – just fuck off and leave me alone! You're not my bloody keeper!'

'Why don't you do as the lady suggests,' said Skellen mildly.

'I'll deal with this, Peter,' cautioned Frankie. 'You're not to mix it with Rod.'

101

Skellen moved a couple of paces so that the light shining from the pub's kitchen was directly behind him. Choosing one's strategic position was sound military practice but Rod was standing well – breathing deeply. Skellen could tell he had been professionally trained. He wondered by whom.

Frankie read the danger signals. 'Look – stop fucking about – the pair of you. Peter, get into the car or the evening's finished, and you too.'

Skellen grinned at Rod. 'Oh I don't know, Frankie. Why not let our friend show us what he can do.'

Although Rod's speed surprised Skellen, he was ready for him. Before Frankie had a chance to intervene, she saw Rod make a dive at Skellen. For an absurd instant she thought that Skellen was bowing – twisting his torso away from Rod. Then she saw Skellen's foot lash out. Rod's jaw and the sole of Skellen's shoe met with a sickening crunch. The force of the impact slammed Rod's head back so that he teetered on his feet for a moment, before his eyes glazed and he crumpled to the ground.

Frankie broke the silence that followed. 'Jesus Christ,' she breathed.

Skellen knelt down beside Rod and lifted an eyelid before dragging him by the armpits and propping him up against the low wall that surrounded the car park.

'Is he all right?' asked Frankie.

'At the moment – no. But he will be in ten minutes and his jaw's going to ache like hell for a few days.'

'It sounded to me like you broke it.'

Skellen walked over to Frankie and took her arm.

'I decided to give him a second chance,' he said, guiding her towards the Porsche. 'But next time he gets in the way, I probably won't.'

Hagen waited until Frankie and Skellen had driven out of the pub's car park before starting the Granada's engine. He followed the porsche's tail-lights at a safe distance.

The poor light in the car park had made it difficult for him to see every detail of the incident from his discreet vantage point, but he had witnessed enough to convince him that Hadley had been employing some typical British understatement when he had told him the Skellen was 'useful'. Hagen was no coward, but he was a survivor and he liked to be damn certain that a few odds were stacked in his favour when embarking on a new venture.

Hagen had a buddy in London who would help with the stacking of the odds. That gave the operation a certain piquancy. It might even help assuage the humiliation Skellen had subjected him to in Wales.

31

Frankie set the wine down and got back into bed beside Skellen. His hands were hooked together at the back of his neck. Eyes closed.

'Worth it?' Skellen asked.

Frankie considered. 'Nine out of ten.'

'Blame the beer in that place,' said Skellen easily.

They fell silent for a few moments.

'What are you thinking, Peter?'

Skellen's eyes opened. 'I was just thinking that this pad and your Porsche weren't paid for by hats passed round at radical floorshows in weird pubs.'

'They weren't,' said Frankie evenly.

'Ah. I've touched a nerve.'

'Not at all.'

'So what's the secret? Or is it a case of poor little rich girl wanting to spit out the silver spoon?'

Frankie regarded him coolly. 'What's it got to do with you?'

'Nothing. Just curious.'

'Well now you mention it, I'm curious about something too,' she said.

'What?'

'You. Who are you, Peter Skellen? Or should I ask what are you?'

'An ex-officer but still a gentleman,' he murmured, winking.

Frankie smiled. 'Who with? The bloody Paratroops?'

'As a matter of fact, you're nearly right. The death or glory boys. Who dares win, etc.' He paused. 'The SAS.'

'Are you serious?' asked Frankie, disbelievingly.

'Deadly.'

She stared at him for a moment. 'So why "ex"?' she eventually said.

Skellen's smile did not detract from the bitterness in his voice. 'Officially, I resigned my commission. Unofficially, the bastards booted me out on my arse.'

'Why, Peter?'

'Because. Because. Because.' He hesitated. 'To save the yellow skins of those cringing wankers at Westminster. They and bastards like them created the Ulster cock-up and they put me and my mates in there to clean up their shit. Trained soldiers. But are we allowed to fight as soldiers are trained to fight? Christ, no. We've got to ride round like fucking human targets and be shot at first. Then we're allowed to shoot back if we're still alive, but we mustn't use too many rounds and there's fucking hell to pay if we do, plus about a thousand forms to fill in. You reckon the Provos do that? Do they hell. They're laughing at us. So are the Yanks. So's everyone. And then the politicians run round in circles, screaming about losing the propaganda war, not giving a tinker's fuck about the poor squaddies and RUCs when they cop it, but going bananas when one of their own does.' Skellen stopped. The anger and frustration in his voice was genuine. His feelings were shared by many serviceman who felt that they had been sent in to do a job with their hands tied.

Frankie propped herself up on one elbow. 'What happened to you, Peter?' she asked softly.

'A lot of things, but it was what happened to a friend that was the final straw.'

'Tell me.'

'We were patrolling bandit country near the border. Our Saracen hit a mine. And then they

105

started sniping at us on three sides. We took cover in a ditch that was booby-trapped. My mate was blown to pieces. I worked my way along the ditch and picked off a guy a mile away who was carrying a rifle. Except that I picked out the wrong guy. Of all things, the crazy goon was a Yank VIP on a shooting holiday in the South. It wasn't a rifle I'd seen him holding. It was a shot gun. He hadn't a clue where the border was and was on his way to see what all the noise was about. I wounded him in the arm and got it in the neck for sending rounds outside the firing zone. They paid the stupid cunt more in compensation then my mate's widow got. That's fucking politicians for you. Then we had one visit our unit. A fact-finding tour he called it. He asked me for some facts and I gave him some – real facts – and what I thought of him and cunts like him. And that was the end of Peter Skellen.'

'Are you married?' she asked, unexpectedly.

'No. Are you?'

'No.'

Skellen grinned. 'Good. You know I've a feeling you and I are going to make a special relationship.'

'A very special relationship, indeed,' agreed Frankie, lightly running a finger across Skellen's bare chest. 'How about trying for ten out of ten this time?'

106

32

Sometimes, thought Powell ruefully, it's just like a jigsaw puzzle for which one has all the little pieces, but none of the important ones.

The little pieces lay on his desk: a stack of files from Registry. Each a dossier a fragment of the pattern, yet none producing a total picture.

Powell sighed. He knew these files by heart. The surveillance reports. The Interpol notifications. The Special Branch memos. The movement reports from immigration. The background notes and loose minutes from MI5. The telephone intercept transcripts. A mass of paper. A stack of covert surveillance reports. But in a democracy it counted for very little. It was, so the law said, everybody's right to undermine the law which gave them the right to undermine it . . .

There was, for instance, the file on Malek. Special Branch kept tabs on him and, as a matter of routine, kept C13 posted. Libyans were always of interests to the Anti-Terrorist squad. Malek, clearly, was a courier. He was bringing funds into the country. Money that would be channeled to certain causes . . .

But there was nothing unlawful about that. In fact, if Powell and his men leaned on Malek too heavily, the Foreign Office types would express their displeasure. They didn't want to antagonize the Libyans.

'Considerations like trade, old boy. And oil of course. Don't want to cut off our nose to spite our face, do we now?'

If one of Colonel Gadaffi's followers was foolish enough to set off a bomb, or assassinate somebody, then C13 would act. But the directing of funds to revolutionaries, the financing of extremists, well, as long as it was done legally . . .

Or take the dossier on the Christian Youth Travel Association. Such an innocuous name. Such a worthy organization, promoting cut rate travel for students. Offering them the cheapest tickets for trips to progressive countries. Countries like Cuba and Libya, Mozambique, even Albania. The chance to see exotic, far-away places. With fares, board and keep subsidised of course.

Security had its own ideas about these trips. How the itinerary sometimes included visits to 'peace' congresses in East Germany, to 'freedom' festivals in Havana. Visits on which contacts were made, acquaintances established, youthful enthusiasm directed into the right, if that was the word, quarters.

But again, C13 had to stay passive. There was no law against providing young people with the opportunity to travel. Or a law which prohibited them spending their time with radicals and revolutionaries in People's Republics who fed them interesting ideas . . .

Frankie Leith had a file all to herself. Sometimes Powell wondered if she fell into the old Patty Hearst

108

syndrome – that she had not so much volunteered, as been pushed. Certainly she was a great one for sloganising. She marched in demos like a latter-day La Passionara, and seemed to find herself in the centre of most extremist demonstrations. The People's Lobby was her current great love. She had latched on to the upsurge of anti-nuclear feeling. Cruise, Trident, Polaris, Neutron were godsends to her. Emotive names that inflamed fear, panic and anxiety, and led thousands to follow the dubious pied piper of 'better Red than dead'.

The trouble with Frankie was that she really was a smart girl. A highly respectable background. Her father, Sir Geoffrey, a pillar of the establishment. A family with plenty of money, Frankie, a girl who wouldn't know a factory bench from a coffee table, who had never wanted for anything, who spent more money on clothes than the average worker had to feed his family, who had never seen privation or endured poverty, was an unlikely revoluntionary. And yet, perhaps not. Look at the Baader-Meinhof crew . . .

There were other files. Bishop Crick had one, but that was very sensitive. If it leaked out that an eye was being kept on the good prelate's more worldly activities, that he was known to associate with people who held life and freedom cheap, despite their prot-estations about these very things, the veritable shit would hit the fan, as Powell's colleagues in the FBI might say.

Crick and his ilk had friends, powerful friends, TV personalities who spouted their philosophy, journalists who thrived on it, Members of Parliament who were thinking ahead, an array of supporters with much influence and tremendous political and economic clout.

Powell knew when he had to watch his step. But he also knew in the days ahead quite a lot of information would be added to these files.

33

Skellen was shaving when he spotted the beige Granada waiting outside the block of flats. He swore.

Frankie joined him and peered down at the car. 'Who are they, Peter?'

'They could be anyone. I've made a few enemies.'

Recalling the way Skellen had dealt with Rod the previous evening, Frankie could well believe him. She turned him around so that he was facing her. 'Are you on the run?'

Skellen gave a savage laugh. 'You can't run from bastards like them, Frankie – they're everywhere.'

'But who are they?'

Skellen dried his face. 'Guess.'

Frankie hesitated. 'You're wanted? By the law?'

'Let's say these are people who would like to shut me up.'

She frowned. 'Why? What for?'

'For Christ's sake, where've you been brought up,

girl? I spent six bloody years in SAS. Doing their shitty work all over the place. Working people over because some high-placed bastard in Westminster or Whitehall took a dislike to them and their views. Even eliminating them . . .'

Frankie took the towel from him and folded it. 'You really would like to hit back, wouldn't you?'

Skellen nodded. 'That's what they're shit-scared of – why these gooks are sitting out there now. With my training I could organize something that could hit them hard. Really hard.'

The front door bell rang. It was Rod. The side of his jaw was badly swollen. He scowled at Skellen who was getting dressed then pointedly ignored him.

'You know what the time is, Frankie?' Rod complained, 'We've got a lot of work to get through today.'

'Be five minutes.' Frankie went up the wooden steps that led to the flat's bedroom and emerged a few minutes later wearing an eye-catching scarlet outfit with matching high boots and accessories. She looked like a model. Frankie enjoyed the effect.

'Okay,' said Rod, deigning to speak to Skellen. 'You've had your sniff at the honeypot, now piss off.'

'Rod . . .' Frankie warned. She moved to the window and looked down without disturbing the net curtains. 'Will they make trouble with three of us present, Peter?'

'I doubt it. Anyway – they're leaving.'

'Will who make what trouble?' Rod demanded. He

111

crossed to the window and stared down at the car park. 'What's going on?'

'You're going on too much,' Frankie commented. 'Peter – have you got a job?'

Skellen shook his head. 'Nope.'

'Okay,' said Frankie firmly, moving to the door. 'You've got one now. You can help out in the office.'

'What!' Rod looked stunned. 'You're not serious! I mean – him!'

Frankie opened the front door to her flat. 'There's a lot to be done – envelopes to be addressed and stuffed. That sort of thing.'

'What sort of office?' Skellen inquired.

'Our office. The People's Lobby,' Frankie replied curtly, taking her car keys out of her bag.

And all the time Skellen felt the venom of Rod's look. A rather frightening look.

34

The offices of the People's Lobby in Soho were on the floor over the Christian Youth Travel Association. A glass door at the foot of the stairs led into the assocation's front office. A girl was pounding away at a typewriter. She was surrounded by lurid wall posters advertising cheap overland safari holidays to various North African countries. The colour pictures showed laughing young people draped over Land

Rovers and hanging over the tailboards of ancient Bedford trucks.

'The girl in the show last night,' Skellen commented, following Frankie up the linoleum-covered stairs.

Frankie turned round while Rod unlocked the door at the top of the stairs. 'That's right,' she said. 'Trisha. She loves helping out when we put on a show.'

Skellen looked curiously around at the seedy suite of offices which appeared to consist of three rooms and a toilet. The desks in the outer office, which served as a print room and reception area, were piled high with political leaflets which appeared to have been printed on the filthy offset-litho machine standing in a corner. A row of battered filing cabinets lined one wall, and the walls were obscured by a mass of Blu-tacked yellowing newspaper cuttings relating to the activities of the People's Lobby – particularly the various rallies and demonstrations it had organized. There were gaudy posters that screamed for the abolition of nuclear arms and for the closure of the Polaris submarine base at Holy Loch. There was a large poster bearing a picture of a smiling Bishop Crick. The captain beneath the photograph proclaimed him as A Man of God – A Man of Peace.

The only modern items were an electric typewriter on a desk in one of the offices leading off the print room, and a telephone answering machine.

Rod gathered up the mail. He gave Skellen a malevolent glance and went into the second office, slamming the door behind him.

'What do you think?' asked Frankie, checking the answering machine.

'Scruffy,' said Skellen shortly. He gestured to the photograph of Bishop Crick. 'Who's laughing boy?'

'Bishop Crick.'

Skellen nodded and waved a hand around the offices. 'I've heard of him. Is he behind all this?'

'Bishop Crick is in front of all this.' Frankie corrected. 'He's the chairman. You could say, our inspiration.'

Skellen grinned. 'Sorry. And you and Rod?'

'I'm the secretary – Rod's the coordinator.'

'Does he co-ordinate as well as I do?'

Frankie gave a frown of displeasure. 'We work together. Nothing more.'

'This is your living?' He sounded incredulous.

'It's my whole life,' said Frankie quietly.

Skelln recalled the intensity that had gone into her performance at the 'Princes Anne' the previous evening and decided that he stood little chance of understanding her. He had met them before: Ulster Defence Association organizers; Provos; Sinn Fein; religious fanatics – men and women of every religious and political persuasion whose fervent obsessions amounted almost to demoniac possession and total alienation from reality.

Frankie perched on the corner of a desk and regarded him steadily. 'You don't approve, Peter?'

'If you think you can change the world by peaceful means – then, in my opinion, you're in for a hell of a let down. But then, it's not your political views I'm interested in.'

114

'The People's Lobby is not a political organization.'

'Sure it is. You want those dummies in Westminster to change their policy on nuclear arms therefore you're a political group.'

'We're not aligned to any political party.'

Skellen shrugged. 'If you say so.' He went over to her. 'Anyway, let's not argue politics. They bore me stiff. The whole bloody lot of 'em. What do I have to do to earn my keep?'

'See those envelopes and letters by the printing machine? The envelopes need stuffing.'

Skellen made a coarse observation. Frankie grimaced at the banality of the remark. Rod's door opened suddenly. He glowered at them – his face a mixture of hostility and jealousy.

'Frankie. A word with you, please.'

Frankie went into Rod's office. He shoved the door shut and turned angrily to confront her. 'Just what the hell do you think you're playing at with that burk?' he demanded, keeping his voice low.

'He's giving me a hand.'

'That's a new name for it.'

Frankie's green eyes blazed. 'Can it, Rod.'

'Christ – you've only got to look at him to see that he's got copper written all over him.'

'How's that?'

'He smells it.'

Frankie sighed. 'He's not the law, believe me. I think he'll be useful. Anyway, we've got nothing to hide, have we?'

Rod changed the subject. 'The donation's come through. It's now in the trading account.'

'How much?' asked Frankie.

Rod opened the door and glanced out at Skellen who was folding leaflets on the opposite side of the outer office. He closed the door again. 'Quarter of a million,' he said softly. 'The first instalment.'

Frankie nodded. 'That means we can go ahead.'

Rod shook his head. 'We've got a problem.'

'What?'

'I wanted to talk to you about it last night but you were too tied-up with lover boy. We're a man light on the team. Number Seven.'

'Trisha said Verna would find a replacement.'

'Verna hasn't come up with one.'

Frankie flushed angrily. 'You tell her it's her job to find them and train – '

'It took long enough as it is, getting the team together. Finding and training a replacement in the time available is going to be next to impossible.'

Frankie thought for a moment. 'Can you reschedule the plans so that we can go ahead without a Number Seven?'

'If we could do that, we wouldn't have had a Number Seven in the first place.'

'Shit,' said Frankie.

'Exactly,' said Rod.

There was a silence. 'Okay,' said Frankie at length. 'Let's both do some hard thinking over the next day or so and see what we can come up with.'

35

'Peter Skellen,' Rod told Trisha as soon as a student making an enquiry about a group trip for his university had left with a brochure. 'That's all I know about him except that he stinks of the law and I'm bloody certain that his shunting of Frankie's car wasn't an accident. Stay with him. Find out everything you can about him.' Trisha frowned. 'Nothing more positive?' She enjoyed her trips on her moped.

'For Christ's sake – no,' said Rod with feeling. 'Frankie will go spare. Get the proof first.'

The promise was enough for Rod. Trisha was reliable. Unlike Frankie, she would never allow a weakness for attractive men to undermine her objectiveness and efficiency for the simple reason, that as far as Trisha was concerned, there was no such thing as an attractive man.

36

Skellen was unhappy about Frankie's choice of restaurant. He enjoyed Lebanese cuisine. The trouble was that a number of his former colleagues had also acquired a taste for Middle Eastern cooking while on overseas service, and the intimate Chelsea restaurant was popular with SAS men in the squadron on standby at the nearby barracks. Skellen had taken Jenny to the same place on a number of occasions before Samantha had been born. He pushed his wife and daughter out of his mind and concentrated on Frankie's conversation.

'Peter, what are you living on?' she was asking him.

'Why?'

'It intrigues me. How does an unemployed ex-army killer with no visible means of support run around in his own car, seemingly with all the time in the world?'

'Good question,' he replied. 'If you want to know I'm just about down on my last tenner. That money I gave you just about finished me. I was tossed out of my digs yesterday.'

'So I was just a bed for the night,' she commented coldly.

'Oh, come on, Frankie. You used me as much as I used you.'

Frankie flushed. 'You can be a first-class shit sometimes, Skellen.'

'I can be a first-class shit all the time,' he replied evenly.

'If you think I'm going to give you back that two hundred and fifty, you can go and piss in the wind.'

'I don't care about the money.'

'What then?'

'I enjoy notching up ten out of tens.'

'Thanks for nothing,' said Frankie, trying to catch the waiter's eye with an American Express card.

'Now, you tell me something,' said Skellen. She waited. 'What the hell are you doing with this crowd you're hanging around with?'

'You sound thoroughly disapproving,' she sneered. 'You remind me of my father. Thinking that people who care what happens to the world are bomb-throwing anarchists. He really believes that everybody who's got long hair and a beard and wears jeans is a threat to the constitution. I suppose you've been conditioned the same way.'

'The people who are going to change this world are the people I've tangled with,' said Skellen. 'Men and women – okay – they're killers most of them – but at least they're prepared to die for what they believe in. They're the ones I can understand. The limp-wristed wankers cranking duplicating machines are the ones who make me sick.'

The waiter brought her the credit slip which she signed.

'It's wonderful to be the guest of a liberated woman,' smiled Skellen sarcastically.

'And your chip gets boring after a while,' Frankie countered. 'And for your information, my money comes from my mother's side of the family and a lot of it goes back into what I believe in. Does that satisfy you?' She frowned. 'Although I'm damned why I should justify myself to you.'

They got up to leave. Then she surprised him.

'Well – if you've lost your room, you could move in with me for a few days,' she said.

'You don't know what you're letting yourself in for.'

Frankie gave one of her unexpected and lovely smiles. 'Yes I do – more ten out of tens.'

37

Joe Steeples had taken part in some odd jobs in his time, but breaking into the offices of a firm of architects was just about the weirdest. Luckily Messrs. Fenwick, Housmann and Blackett went in for modern premises with fancy aluminium windows that presented no problems. Joe finished boring through the soft metal with a hand drill and pushed a bradawl into the hole. He carefully levered the tool up and grinned cheerfully at Rod when the catch released with a soft click.

'There we are, guv,' Joe whispered, sliding the window open. 'Like I said – no trouble. And no one will ever notice a three mill hole.'

The two men dropped silently into the corridor and entered the main drawing office. Joe sat on a high stool at a draughtsman's board while Rod searched through the plan chests with the aid of a penlight.

Joe picked up a glossy presentation folder and

examined photographs of tastefully-designed Regency and Edwardian style houses. Some were palatial affairs – twenty bedrooms plus and set in several acres of landscaped gardens. The sort of homes that Joe would never dream of tackling because they were invariably bristling with every alarm system going.

'Looks like they design some fancy pads, guv,' he commented wistfully.

'They specialize in them,' said Rod, finding what he was looking for and pulling two large scale drawings out of a plan chest's top drawer. He unzipped the bag he brought with him and produced an expensive Pentax camera and a tripod. 'You can unlock those filing cabinets.'

'All of them, guv?'

'All of them,' Rod confirmed.

Joe pulled some tightly-packed bunches of keys from his pockets and set to work without complaint. He had nothing to complain about. Not at £10,000 for breaking into a suite of offices that had no security system worth speaking of. Unlocking the dozen steel filing cabinets took him less that ten minutes.

Rod checked that all the venetian blinds were closed before taping the first drawing to the wall by its corners and training a tablelamp on it. He quickly set up the tripod and camera in front of the drawing, adjusted the focus and took several pictures at a selection of apertures to be certain of getting at least one good exposure. He repeated the process with the second drawing.

'Ready when you are, guv,' said Joe, standing by the unlocked filing cabinets.

Murphy's Law – also know as Sod's Law – dictated the building specification that Rod was searching for was in the last cabinet. He repeated what he had done with the drawings – taping the typewritten pages to the wall one at time and photographing them, pausing only to reload the camera with a new film cassette.

'Okay,' said Rod, returning the camera to his bag. 'That's about it. We've got to put back everything as we found it and then we're through.'

'You gonna be doing a stately home, guv?' asked Joe as he relocked the filing cabinets.

'Something like that,' said Rod, noncommittally.

38

Hagen was waiting in the unlit car park outside Frankie's flat with his buddy. To describe Hagen's buddy as a gorilla would be unfair on the largest members of the primate family because gorillas are essentially gentle creatures, not given to violence. But Hagen's buddy was not only given to extreme violence, but was gift-wrapped for it. He owned a nose that had been broken in several places for which some of the pieces had been mislaid during repairs; a face that had been involved in an altercation with a bottle bank and had won; and fingers that would not have looked out of place on a banana tree. Yet in Ranger uniform, he could look quite smart. On this job, however, instructions were specific – only rough civilian clothes to be worn.

'Hi,' said Hagen affably, stepping out of the shadows as Frankie was locking her car.

Skellen froze. 'Frankie!' he hissed. 'Get out of here! Move!' He thrust her forcibly to one side.

The instant's distraction was all that Hagen needed. The American's forward movement was followed through by a blur of a hammer punch that sank into Skellen's jaw.

Considering his size, Hagen's buddy could move like a cat; he came up behind the SAS man and drove a fist at the back of his neck – but Skellen was no longer there. He rolled to one side, hooked his feet round the gorilla's ankles and brought the giant crashing down across the bonnet of a Metro – turning convex metalwork into concave.

It was Hagen's turn. He lunged at Skellen but his opponent suddenly whipped round and laid his cheek open with the jagged end of a broken wiper blade torn from the Metro. The American swore. Gorilla swung a wide punch at space that Skellen had suddenly stopped occupying. Gorilla's fist went crashing through the Metro's side window causing him great displeasure. He threw himself at Skellen. The SAS man used his opponent's momentum to toss him onto the Metro's roof which responded to the treatment by caving in. Its front and rear wind-screens popped from their rubber mouldings like seeds from a pomegranate stepped on by a rhinoceros.

Skellen's resistance ended when a double-fisted, driving uppercut from Hagen connected with his jaw.

Frankie began to watch with interest. What little science there had been in the brawl was suddenly over; Gorilla held the limp body upright from behind while Hagen worked his fists rhythmically from Skellen's face to groin and back again. Gorilla let the still form slide to the ground and the two men went to work with their boots.

'Okay,' said Hagen after a minute's work. 'Guess that's enough to be going on with.' The US Ranger stepped over Skellen and moved unsteadily towards Frankie, blood streaming from his gashed cheek, his knuckles torn and raw.

Frankie shrank away at his approach but the American seized hold of her arm. 'Message for boy-friend when he wakes up, honey,' he said thickly. 'Tell him . . . Not only a present from me, but from the tiptoe boys as well. Tell him.'

39

Rod looked incredulous. 'He said what!'

Frankie turned to him and said: 'They were SAS. They were warning him off.'

Rod gaped at her.

'What the hell are you talking about?'

'They're paying him back.'

'You don't make sense.'

Frankie stopped bathing Skellen's face and came out with it.

'Peter's ex-SAS. He was with them until recently, then they parted company. He was a captain in the SAS.'

'*He was what!*' cried Rod. He stared at her as if she'd gone crazy. 'What the fuck are you playing at? Don't you know what they are? They work undercover. Jesus Christ, they're probably infiltrated him. You're nuts.'

Frankie resumed dabbing Skellen's wounds while she related everything that Skellen had told her about his involvement with the SAS.

Rod shook his head slowly when she had finished. He stared hard at the mass of battered, raw flesh that bore a vague resemblance to Skellen's face. His eyes had virtually disappeared into the swollen cheeks and the sheet bound round his arm was turning red. 'Jesus,' he muttered at length. 'They must hate him pretty bad.' Then he added, thoughtfully: 'If this is for real.'

'Sure they hate him, but not as much as he hates them,' said Frankie. 'We've got to get him to a doctor.'

Rod glanced at Skellen's unconscious form. 'It's too dangerous,' he said. 'A quack will take one look at him and get straight onto the police. We can't risk the police asking questions. Not this close to the deadline.'

'No doctor,' mumbled Skellen.

'Peter, thank God,' Frankie whispered.

Rod's eyes narrowed.

Skellen pushed himself up on his elbows. 'No doctor,' he repeated through torn lips. 'Don't want police onto me. Help me up.'

Frankie helped Skellen into a sitting position and rearranged the cushions behind him. Rod found it incredible that Skellen could even talk let alone move after such a working over.

'Peter, listen,' said Frankie urgently. 'Your arm's badly cut. Really deep. I've cleaned it up but we must get you to a doctor. Do you understand?'

'No doctor,' muttered Skellen stubbornly. He lifted his arm and swore at Frankie's dressing. 'Bandage. Get it off.'

Frankie started to remonstrate but Skellen cut her short. She untied the bandage. The ugly long wound in his forearm yawned open and started bleeding afresh. She tried to staunch the flow.

'Let it bleed. Clean. Need whisky, bowl, needle and thread. Strong thread.

Frankie was back a minute later with the requisite items. 'What are you going to do?' she asked, half-guessing the answer.

'Whisky.'

Rod removed the top from the whisky for Skellen, thinking he wanted to take a swig from it, but Skellen splashed the spirit liberally over the open wound.

'Thread the needle,' said Skellen, beginning to

speak more coherently. 'Give me one of those oranges.'

Puzzled, Frankie gave him an orange from a silver fruit bowl. Skellen tucked it under his left armpit and the flow of blood stopped. 'Presses on artery,' he explained. He held out his hand. 'Needle.'

Frankie handed it to him, horrified.

Skellen's bruised and swollen lips twisted into the nearest he could manage to a grin. 'Gonna show you one of the more useful tricks I learned in the mob.'

Frankie and Rod looked on, white faced, as Skellen began stitching up the gash.

40

Skellen woke at ten o'clock the following morning with a thousand out of sync orchestras playing the 1812 overture in his skull, and a mouth as dry as a Persian brickyard. A demon, armed with a hellish bone-welding machine had gone on a grand tour of his body, locking all his joints while he had been asleep.

Frankie had left a note saying that she would be back at 6pm and that he was to take it easy for the day. She said that his car had been collected from the 'Princess Anne' car park and was outside.

He peeled back a corner of the sticking plaster on his arm and had a vague recollection of stitching the wound the previous evening.

After a whisky that stung his cut lips, a hot bath and some scrambled eggs, he didn't think his jaw could cope with anything else, he began to feel slightly better.

Ryan. He had to get in touch with Mike Ryan. Thankful that he had committed Ryan's number to memory and not left any incriminating slips of paper in his pockets that Rod would have certainly found, he picked up the phone. He changed his mind in case there was an intercept on her line. Skellen knew how the massive tapping operation worked. A computer in a South London centre had been programmed to 'recognise' up to a hundred key words that passed through the 10,000 telephone circuits it was monitoring. Every time one of a 100 key words, such as 'Gun', 'Bomb', 'Ransom', 'National Front', etc., was identified by the computer, the tape reels on the bank of Neal-Ferrograph logging recorders would begin turning. At the end of each 24-hour period, the computer would obligingly provide frequency counts – print-outs that gave the telephone number of the source line the keyword was heard on, the time it was heard and a running total on the number of keywords used. The lists were studied by the various intelligence-gathering agencies and decisions were taken on which lines warranted a direct tap with human eavesdroppers. In a growing number of extreme cases, not only was that particular line tapped, but the lines of every public phone box within a kilometre radius of the 'source' telephone.

From a shaky start in the late 70s, the operation

was now so sophisticated that the computer could recognise keywords in five languages including Arabic, and the overworked London centre had been joined by another in Birmingham, and one had recently been opened near Liverpool to monitor the mainland-Ulster telephone traffic.

Skellen decided to call Ryan from a phone box at least three miles from Frankie's flat. He didn't feel up to driving so he called a taxi which picked him up ten minutes later. Skellen sat well back in the seat as the taxi pulled away so that he wouldn't be seen by the forlorn owner of a Metro, who was standing by his wrecked car discussing his problems with two uniformed policemen.

Trisha followed the taxi at a discreet distance. An open duffel bag was slung from her moped's petrol tank and the tinted visor on her crash helmet made it impossible to see her face.

Skellen pushed the coin into the slot when he heard Mike Ryan's atrocious accent.

'Ryan. It's Tiger's Eye. I want to talk to you.'

'How urgent?' Ryan asked.

'Like right now urgent.'

There was a pause then Ryan said. 'I feel like a breath of fresh air. A walk will be doing me the world of good, so I might be passing Cleopatra's Needle around 12.30. Say an hour's time.'

'I'll be there,' Skellen promised, and hung up. He returned to the waiting taxi and told the driver to drop him off at the Victoria Embankment.

*

Rod was ten minutes late arriving at the pub behind the Strand. The mousey-haired girl was beginning to look anxious. But when she spotted the tall, lanky figure coming towards her, she made no attempt the disguise her relief or pleasure at seeing him. Mary Tinker did not have much of a social life and she had been much struck by this gruff, surly man when she had first met him. They had been out a couple of times, but she hadn't seen much of him lately. Then, to her surprise, he'd phoned that morning and said he wanted to see her urgently.

Typically, Rod went to the bar first and bought himself a drink. He didn't ask her what she wanted, but sat down and gave her a nod.

'How's tricks?'

'I'm all right,' replied Mary. 'How have you been?'

'Busy,' said Rod, but didn't amplify. She waited, intrigued, for him to continue.

Rod was watching her closely. 'Feel like doing something for me?' he inquired, and the way he said it she knew that she didn't have to, but if she refused that would be the end of their relationship. And Mary was anxious to cling to what she had, however little it was.

'Me?' She was genuinely puzzled. What could she do for him.

'Won't take you a minute, love.' explained Rod. 'Just want you to check on something for me. Find out about a bloke. It's quite simple. I want to know about an officer. If he's still in the army. A guy called Skellen. Captain Peter Skellen of the SAS.'

She felt herself going pale. She was a very minor

and unimportant clerk in the Ministry of Defence but she'd had to sign the Official Secrets Act. She didn't know that the little blue form was a psychological device. All it said was that she had read the relevant sections of the two Official Secrets Acts and that she understood them. As a legal document, it was meaningless and was never produced in court simply because the law applied to everyone in the land whether or not they had signed a piece of paper.

'Oh,' she said. 'I don't think I should . . .'

Rod was annoyed. 'Nothing to be scared about. He's either in the army or he's not. If he quit it will be on the records. It's not important but it matters to me. Of course if you can't be bothered . . .'

She gulped. 'I think I'd like a drink.'

But Rod didn't move. 'Won't take you a minute, will it?' he persisted. His eyes were almost challenging. 'I'd be very appreciative, love. Really grateful.'

Mary hesitated. Then she nodded. 'That's all you want?'

'Absolutely.'

'Okay,' she murmured. 'I'll see what I can do, but I'm not promising anything.'

'That's my girl,' smiled Rod. 'Now I'll get you that drink.'

This time Trisha wasn't a 'knowledge boy' but just another tourist. She was idly leaning on the parapet of Waterloo Bridge, picking out landmarks with her binoculars. Only someone watching her with a more than casual interest would have noticed that her binoculars kept returning to Cleopatra's Needle.

Like her, Skellen was leaning on the parapet. He was staring down at the river. The benches along the embankment were beginning to fill with clerks from the nearby Ministry of Defence offices taking advantage of the warm early summer sunshine to eat their lunchtime sandwiches. A few couples were hanging about. It was all very normal. A red-haired man stopped a few yards from Skellen and lit a cigarette, cupping a hand over his mouth. Perhaps he spoke to Skellen while his mouth was covered – Trisha couldn't be certain. And then the red-haired man moved closer to Skellen and seemed to strike up a conversation with him. Trisha decided to get closer. She dropped the binoculars into the duffel bag and wheeled her moped onto the road.

'No one said anything about you having to declare a Third World War,' said Ryan, commenting on the appearance of Skellen's face. 'Or did her husband catch you?'

'Those leads,' said Skellen. 'Frankie Leith and Rod Walker.'

'Any good?'

'Maybe. Maybe not.'

'That's helpful,' Ryan observed.

'But I'm inclined to the maybe.'

'Ah. Reasons?'

'Last night when I was coming round, Walker was jumpy about calling a doctor to see me. His exact words to Frankie Leith were, "we can't risk the police asking questions – not this close to the deadline".'

Ryan digested the information. 'Interesting,' he observed noncommittally.

'I knew you'd be knocked out.'

'No idea what the deadline could be for?'

'Not yet.'

Ryan considered for a moment. 'Okay. I'll pass it on.'

'Do I stay with them?'

'It's not for me to say, but I think you'd better. How are you making out with the Leith girl?'

'Making out,' said Skellen evenly.

'It must be your dazzling good looks. Let's hope she's not too put off by your present appearance.' Ryan turned away from the parapet. 'I'll let you get back to work.'

'Cheers,' Skellen muttered.

Ryan paused. 'There was one thing. The grand I gave you. Keep a mental note of your expenditure, because it'll all have to be accounted for.'

Skellen invited Ryan to do something that would have got Ryan arrested had he attempted it on the street.

Trisha was 300 feet away when the two men separated. She was in a quandary: she guessed that Skellen would be returning to Frankie's flat, therefore it might be more fruitful if she followed the man he had been talking to. Rod had told Trisha not to do anything 'drastic' about Skellen, which was a pity, but he had said nothing about isolating him from his contacts – assuming that the red-haired man was a contact. Trisha decided that he was.

The red-haired man was less successful than Skellen in hailing a taxi. Trisha was 50 feet from him when he broke into a run and boarded a bus. Being a smoker, he climbed the stairs to the upper deck. Trisha went ahead of the bus to its next stop, where she padlocked her moped to some railings, tucked her crash helmet under her arm, grabbed the duffel bag, and boarded the bus when it stopped. The conductor issued her with ticket before she climbed the stairs to the upperdeck. The red-haired man was sitting right at the front. He was the only occupant.

Trisha sat behind him.

Ryan glanced round and saw a brunette gazing out of the window.

She smiled at him. It was a nice inviting smile. 'Excuse me,' she said, 'do you think I could have a light?'

She held the cigarette ready, and Ryan swung round to offer her his lit Marlboro.

Trisha held her cigarette in her left hand. Her right arm moved very quickly. Ryan actually had no idea what was happening. He felt a sudden, sharp pain but by that time the thin, razor-honed blade was deep inside him.

It hurt. It hurt badly.

'Jesus,' moaned Ryan, and then he coughed, and the blood came through his shirt. It was an eight inch blade and Trisha had thrust it into his body, almost to the hilt, so that it cut and severed vital organs. Verna had trained her well.

Ryan tried to move, but it was impossible. He

croaked something, and then his eyes glazed and he was still.

The bus stopped, but Trisha waited patiently. She hoped nobody would climb onto the upper deck, but even if they did they would only see a man sitting slumped.

The conductor sounded the buzzer, and the bus started up again. Nobody came up the stairs. Trisha was cool. Very calm.

She pulled the knife out of Ryan's body – no need to leave the police unnecessary clues. She wrapped a handkerchief around it and put it in the duffel bag. Then she reached inside Ryan's coat, took out his wallet and went quickly through his pockets.

She stood up, walked along the upper deck, and went down the stairs. On the platform below, the conductor gave her a hand to steady her, because she was loaded down with the duffel bag and crash helmet.

'Don't want no accidents on my bus,' joked the conductor genially

Trisha smiled her thanks. The conductor wished she made the journey every day. She got off at the next stop.

Two schoolboys found Ryan two stops later. They had clambered upstairs for a clandestine smoke and had found the body sprawled on the floor.

It didn't need a doctor to know that the red-haired man was dead.

Fifty minutes later Trisha was sitting in a coffee bar examining the contents of Ryan's wallet and pockets.

There was nothing that identified her victim. She decided that that in itself was suspicious. The cheap wallet contained £15, a laundry ticket, a folded scrap of paper and that was all. The most interesting find was the creased square of lined paper that bore a hastily scribbled address: 17 Ringwood Road, SW17.

She located the street in a dog-eared A to Z dragged from the depths of her duffel bag. Once she had carefully gathered up all items that had belonged to her victim, she paid her bill and left.

Mary Tinker phoned Rod and gave him her news.

'That army captain you asked about. Peter Skellen. Yes, he was SAS but he's out of the service. Resigned his commission.'

'Thanks,' said Rod. He was disappointed. Skellen's story stood up. He'd hoped for better news.

'Rod,' asked Mary tentatively. 'Will I see you sometime?'

'If I get a minute,' said Rod brusquely. 'Cheers.'

He put the phone down. She had served her purpose.

41

The car pound was one of few places that could accommodate a London Transport double-decker bus. Its presence caused some ribald comments about over-zealous bobbies from drivers who had come to collect their illegally parked cars. The uniformed constable guarding the bus's boarding platform saw nothing funny about the jokes.

Commander Powell and Major Grant waited until the fingerprint experts and police photographers had finished before they entered the bus's upper deck.

'Yes,' said the dapper SAS officer expressionlessly, when he had examined Trisha's handiwork. 'He's one of our men. Sergeant Michael Ryan.'

'Would there have been anything on him to identify him?'

'No,' said Grant emphatically.

'And yet they knew who he was.' said Powell. He studied Ryan's face for a moment and looked quizzically at Grant. 'Had Ryan worked his way close to anything interesting?'

'That wasn't his job,' said Grant. 'He was a go-between – just a messenger.'

'And yet they decided to kill the messenger,' Powell observed.

'So it would seem,' Grant replied expressionlessly.

Once again Powell wondered if Grant was really human.

42

Trisha cut her moped's engine and dismounted. She surveyed Ringwood Road. The terraced houses had virtually abandoned the struggle of clinging to vestiges of respectability. The rash of estate agents 'For Sale' boards and cards in windows advertising rooms to let was an indication of the state of the economy. It was the sort of street that was the first to feel the bite of a recession and the last to recover. She wheeled her machine along the neglected pavement, looking at the house numbers, and eventually came to the house she was looking for. It was an end of terrace two-up and two-down – slightly smarter than its neighbouring dwellings. A child's discarded toy lay on the tiny front lawn that was hemmed in by a neatly-trimmed privet hedge. An empty milk bottle, with a note for the milkman thrust into its neck, stood on the front doorstep.

A few doors away she saw the postman. Trisha could be charming when she wanted to. 'Excuse me,' she called as she approached the postman with a warm, friendly smile. 'I'm looking for some friends of mine called Skellen . . .'

'Number seventeen,' said the postman helpfully, nodding to the end of terrace house.

'I thought that was the number. Thank you so much.'

Trisha walked back to her moped thinking what a particularly fruitful day it had been.

And it wasn't over yet.

43

The eight members of the SAS troop were led by Captain Robert Hagen of the US Rangers. They were shrouded in black and wore Balaclava helmets and NBC gasmasks. They checked the Dacron ropes that passed through their karbiners. On a signal from Hagen, they abseilled down the ropes from the roof of the house and landed on the first floor balconies. Windows were smashed, stun grenades were fired. The SAS men disappeared into the house with their submachine-guns at the ready. There were several short bursts of gunfire from inside the house. A Range Rover screeched to a standstill outside the house. Four more SAS men leapt from the rear of the vehicle before it stopped moving and demolished the lock on the front door with their submachine-guns. There was more firing inside as the four men burst into the house. A truck, piled high with a wobbling mass of foam rubber high jump mattresses, pulled up beside the Range Rover. Soldiers vaulted over the tailboard and began piling the mattresses to a depth of a metre on the ground under one of the first floor windows. A whistle was blown. Hagen appeared at the window, glanced down at the mattresses and signalled to someone inside. Hagen grabbed a girl by the arm and launched her unceremoniously from the window. She screamed as she plummeted down. She landed on the mattresses, providing the visiting dignitaries with an immodest display of underwear, and was immediately grabbed by a waiting soldier and snatched clear just as another terrified girl hit the mattresses. In the following twenty seconds, several more men and women were tossed out of the upstairs window. They were forced to lie in a row on their stomachs while two hooded soldiers covered them with submachine-guns. One girl rose to her knees to protest at the cavalier treatment, but quickly threw herself flat again when her objections were answered by a burst of fire that kicked up clods of turf near her feet. The SAS soldiers who had gone into the building also jumped down onto the mattresses. The last one scrambled off the foam rubber mountain just as a series of small explosions in the house blew out the downstairs windows. Hagen pulled off his gasmask and Balaclava helmet and crossed to confer with Colonel Hadley.

'Two minutes, thirty-two, gentlemen.' Hadley announced to his visitors. 'Not bad – but not good. This is Captain Robert Hagen of the US Army Rangers. Captain Hagen is with us under the NATO joint-service training scheme.'

The 'hostages' were ordered to their feet and led away. The girl who had risen to her feet was arguing forcibly with her captors.

'What would you call good?' asked one of the visitors, a chief constable.

'We once got thirty people out of a building in under two minutes, twenty,' Hadley answered.

'Who are the girls?'

'WRAC volunteers.'

Another visitor chuckled. 'Weren't they told that they'd be thrown out of an upstairs window?'

'No,' Hagen replied. 'Otherwise what would be the point of the exercise? Under real conditions there wouldn't be time to explain that the terrorists had told us they'd wired the ground floor with explosives and that the detonator was on a timer.'

Major Grant's Subaru stopped near by. The dapper little major got out of his car and nodded to Hadley.

'Where are the "terrorists"?' asked a Home Office official.

'Inside the building playing dead,' said Hadley simply. 'If you would excuse us for a minute, gentlemen. Lieutenant Stevens will look after you,' Hadley handed his guests over to the SAS officer. He and Hagen walked across to Grant.

The Major came straight to the point.

'Ryan's dead, sir. Found stabbed on a London Transport bus.'

Hadley swore softly and listened intently, while Grant sketched in the details – including the fact that Ryan had been thoroughly searched by his killer.

'What are the chances that Ryan had anything on him that might jeopardise Skellen?' Hagen fired at Grant.

'Very slim. Ryan was a shrewd operator.'

'Obviously not shrewd enough,' said Hadley acidly. 'The fact that this has happened even before Skellen got information to him must mean that Skellen's cover, if it hasn't been blown, is now very shaky.'

Grant said nothing.

'And if it isn't then it's not much use to us anyway, unless he risks contacting us directly,' Hadley continued.

'Unlikely, sir. He'll clam up once he discovers that Ryan's no longer active. And he'll never go near his wife in case he leads them to her.'

'Maybe,' said Hadley thoughfully, but let's not take any chances this time.'

'Sir?'

'Put at least two men onto watching his wife. Do it now.'

Major Grant turned to leave.

'And, Eric.'

'Sir?'

'A round-the-clock watch, please.'

44

Frankie and Rod were in the office, running off handbills, when Frankie returned to the subject of Skellen.

'No,' said Rod, taking the same stance he'd taken that morning.

'But think how useful he'd be to us,' Frankie persisted.

'His knowledge of SAS tactics. Their training –'

'No.'

'But he wants to hit back at them, Rod. We'd be crazy not to exploit that chip he's carrying around. And we're a man short anyway.'

Rod stopped work. 'I don't trust the bastard. It's as simple as that.'

'Or is it that you're jealous?'

Rod began to get angry. 'I'm not likely to be the one whose emotions are going to screw-up this operation,' he snapped.

'Then what have you got against him?'

'For Christ's sake, Frankie, he's SAS. Isn't that enough?

'But he's admitted that. How they threw him out. It's not as if he's trying to hide anything from us!

Rod sighed. 'We've only got his word for it that they threw him out. For all we know, he could still be an SAS captain drawing full pay. They could have doctored the records.'

'You checked?'

'Of course I did. Somebody has to around here.'

He broke off when a buzzer sounded. The simple alarm was operated by a pressure-sensitive switch under the stair covering. It was Trisha. She was carrying her crash helmet under her arm and was looking pleased with herself.

'Did you get the prints off to Verna?' asked Frankie.

Trisha nodded. 'The courier should be there by

143

this afternoon.' She glanced questioningly at Rod. 'I carried out your errand, Rod.'

Frankie was suspicious. She knew about Trisha and her 'errands'. 'What's this about?' she demanded. She rounded on Trisha – her eyes blazing. You haven't touched Peter have you? Because if you have – '

'Now calm down,' muttered Rod. 'What is it, Trisha?'

'I've found out where Skellen lives – or lived. He's got a wife and a kid.'

There was a silence. Rod smiled at Frankie's stunned expression. 'Did lover boy tell you that as well?'

45

Verna pinned the plans of the imposing mansion to the blackboard and turned to eager pupils – a team of ten alert young men with the light of revolution shining in their eyes. She tapped the plans with a pointer.

'Comrades – the target,' she announced. 'We now have all the dimensions we need end later we shall set up the partitions in the training building to duplicate the real thing as close as possible. In the meantime we shall go over all the entrances and the positions of the windows. Bring your chairs closer.'

The young men formed themselves into a tight semi-circle around the blackboard. Verna smiled benignly at them. She was proud of them. They were good boys, prepared to work hard for a new future which would see the corrupt edifice of capitalism crumbling to dust.

'We shall have ten days, she said. 'Therefore for the next nine days we shall have to work extra hard. Any questions?'

A hand went up. It was Neilson – a quick-witted young man whom Verna had selected as an assault leader.

'Yes, Neilson?

'We're still one short, Verna. When do we get a replacement? With only nine days training left – '

'I have been assured that there will be a replacement as soon as possible.' Verna replied. She rubbed her broad, powerful hands together. 'Now, comrades. Time is short. From now on there will be no more free periods; no time for playing around. Is that understood?'

It was understood. Not one member of the team raised objections.

46

Trisha went through the files of the Christian Youth Travel Association and found the letter she was looking for. It was an inquiry about block bookings from the Soldiers' Sailors' and Airmen's Families Association which she remembered receiving a few months previously. It was a stroke of luck because the letter heading was exactly what was needed.

She masked the text of the letter with white paper and fed it through the photocopying machine. The result was a clean sheet of SSAFA stationery. She fed it into the electric typewriter and typed an appropriately-worded letter.

Jenny was settling Samantha down in her cot for her afternoon sleep when the front door bell rang.

'Mrs Skellen?' enquired Trisha politely.

'Yes?'

'Good afternoon, Mrs Skellen. I'm Paula Hamlyn from the local branch of the Soldiers' Sailors' and Airmen's Families Association. May I have a word with your husband, please?'

'I'm sorry but he's not at home. He's away on business.'

Trisha frowned. 'Oh dear. And I've come miles.'

'I'm sorry,' said Jenny. 'You'd better come in.'

She led Trisha into the front room, apologising for the mess and placing responsibility for it on Samantha's shoulders.

'Perhaps I can help, Miss Hamlyn?' Jenny suggested when they were both seated.

'Actually, perhaps we can help you.' Trisha opened her bag and unfolded the letter so that Jenny could see the printed heading. 'We look after ex-service families, help them to adjust to civilian life, that sort of thing. Perhaps we can be of assistance to you . . .'

'I had no idea that Peter had been to see you about it,' said Jenny.

'He hasn't,' said Trisha. 'That's why I'd hoped to see him.'

Jenny smiled. 'Well. I'm sorry you've missed him.'

'When are you expecting him back, Mrs Skellen?'

Trisha watched Jenny's face carefully and noticed the fleeting look of anxiety. Or could it have been sadness.

'I don't know,' Jenny admitted.

Trisha smiled and stood. 'Well, not to worry, Mrs Skellen. If he's got a job, it looks as if he's found his feet without our help. I'll come again another time.'

Trisha was back at the office by 4:00 pm. Rod and Frankie listened to her account of her meeting with Skellen's wife.

'Did she say anything about when Peter would be back?' asked Frankie, when Trisha had finished.

'She didn't seem to know. I think she was covering up the fact that he had left her. Most wives must have some idea when their husbands are coming back from a business trip.'

Frankie turned to Rod with a little smile of triumph. 'That proves that he was telling the truth.'

Rod thought for a moment and nodded. 'All right,' he said in bad grace. 'Maybe we can use him after all. But I'm still not one hundred per cent convinced. We don't give him the full details.'

47

While Sergeant Clegg filled in the tenancy agreement, the estate agent examined the documents that the man had given him. 'These are excellent references, Mr Clegg.'

'So why can't I have the house from now? It's empty, isn't it?'

'Yes – of course it's empty. But this bank reference has to be confirmed,' said the estate agent. 'It's most unusual to grant possession of a property at such short notice.'

'I didn't know I was being sent to London at such short notice,' said Clegg laconically. 'And my wife can't stand hotels. Okay – so if it's a month's minimum rental – I'll pay two months in advance.' Clegg opened his wallet and counted out two month's rent. He dropped the banknotes on the estate agent's desk.

The estate agent thought for a moment. There were more empty houses in that particular street than there were takers, and takers were rare birds nowadays. He scanned through the completed tenancy application form. Hugh Clegg. A Ministry of Defence civil servant. 34-years old. Built like a bank vault door. Short haircut. Well-cut safari suit. Not what one imagined a civil servant looked like but respectable-looking nonetheless.

'Very well, Mr Clegg,' sighed the estate agent, opening a drawer and tossing a bunch of keys on his desk. 'I'll make out a receipt, and number forty-six is yours.'

Sergeant Clegg of the SAS left the estate agent's office twirling the bunch of keys on his little finger. He gave Trooper Mike Dowsett in the waiting Range Rover a triumphant grin and leaned on the door. 'Get onto Mr Douglas at British Telecom and tell him we want a phone installed in the house. Tell him we want it by yesterday or sooner.'

Two hours later the two SAS men settled down to keep watch on the Skellen's house from the vantage point of the upstairs bedroom of a house some 100 yards along Ringwood Road on the opposite side of the street.

'Rather be a bit closer, Hugh,' observed Dowsett, peering through the lace curtains at his objective. 'It'll take us best part of ten seconds to get across there in a hurry.'

'You'll do it in five with me behind you,' growled Clegg from the bed, where he was sprawled like a pole-axed bear. He was reading a copy of Goethe's *Werthers Leiden* in its original German. Clegg was one of those men who were difficult to categorize.

48

'Tell me about your wife,' said Frankie, as they lay in bed in the dark.

There was no sudden tension; Skellen maintained his relaxed breathing.

'There's not much to tell. We met. We married. We split.'

'Why didn't you tell me?'

Skellen stroked her hair. 'The answer to that's a cliché, but correct – you never asked.' He added quietly, almost indifferently: 'How did you find out?'

'Never mind. Why did you split?'

'She hated the mob even more than I did. I was prepared to try and make a success of the SAS but she wasn't. The few times I was home, we fought. So in the end we decided that there wasn't much point in me being at home. Also I can be a right bastard to live with.'

'That I can believe. Any children?'

'Hey. What is this?'

'Just curious.'

'A kid. She's eighteen months old now.' Skellen's calm tone cloaked his unease. He didn't like the questions.

'Don't you miss her?'

Sometimes. But I prefer the women who keep me awake at night to be nearer your age.'

They made love again, but Skellen's thoughts were with Jenny.

49

Arif looked up at the lanky young man and smiled warmly. Arif smiled warmly at all his customers and always made them welcome.

'Yes, sir? Can I be of assistance?'

'I need a closed circuit TV system,' said Rod. 'A camera and power supply and a monitor set. You've got a camera in the window . . .'

Arif nodded enthusiastically. 'Ah yes, sir. A very good camera. Very good indeed. And you will be wanting a video recorder to go with it?'

'Just the closed-circuit system,' said Rod.

Arif retrieved the camera from his window. He was about to demonstrate it but Rod cut him short. 'I want it for viewing wild life at night for some research I'm doing. Can you fix it up with an infrared lens system?'

'Yes, indeed, sir. It is no trouble, but it will take two days.'

'I'll pay cash now and collect it the day after tomorrow if that's okay.'

Arif was pleased. 'Very good, sir. It will be ready, I assure you.'

'And I'll need a universal mounting clamp so that I can fix it up on trees and things.'

Fifteen minutes after leaving Arif's shop, Rod walked into another Asian-owned electrical retailer, placed exactly the same order and paid cash. By the end of the morning he had visited a further ten stores and ordered the same equipment from each one. He selected Asian traders as the beneficiaries of his £15,000 spending spree because they were invariably anxious to please their customers and could be relied on to keep their word. To have ordered all the closed circuit television systems from one supplier would have aroused suspicions, and would have made him remembered.

Rod's last call was to a Honda dealer, where he purchased a compact 2-kilowatt petrol-engine generator and a 100-metre length of supply cable. The assistant showed Rod how to operate the machine and the two of them carried it out to Rod's hired car.

50

In terms of attendance figures, the rally organized by the People's Lobby was a resounding success. The Albert Hall looked like the last night of a promenade concert season – the main auditorium was crammed and the tiers were packed to capacity. The difference was that the main entertainment was being provided by a rock group, and the mass banners being waved by the chanting crowd bore slogans such as, 'Sanity In – Nukes Out!', 'Cruise Missiles Off British Soil!', 'Yanks Go Home – Take Your Cruise Nukes With You!'

It seemed remarkable to Skellen that the owners of the Albert Hall were happy to place the dignified building at such risk, not from the crowd, who were obviously enjoying the free concert, but from the ground-shaking, mind-numbing gargantuan amplifiers and banks of speakers belonging to Naked Aggression – the group who only appeared on television during the late hours, and who had earned notoriety by their near-nakedness and their aggression – the latter being directed at their instruments during the finale of their act.

Even more incomprehensible to Skellen was Frankie. She was moving her body in time with the pounding, insidious beat and the blinding, disorientating strobe lights. She was twirling her long hair from side to side, oblivious of him and the crush and the surrounding near hysteria, and enjoying every minute of the experience.

He cupped his hands to her ear. 'Got to go for a pee!' he bellowed.

'Don't miss the finale!' she yelled back. 'And the bishop's on afterwards!'

'Wouldn't miss him for the world!'

Skellen fought his way out into the fresh air and breathed deeply. Not so much because of his relief at

153

escaping the insane uproar and the blinding strobes inside the hall but because it was the first time in several days that he had managed to get away from either Rod or Frankie. Frankie had insisted that he go into the office with her every day and that they take all their meals together. And if Frankie hadn't been with him, there had always been Rod. Watching, suspicious and hostile, willing him to put a foot wrong.

Skellen narrowly escaped being mown down by a car as he crossed. He wondered if his hearing and vision would ever be the same again.

He found a phone box and called Ryan's number. The voice that answered wasn't Ryan's voice.

'Hello?' said the voice. 'Who's that?'

Skellen froze. He held the handset to his ear and listened to the other end of the line, not breathing, waiting for the voice to speak again so that he could be doubly certain.

'Hello?' said the voice again. 'Who's calling, please?'

The speakers may have messed up his hearing temporarily but the voice definitely wasn't Ryan's. Skellen slammed the handset down. He debated with himself for a moment, wondering what the hell to do next and who the strange voice belonged to.

He pushed the phone box door open.

Rod was standing there smiling at him. 'Wrong number?' the lanky young man inquired.

Skellen shrugged. 'She's probably out with her boyfriend.'

'Who?'

'None of your bloody business. But as you're so

curious, my wife. I want to know what my kid needs for her birthday. Satisfied?'

'You're missing out on all the fun.'

Bishop Crick had one thing in common with Christ and Hitler – he had a God-given gift of oratory. For twenty minutes his persuasive voice boomed at the faithful from the speakers. He used no notes or rostrum. His style was the radio microphone and the speech committed to memory so that he could move about the stage – addressing groups in the audience – sometimes individuals – sometimes raising his arms to heaven and addressing a higher authority. His message was nuclear disarmament; an end to the arms race. 'So that there will be world Peace!' he cried. 'Not only in our time! But in our children's time! And in their children's time!' With every pause for breath the most devoted in the crowd, who had pushed their way to the front, roared and stamped their approval and renewed their feverish banner waving.

Skellen noticed that Frankie was hanging onto every word even though a copy of the bishop's speech had been floating about the office for the past week. Her eyes were shining with the light of battle. She joined in the screaming and cheering with enthusiasm like a teenage kid at a pop concert. Skellen realised how little he understood her, but the irrational, by definition, would always defy understanding. One evening a sophisticated rich girl eating lobster thermidor in an expensive restaurant, and the next a screaming banshee in the midst of a sweaty, raving throng of students and militants with whom she had little in common. For the hundredth time that week Skellen wondered if there hadn't been a glorious cock-up somewhere along the line and that the People's Lobby were no more than a bunch, admittedly a well-organized bunch, of harmless idealists. Then he thought of Andy Wilcox, murdered outside the Houses of Parliament, and the telephone that hadn't been answered by Ryan. The trouble was if the People's Lobby were planning something big, where was the evidence? Where were the fanatics who would be taking part? If motivation in itself was enough, then Frankie and Rod had sufficient between them to blow up Aldermaston, but two people could only do so much – maybe an aircraft hijacking, and that was about all. Nothing that would set the world on fire.

Nothing added up.

Bishop Crick had launched into his stride, speaking with passion and eloquence. 'Brethren, we must lift the shadow of death from mankind. Remove the fear that hands over us all. I want children to grow up in a world of peace, not haunted by the four-minute warning.'

Dramatically he paused.

'If Christ walked among us now, I know whose side he would be on. What badge he would wear. I know what *they* would call him too. Left-winger. Unilateralist. I know they'd put him in jail. Well, I tell the cowboy in the White House, we don't want your bombers and your missiles, we don't need them. And they will soon discover that our will, the will of the peoples of the world, is stronger than the Pentagon, or Wall Street.'

The hall echoed with applause, but scuffles had broken out too. A group of skinheads were stamping their feet. A couple of them started fighting. Armbanded stewards rushed down the aisles to calm the uproar. One had knocked a heckler down, and was kicking him.

'Some pacifist,' snorted Skellen.

But Bishop Crick handled it like a master. 'Take no notice, my friends,' he shouted, his amplified voice echoing round the hall. 'Pity them. Be kind to them. They don't understand. These people come to provoke us. Don't give them satisfaction. Ignore them.'

The meeting roared its approval.

One heckler yelled; 'Why don't you go and demonstrate in Red Square?'

Frankie had half risen, fists clenched, her face flushed. 'Bastards,' she cried, 'Nazi pigs . . .'

Skellen regarded the skinheads contemptuously. One group was waving a Union Jack. In another time, another place, he would have ripped it from them. Instead, he said coldly: 'Don't get so worked up. That scum isn't so much different from your lot . . .'

She turned, furious, eyes flashing.

'Nazis, red Nazis, black Nazis, they're all the same breed,' added Skellen. 'A Nazi is a Nazi, wouldn't you say so, Rod?'

And he smiled coldly at the man who was sitting on his other side.

'Shut up,' snapped Frankie.

The commotion had subsided. Some of the bovver-booted thugs were being escorted from the meeting by policemen who had appeared at the exits. Bishop Crick had completely regained control. He raised his arms high, like a Messiah come again, and declaimed: 'Let us fight the good fight. Not the kind of war they plan that will destroy mankind, but *our* fight – the glorious fight for peace. It is a fight that we the People will win! It is a fight we *must* win. And win we shall, my friends, with the Lord's help, with the strength of our united movement. We will win, I promise you, by fair means or foul, because this is one battle humanity cannot afford to lose.'

Fair means or foul. That phrase intrigued Skellen. It hadn't been in the text that he had read in the office.

The crowd exploded with delight. Flowers were hurled onto the stage, and Frankie joined in enthusiastically with the delirious uproar of applause and chanting.

It was a triumph.

'What did you think of it?' Frankie asked, as Skellen drove the two of them home in his Cortina. They had dropped Rod off outside his digs.

'What am I supposed to think of it?' Skellen demanded. 'If you want me to say that it was a resounding success I won't because it wasn't.'

He glanced in the mirror. A car with a blown sidelight bulb was on their tail.

'Don't be ridiculous,' said Frankie. 'Look at the size of the crowd.'

Skellen snorted. 'You provided a free rock concert at the Albert Hall. Of course there was a good turnout. They went to see a pop group, not Crick the Prick spouting platitudes.'

'He's standing up for what he believes in.'

'Like all good pricks,' growled Skellen. 'Look, Frankie – don't get me wrong. I don't want to see this country incinerated. If I thought all this hot air would do any good, I'd be right up there on the platform. But we've had it all before. CND. Marches. Demonstrations. A waste of bloody time. Who takes a blind bit of notice?'

'Christ, you've been well brainwashed,' said Frankie bitterly.

'No, I'm just a realist. I don't kid myself.'

'So!' she challenged him. 'What's your solution?'

'Direct action,' said Skellen quietly.

She stared at him.

'That's the only way to get results,' he went on. 'Direct action. All those dirty little wars I've fought in the SAS taught me one thing.'

'Taught you what?'

He paused. 'That bullets speak louder than words.'

Frankie sat frozen in her seat, not speaking. Skellen glanced sideways at her. He sensed her tension.

Skellen swung down a side street. The car with the missing sidelight followed.

Frankie asked softly. 'Do you mean that. Peter? Really mean it?'

He banged the steering wheel impatiently. 'Of course I bloody do. That's what my mob always used. Direct action. It always worked and it always will work. It's your futile way of going about it which I think is so crazy.'

'Direct action if it meant changing sides?'

'If you mean, do I believe in violence as a means of achieving political objectives, the answer's yes. Because it works and I've seen it work; and because violence is the one thing governments fear above all else. That's why they like to have a monopoly on it.'

Frankie considered her next question very carefully. 'Would you be prepared to fight for what you believe in, Peter?'

'He gave her a twisted smile. 'Sorry, love, I've seen all the fighting I want.' Then he frowned. 'Unless . . .'

'Unless . . .' she prompted.

Skellen hooked the Cortina unexpectedly back onto the Victoria Embankment. Frankie saved herself from being thrown against Skellen by hanging onto a grab handle.

'Hey, Peter. What are you doing? This isn't the way.'

'We're being followed.'

Frankie turned round. 'The car with the busted light?'

'That's the one. It's been with us since we left the Albert Hall.'

'The police?'

He shrugged. 'He must've spotted me at the rally and decided to find out where I'm living. Except that he's not going to find out.'

Skellen drove on at moderate speed. It was gone midnight and there was little traffic about.

'You won't lose him driving at this speed,' Frankie observed as they drove past Tower Bridge.

'Who said anything about losing him?'

They drove in silence along Wapping High Street. The car with the broken sidelight maintained a discreet distance behind them. Skellen turned towards the Thames, threading the car along deserted backstreets between the brooding bulks of disused warehouses. He slowed down as they juddered over the cobbles and turned the car into a dead end that ran parallel with the river. The Cortina stopped where the road ended at the dark alleyway with the Thames on one side and a warehouse on the other.

'Come on. Let's walk.'

Frankie started to protest but Skellen cut her short. They got out of the car and were just entering the alleyway when the car turned into the dead end, swinging its headlights towards them.

'Nice timing,' said Skellen.

'Peter – what the hell are you planning?'

'Direct action, my precious. I'm going to give that bastard, whoever he is, a little lesson in my sensitivity to being followed.'

Skellen took Frankie's arm and guided her further along the dark alleyway. A tug's lights moved in ghostly silence on the sluggish oil-black water. They both heard the car stop and one of its doors open and slam.

'Okay. Wait here,' said Skellen tersely.

He left Frankie and doubled back, crouched low, moving like a cat.

*

Detective Sergeant Pope nearly cannoned into Skellen when the SAS man unexpectedly materialised out of the gloom.

'Well now,' said Skellen amiably. 'I do believe it's my trusty shadow from Gough Square. It's just not your month, is it, Sergeant Pope?'

Frankie peered back along the alleyway. She thought she could hear two men's voices. Then there were noises that sounded suspiciously like punches. A man's cry was followed by a heavy splash.

'Peter!' Frankie ran back. A man's arms suddenly went round her and a hand covered her mouth.

'Shh!' said Skellen warningly.

'Peter! What happened?'

'Nothing. Let's get back to the car.'

The car with the dud sidelight was parked behind the Cortina. Skellen reversed past it and drove back towards Wapping High Street.

'Who was he?' asked Frankie after they had driven in silence for ten minutes.

'A copper.'

Frankie was shaken. 'How do you know?'

'I looked at his warrant card before I dropped him in the river. Don't worry. There won't be any evidence.'

'As long as you're sure,' said Frankie, giving a little shiver.

'Relax,' Skellen assured her. 'They haven't found quite a few of the people I've eliminated.'

51

For Malek too it had been an interesting evening. He had sat inconspicuously in an upper tier, watched the crowd, listened to the rock group, and attentively followed Bishop Crick's words.

He took care not to stand out. It was easy to merge in the big gathering. He knew that, here and there, dotted all over, were Special Branch eyes, and that if he was recognised, it would be noted. Not that there was any reason for him to conceal himself; as a legitimate tourist, he was entitled to attend public functions. But Malek did not like to draw attention to himself.

He would make a report of what he had seen. His masters liked to know how effectively their funds were being used. They had no cause to complain. The People's Lobby had done a fine piece of organizing.

In the throng packed into the venerable hall it was difficult to spot the individuals who mattered, but his sharp eyes picked them out. The Leith girl, Rod Walker. The revolutionary cadre. The key activists. Malek kept away from them, but he knew them well by sight.

Malek didn't mix work with pleasure, but the Leith woman attracted him. If it wasn't for the rigid code by which he had to operate, he would have been happy to pursue the possibility of making a closer acquaintanceship. She wasn't a believer, of course. And he knew well the Koran's caution: 'Verily a maid servant who believeth is better than an idolatress, although she please you more.'

Frankie, by the standards of his world, was definitely a pagan. She dressed shamelessly, and was clearly not averse to flaunting her physical attributes. Also, judged by the women of his kind, she was strident, pushing.

But she was still very attractive. Malek sighed. The discipline of his work, and the good Book between them were hard taskmasters.

Then the fight broke out below. The skinheads started swinging at some of the spectators, policemen rushed in, men fell. There was brief uproar. It was time to go.

Malek slipped out of a side exit just as a couple of police vans drew up with reinforcements. He had timed it just right, and walked away from the meeting via a side road.

The Mercedes was waiting by a parking meter.

'Finished already, sir?' enquired Curtis, holding the car door open.

'As far as I'm concerned, yes,' nodded Malek. He had got to like the chauffeur. He found the man intelligent and discreet, qualities that seemed to be sadly lacking among so many of the English these days.

'Where to now, sir?' asked Curtis.

Malek glanced at his heavy gold watch. It was still

early. 'A little relaxation would not be unwelcome,' he murmured.

'Of course, sir,' said Curtis impassively. 'Were you thinking of a night club, perhaps?'

Malek considered, then shook his head. 'It's not much fun on one's own.'

'Perhaps a companion . . .'

Malek stared at him, his eyes hard. 'Not tonight.'

'No, of course not,' said Curtis blandly. He sensed that beyond a certain point this smooth, suave man was always on his guard.

'You mentioned something about a casino . . .'

'Any time, sir.'

Of course the Koran said that gaming was 'an abomination, the work of Satan,' but a little sin could surely be forgiven. If necessary, he would fast three days and feed ten poor men when the next opportunity to atone arose. That would satisfy the Book.

'You know a good place?' asked Malek.

'I'll take you there, sir,' said Curtis steering the purring Mercedes in the direction of Knightsbridge.

For the next three hours Malek was entertained by a little ball bumping around a roulette wheel. By the time he left he was £21,000 poorer, but he'd had a most enjoyable time, and the casino supplied endless free cups of excellent coffee. He had had a most pleasant evening, and was quite surprised to discover that the crazy English laws forbade him giving the pert little redhead female croupier a tip.

So he gave the £500 to Curtis instead. The man had, after all, had a long wait.

The £21,000 was easily accounted for. The Colonel

gave Malek an extremely generous expenses allowance. He never asked how he spent the money.

Once back in his sumptuous flat Malek made a long Telex report in code about the evening, but he didn't mention the casino visit.

52

'Police have not so far released the name of the drowned officer,' said the radio newsreader. 'But they have said that he was on special duty. The theory is that he slipped and fell when following a suspect.'

Frankie and Rod listened to the interview with a police spokesman that followed the bulletin. The spokesman had little to add to what the newsreader had already said.

'He's a killer,' said Rod. 'Just like Trisha. We don't use Skellen for the same reason that we're not using her.'

'He's a hundred times more disciplined than Trisha,' pointed out Frankie. 'We need him – therefore we use him.'

Rod decided not to argue. Frankie was right: they needed Skellen. They'd just have to watch him.

'Okay,' he agreed slowly. 'We'll talk it over with him tomorrow.'

'We'll *brief* him tomorrow,' said Frankie firmly.

53

The stocky man with the bald head made his way through the blue haze of the public bar and leaned on the counter beside Rod. 'Walker?' He spoke with an East End accent.

Rod looked down at him. 'Yeah?'

'Come with me.'

Rod followed the man into the Bermondsey street. It was dark and a steady drizzle had started.

'They said you'd be the tallest man in the pub,' said the bald man. 'Where's your car?'

Rod pointed to his elderly estate car.

'Give us the keys.'

Two men appeared from the shadows and pushed Rod into the back of his car. He made no attempt to struggle as one of the men pulled a reversed Balaclava helmet over his face. He was thrust onto the floor. The two men sat on the back seat with their feet pressing none too gently into his back.

'Sorry about this, squire,' said the bald man, starting the engine. 'But we gotta be careful, know what I mean?'

'Yeah,' mumbled Rod. 'But does that mean using me as a doormat? Call your friends off.'

The bald man laughed good naturedly and let in the clutch. They drove for fifteen minutes. Rod lost track of the turns the car made but the journey ended with the gearbox whining in reverse and the clatter of an electrically-operated door closing. Rod was allowed to climb out of the car and the Balaclava helmet was whipped off. His eyes adjusted to the bright lights and he saw that he was in a warehouse. The bald man was grinning at him.

'The goods are on their way, squire.'

An electric forklift truck with a packing crate resting on its fork moved under the lights and lowered its burden to the floor. It was driven by one of the men who had bundled him into the car. He gestured to the crate.

'Take a look.'

Rod lifted off the crate's cover. He opened one of the Interarmco-stencilled boxes inside the crate and picked up one of the heavily-greased Sterling sub-machine-guns. He examined it critically.

'I was promised Uzis.'

'You was told wrong, squire,' said the bald man, sitting on a packing case and picking his teeth. 'Uzis are scarce right now. Too trendy.'

'I'm not paying a grand each for these.'

'Oh, but you are, squire. Those gizmos are made in Spain. Not genuine Sterlings. Reproductions with a lot of improvements. But the risks of getting them here were the same. They don't have no serial numbers. And they work a treat. There's a dozen there – count them.'

'I'll take your word for it,' said Rod in bad grace, putting the submachine-gun back. 'And the rounds?'

The bald man nodded to three foil-covered ammunition boxes. 'Three Gs a box, squire. Catch.'

Rod caught the grenade. It was an old British Army pattern but it had been well preserved.

'How about some of those while you're at it, squire? Only a hundred each or a grand a dozen.'

The bald-headed man could have been selling cabbages on a street corner.

'I'll take a dozen,' said Rod.

'And the ten Brownings are five each. You got the readies with you, of course?'

Rod nodded. He was thinking that with the haul from the barracks they now had a sufficient arsenal.

'Old ones?'

'As old as some of this crap you're flogging me.'

The bald man grinned and continued to pick his teeth. 'I make that twenty-seven, squire. Plus a twenty per cent handling charge. Let's say thirty the lot with the hand grenades thrown in.'

Rod was the only one who didn't fall about at the joke. 'The deal was twenty-five,' he said sourly.

'Yes, but there's something you ought to know.'

'Like what?'

'We're a bunch of crooks, squire.'

'What's the importance of next Saturday?' asked Skellen over breakfast.

Frankie's eyes opened wide. She carefully put down her coffee cup. 'Why do you ask, Peter?'

Skellen waved a knife at a wall calendar. 'There's a ring round that date.'

Frankie nodded. 'Oh that – It's my father's birthday on Sunday. I must get him something.'

'Only four more shopping days,' remarked Skellen.

'That's right,' Frankie agreed. 'Only four more days.'

The morning papers lay on the table in front of them. Frankie always skim read them with her first cup of coffee.

'You know there's something that bothers me a bit,' she said. 'It's about that copper you killed.'

'What about him? There's hardly anything about it in the papers.'

'Exactly,' said Frankie. 'A CID man is murdered and it doesn't make the front page. I wonder why?'

Skellen felt her eyes on him. It wasn't a comfortable feeling.

55

They came to the city.

Ten superbly fit and well-trained young men, all eager for battle. With money in their pockets and revolution in their hearts. They came by different routes at different times. Some arrived at Heathrow Airport; some arrived at Gatwick; two passed through the formalities at Luton Airport, and one even turned up on a cross-Channel ferry at Newhaven. Some hired cars and some used public transport. But in all cases their destination was the same.

London.

Some found cheap hotels, two found an expensive one overlooking Hyde Park. A few materialized, all grins and souvenirs, on parents' doorsteps, and one even shacked-up with a girl he met on the train. One arrived at Euston Station in the custody of the transport police for playing a duty-free ghetto-blaster at full volume to the annoyance of the other passengers. He was handed over to one of the hordes of marauding social workers in search of case histories who haunt Euston Station like the ghosts of steam locomotives. He ended up in the clutches of a social worker who was as bent as a bedspring and who had enough hang-ups to start a cloakroom. The young man escaped by boring the social worker senseless with nonstop talk about the coming revolution. But no matter where they ended up, they all called the same telephone number when they were settled in.

One by one, Trisha ticked their names on her passenger list. Michael Harvey was down as Mr and Mrs M. Harvey. Joe Belchamber was down as Mr and Mrs J. Belchamber, and so on. It was a very simple system.

At 4:30 pm on Thursday she called Rod on the intercom that linked her office with his.

'They're here, Rod. Every one of them.'

56

They arrived in England.

They touched down at Mildenhall Air Base in United States Two – the white Boeing in which those ranking immediately below the president travelled.

A cavalcade of official limousines, flying the Stars and Stripes, swept towards it as the steps were wheeled up.

TV camera lenses tightened on the VIPs as they left the aircraft; reporters talked into lip microphones; movie film whirred through camera gates. Shutters clicked. Flashes flashed.

They were the target.

'Christ,' muttered Trooper Dowsett, yawning. 'How long is it going to last, that's what I want to know.'

'Stop bitching,' said Sergeant Clegg from the bed where he was engrossed in Immanuel Kant's *Perpetual Peace*. 'Just watch the house and stay awake.'

But despite his complaints Dowsett had never stopped watching the Skellens', even though this was his fourth on-duty period in the empty house with Clegg. The bedroom had been transformed by the other SAS men, who took it in turns to keep the house opposite under continuous observation. There were magazines scattered all over the floor and the inevitable pin-ups had appeared on the walls. In the corner stood a reel-to-reel Teac tape-recorder that started automatically whenever the Skellens' telephone was picked up or whenever their number was called. The pad on Dowsett's knee recorded every arrival and departure at the Skellen's house. Even the milk deliveries were noted. The SAS trooper yawned again. It was all so bloody boring.

The telephone rang. Clegg answered it 'Yeah?' A pause then: 'Yeah.' Another pause, another 'yeah' and Clegg dropped the handset onto its cradle. The back of the house is now under observation,' he informed Dowsett.

He didn't look happy. It was all going too smoothly.

58

At 10:00 pm, Frankie's video recorder switched itself on and began recording the news. It was still on an hour later, churning its way through a movie, when Frankie, Rod and Skellen entered the flat. All three had been celebrating but Skellen had no idea what they were supposed to be celebrating. Even so, it had been an enjoyable evening and even Rod had been less taciturn than usual.

Rod switched the video recorder off and rewound the tape while Frankie poured drinks for all of them.

'To success,' she said, raising her glass.

'We're not there yet,' cautioned Rod. He switched on Frankie's television and fast-searched through the news until he found what he was looking for.

'Mind telling me what you're on about?' asked Skellen.

'Watch the box,' said Rod curtly, starting the tape.

The picture showed the white Boeing touching down on the flightline. Rod skipped some tape until the VIPs were seen descending the steps from the aircraft and shaking hands with their official greeters: US ambassador, Harrison Franklin and the British foreign secretary, Lord Staunton.

Rod stopped and started the tape, identifying each man in turn while they were frozen on the screen. 'Secretary of State, Arthur Curry,' said Rod, reeling through the VIPs. 'The head of Strategic Air Command.'

It was a formidable delegation, high powered and all heavy brass. A couple of top senators, a group of Air Force generals plus their aides. The silver stars shone and the medal ribbons were six deep.

Rod also stopped the tape a couple of times to look at some other faces in the background. The faces of anonymous looking men in raincoats with walkie-talkies. Security men. Charged with protecting the VIPs.

They seemed to be of particular interest to Rod.

'Quite a party,' Skellen observed when Rod switched off the television and the recorder. 'Enough scrambled egg to make ten omelettes.'

'There's to be a series of conferences on defence strategy and they're going to inspect about a dozen potential cruise missile sites,' Rod remarked.

Skellen twirled his glass disinterestedly by its stem. 'And what's your interest in their visit?'

Frankie sat cross-legged on the floor and glanced at Rod. 'Shall I tell him or you?'

Rod shrugged. 'It's your idea.'

'We're going to demonstrate against the cruise missiles,' said Frankie.

Skellen smiled lazily. 'Extra large banners this time?'

Frankie flushed angrily. 'You were the one who talked about direct action.'

'Well?'

'We're going to take them.'

'What do you mean?'

'Take them hostage,' Frankie stated coldly.

So this is it, thought Skellen. He maintained his lazy, indifferent smile. 'You're crazy!'

Frankie hesitated when she caught Rod's warning expression. 'You think so?'

'Just the two of you? I wish you luck.'

Rod went up the steps leading to the bedroom level.

'Thirteen of us,' said Frankie. 'That's including you.'

'The hell it does,' said Skellen. 'Amateur dramatics aren't my scene.'

'How about acting with one of these, soldier?' said Rod.

Skellen looked up. The lanky young man was leaning on the low balcony overlooking the living-room and was holding a Sterline submachine-gun. He tossed it to Skellen who caught it expertly.

'Neat,' murmured Skellen, examining the weapon with a professional eye.

'Well, soldier?'

Skellen held the submachine-gun by its open stock and looked quizzically at Frankie. 'You're kidding, of course. You? Handling one of these?'

Frankie took the weapon from Skellen without saying a word. She quickly dismantled it and reassembled it, expertly checking the action when she had finished. She got up and stood with her feet slightly apart, holding the Sterling in the correct stance – the muzzle pointing at the floor in front of

Skellen. Her expensive, well-cut trouser suit could well have been a chic combat dress. She looked like one of the idealised freedom fighters to be found adorning the covers of the extremist magazines in the Charing Cross Road bookshop. Her green eyes were fixed defiantly on Skellen.

'Satisfied?'

Suddenly Skellen realised that he was looking at a woman prepared to kill. He had seen the same, fanatic eyes staring at him from the face of a gun-girl in Aden just before she blasted an SAS jeep. Suddenly, he knew what Frankie was.

'It looks like I've been wrong about you and the People's Lobby,' Skellen finally admitted.

Frankie nodded. 'You could say that, Peter.'

'Okay – so you're going to take hostages. What sort of demands will you be making?'

Rod sat down, not taking his eyes off Skellen for an instant. Frankie hesitated a moment as if she was going to reveal their plans. But then all she said was: 'You'll see.'

Skellen shook his head in disbelief. 'You're dead,' he said softly. 'Both of you – and anyone who's involved.'

'Why?' asked Rod.

'Because my old mob will kill you, that's why.'

'Your job is to tell us how not to let that happen,' said Rod.

Skellen crossed to the drinks cabinet and poured himself a whisky. It gave him time to think. 'I can't do that.'

'Why not?' Rod inquired.

'I can't judge a situation I know nothing about unless I take part.'

Frankie walked over to him and slipped her arm through his. 'So you'll have to take part, Peter, won't you? And I'll promise you one thing – you won't regret it.'

And she kissed him hard on the lips. Skellen glanced over Frankie's shoulder at Rod. The lanky young man just stood looking at them. He was very thoughtful.

59

Rod headed the estate car south over Putney Bridge and onto the A3. He drove through Kingston-upon-Thames and parked outside a rundown warehouse on the outskirts of the town off the Portsmouth Road. A faded board on the side of the building advertised secure storage space to let.

'Give us a hand,' said Rod, opening the car's tailgate. Skellen helped carry several cartons into the warehouse. They were marked 'Guido Benno – Theatrical Costumiers'. Inside the building they were piled on trestle tables.

Stacked against a wall were some boxed closed-circuit television cameras plus an equal number of TV monitors, also in their makers' boxes. There was also a bright red Honda petrol generator.

'Thinking of making a television spectacular?' asked Skellen.

Frankie was about to explain but Rod cut in. 'You'll be told when we want you to know. Okay?'

A young man clattered down a flight of wooden stairs. Frankie introduced him to Skellen as Joe Belchamber. 'Peter's one of the team, Joe. So you'd better get to know one another. Where's the team?'

Joe jerked his head upstairs. 'Watching a movie. Windows taped-up so no-one knows we're here. No coming and going.'

'How are they taking it?'

'As they were trained to take it,' Joe replied. 'All keeping quiet and all doing as they're told. A good crowd.'

Skellen could hear movements upstairs. He wondered how many were in the team. The question was answered a few minutes later when they opened the cartons and started unpacking the contents – thirteen USAF uniforms. Each uniform was labelled and numbered.

'This one is yours,' said Frankie.

Skellen stared at the garments, nonplussed.

'Go on, Peter. Try it on. It's not the first uniform you've worn.'

It fitted him perfectly. She had obviously taken the trouble to find out his size.

'Smart,' Joe Belchamber commented. 'Hope mine fits as good.'

Frankie smiled. 'I think Peter would look good in any uniform.'

'Uncle Sam's proud of you,' sneered Rod.

'So what's this fancy dress for?' asked Skellen.

'You'll find out tomorrow.'

They told him to take the uniform off and change into his street clothes again. The thirteen uniforms were carefully hung so that they wouldn't be creased and then shrouded in polythene covers.

'Wouldn't do to be untidy on parade, eh?' grinned Rod.

Skellen had noticed that Rod particularly enjoyed taking the piss out of anything military. He felt curiously set apart from the group. He wondered if he was imagining it, but it seemed as if one of them was always watching him. At one point, the trio stood in a little group talking in low tones among themselves.

'When does the hardware arrive?' he heard Joe inquire.

'Tomorrow,' said Rod shortly. His look silenced any further questions.

'You need a drink, Peter,' said Frankie, noting Skellen's interest. 'Let's go.'

The three of them stopped off for lunch at a busy pub on their way back to London.

Rod, carrying two brimming pints of beer and a half for Frankie, picked his way out of the crowd packed round the bar and set the drinks down on the corner table.

'Where's Skellen?' he snarled.

'For God's sake, Rod,' said Frankie irritably. 'He's gone to make a phone call to his kid.'

'We agreed never to let him out of our sight!'

'It was your idea. I didn't agree to it. What the hell's the matter with you, Rod? Peter's got more reason to be committed to this than any of us.'

Rod turned on his heel and pushed his way angrily past the pub's customers towards the door with the payphone sign.

Skellen thrust a coin into the slot as soon as the ringing tone stopped.

'Tell Grant the Tiger's Eye wants to speak to him,' he rasped, watching the door leading to the saloon bar. 'It's very urgent.'

There was a brief pause then Grant's voice came on the line. 'Grant speaking.'

'Listen. This is Tiger's Eye. The PL are pulling something big tomorrow. I don't know where or when.'

The saloon door burst open. Rod's face was twisted with rage as he strode towards Skellen.

'Okay, darling,' said Skellen, changing his voice to a gentle tone. 'Daddy promises to bring you back the biggest teddy they'll let me take onto the aeroplane . . . Yes – that's a great big promise, poppet. Tell mummy I rang – '

Skellen broke off as Rod snatched the handset out of his hand and banged it down. Skellen rounded furiously on his antagonist. 'Listen, you prick – that was a private conversation.'

'Which was just ending,' Rod grated. 'You're the one who listens, Skellen. I'm not going to have a year's planning screwed-up by a psychopathic peas-ant of an ex-soldier who's never heard of security.

Until this job is over, you don't even fart without my say-so. Understand?'

For a brief moment Skellen's considerable resources of self-control were put to a severe test. The confrontation ended with the SAS man moving past Rod and returning to the bar.

In the Chelsea Barracks, Major Grant of the SAS put down his telephone handset and was lost in thought for a moment. He made two calls: one to Commander David Powell at New Scotland Yard and the other to Colonel Hadley at Hereford.

Things began to move fast.

60

The Army's *Mobile One* was made ready. The huge airconditioned cabin was a portable command centre, equipped with the most advanced communication systems in the world. It could be moved by road or by air when slung beneath a Sikorsky helicopter. The cabin's fibre glass shell could be hermetically sealed from the outside world. It could float, and it could even be deliberately buried – in such circumstances access would be through a hatch in its roof. It could operate from an external mains electric supply; failing which, it had two generators. If they failed, it could always resort to the bank of nickel-cadmium batteries beneath its floor.

There was little that the technicians checking over *Mobile One* had to do because the centre was kept in a permanent site of readiness. They ensured that the coloured telephones were in perfect working order, especially the red one that provided constant link with the prime minister. They tested all the radio channels and the miniature 'Monarch' exchange that patched the command centre into the civilian telephone network. The Creed teleprinters were checked and the row of Muirhead facsimile machines. There were the more mundane items to be checked: making certain that there was an adequate supply of pens and pads, that the water tank was flushed and replenished, that the microfiche viewers for examining large scale maps of the entire United Kingdom were in working order, that the hot drink vending machine was filled with cups and fresh ingredients. The last items to be tested were the external surveillance systems. These included a motor-driven telescopic mast with remote-controlled television camera on top that could be extended to a height of 35-metres, providing the men in the cabin with a birds-eye view of the surroundings.

Part of *Mobile One*'s support was a vehicle that resembled a furniture van because that was what it had been in civilian life. The new owners had not even bothered to remove the original name. Nor had it been issued with an army registration number. The large van was essentially a mobile storeroom, although the army preferred to refer to it as a mobile logistic support centre. The vehicle was crammed with over a million pounds' worth of specialist military supplies in particular those that would be needed in terrorist-instigated siege breaking. In short, both vehicles, and more importantly, the two squadrons of SAS men on permanent standby in the London area, added up to a formidable anti-terrorist task force.

Mobile One's facilities were demonstrated to Commander Powell by Major Grant.

'Impressive,' the senior police officer commented. 'Only one problem.'

'What's that?' Grant asked.

'Where the hell do we send the damned things?'

61

Trisha walked past Skellen, who was reading an evening paper, and entered Rod's office.

'Have you finished for the day?' asked Rod.

Trisha nodded. 'How's everything going?'

'Perfectly. Frankie's moving the rest of the hardware to Kingston.'

'I wish there was a job for me.'

'There is, Trisha.' Rod nodded to the door and lowered his voice. 'I don't trust him.'

'But Frankie said – '

'Fuck what Frankie says. I've always gone by my

gut reactions to people and situations. Skellen worries me.'

Trisha's eyes gleamed. 'So what do you want me to do?'

'Make certain he can be trusted until noon on Sunday . . .'

'How?'

'He's fond of his kid.'

She smiled briefly. 'That makes it easier,' she murmured.

'You'll need help.'

'There's Mac,' said Trisha. 'He wants to help somehow. It's a chance for him.'

Rod considered. MacIntyre was an excitable Scot with a tendency to break into a rage when under pressure or when things didn't go his way. He was one of the movement's most fanatical followers, but his mercurial temper had made him an unsuitable candidate for the weekend's work. He allowed hate to colour his judgement. More than that – the man was psychotic looney. For this job that could be an asset.

'Okay,' agreed Rod. 'Take Mac with you.'

'Starting this evening?'

'Starting this evening,' Rod confirmed. 'And Trisha. You'll be in the house until Sunday, so take plenty of food with you, just in case she hasn't got much in and usually does the shopping on a Saturday morning.'

Trisha nodded. 'Good thinking.'

Rod smiled sourly. 'I'll get Skellen to call his home some time after ten this evening. Give him a chance to know the score.'

62

Dusk was settling when a taxi drew up outside the Skellen's house. Clegg tossed a volume of Kant onto Dowsett's sleeping form.

'Taxi stopping,' remarked Clegg laconically. 'Wake up, sweetheart.'

The two soldiers watched as a man, carrying two bulging Safeway carriers, and a woman holding a duffel bag paid off the cab and rang Jenny's doorbell.

'Looks like she knows them,' Dowsett commented.

Clegg relaxed. 'Yeah. Looks like it. Sorry, Mike – you can go back to sleep.'

'This is Mac, my boy friend,' Trisha explained. 'We've been to look at a flat just round the corner and I thought you wouldn't mind me looking in to see if your husband's back yet.'

'He's still away,' said Jenny. She felt lonely. She was glad of a chance for some company. She held the door open wider. 'But won't you come in for a moment? I was about to make myself some coffee. You'd be very welcome to some.'

'That's very nice of you Mrs Skellen,' said Mac, Following Trisha into the hall and setting down his two carrier bags.

Jenny closed the front door. Her smile of welcome

froze when she came face to face with the automatic that Trisha was pointing at her.

'Not a word from you, Mrs Skellen,' warned Trisha icily. 'We would like that cup of coffee, but first I want you to draw all the curtains.'

Sergeant Clegg looked at his watch. It was 9:30. Jenny's visitors were still with her. He noted that in his log book.

63

At 10:05 Rod placed Frankie's telephone on the coffee table in front of Skellen.

'What's that for?' asked Skellen.

'You're going to make a phone call.'

Skellen glanced at Frankie who was looking at Rod in surprise.

'Dial your wife,' ordered Rod.

Skellen met Rod's cold, unsmiling eyes. 'Why should I?'

'You were keen enough to call her at lunchtime.'

'If you must know, I wanted to hear my child's voice.'

'Well, now I'm giving you a chance to hear it again.'

'What's going on, Rod?' demanded Frankie.

'I want soldier boy here to call his wife.'

Skellen shrugged, picked up the handset and dialled Jenny's number. Jenny answered, but even before she spoke, Skellen sensed that something was wrong.

'Hello, Jenny . . .'

'Peter!' Jenny broke in hysterically. 'There's two of them! They're going to – '

There was the sound of the phone being grabbed from Jenny. Trisha's voice came on the line. 'Hello, Peter. Nice of you to ring. Be a good boy.'

Then the line went dead.

Frankie plainly heard what happened but remained silent. Rod took the handset from Skellen and replaced it. Skellen's face was ashen. He stared at Rod.

'What's all that in aid of?' Skellen inquired evenly.

Rod smirked. 'I think you can guess, soldier boy. Insurance. Life insurance that is. Just to make sure that you don't step out of line, otherwise your daughter . . .' He left the sentence unfinished.

'You know what your trouble is, Rod?' said Frankie. 'You've seen too many second-rate movies. Peter's one hundred per cent with us.'

'In that case he's got nothing to worry about, has he?' said Rod, not taking his eyes off Skellen for an instant. 'Presumably there's a radio or television in your house?'

Skellen nodded.

'So if Trisha sees that everything has gone according to plan by noon on Sunday, she'll leave your wife and kid alone. Fair enough?'

There was a brief pause before Skellen answered.

When he did, his voice was flat, devoid of expression. He merely shrugged and said: 'Fair enough.'

64

Major Grant listened to the tape-recorded conversation between Skellen and Trisha for a second time. He picked up the night-sight binoculars and studied the Skellens' house again.

'The odd thing, Hugh,' said Grant, 'is that you say Jenny recognised them when she answered the door?'

'Well that's how it looked to me,' said Clegg.

Major Grant was still watching the house through the binoculars. 'What's the name of the neighbours in the adjoining property?'

Dowsett consulted an electoral register for the street. 'A couple – Martin, Alan C. And Martin, Christine J.'

'Okay,' said Grant. 'Let's pay Mr Martin a visit.'

Alan Martin was balding, and middle-aged. His wife was visiting her sister in Wolverhampton and he seemed quite pleased at the thought of some unexpected callers, even though he was not really quite clear just exactly who these men in civilian clothes were. Police? Home Office? Army? Something to do with the authorities anyway. They may have used the word security.

He gaped a little when Major Grant explained that there was what he termed 'a hostage situation' in progress next door and that they would be grateful for his co-operation.

What that co-operation would entail he was due to find out, and a lot of it would provide a topic of conversation for a long time ahead.

'Are these people armed?' he asked a little anxiously.

'There's nothing to worry about,' Major Grant reassured him. 'Everything is under control.'

Inwardly, Grant wished it was. He had a growing feeling that they were about to confront a major crisis.

'Please,' said Martin, glancing anxiously at the dividing wall as though he expected bullets to come smashing through the ancient plaster. 'Do whatever you have to.'

'Do you normally watch television at this time, Mr Martin?' asked Grant.

'Yes. The Friday night film.'

'Then keep your television on.'

There were three gentle taps on the front door. Dowsett entered carrying an audio amplifier and a box of assorted microphones.

'We think they're in the front room,' Grant informed Dowsett.

Dowsett nodded and selected a microphone that was fitted with an inverted dish. Clegg held the microphone against the wall while Dowsett pulled on a pair of headphones and switched the amplifier on. He adjusted the controls and listened intently. Clegg repositioned the microphone several times in response to Dowsett's gestures. He listened again and took the headphones off.

'They're in the front room all right. The man's quite close to the wall. I can't make out what they're saying but they're not moving about.'

'Okay,' said Grant briskly. 'Let's get down to work.'

65

It was almost like being back in the regiment, thought Skellen surveying the row of campbeds in the room above the warehouse. A bronzed, fit-looking man was standing to attention beside each bed. They looked very smart in their snug-fitting uniforms.

'Okay, stand easy,' said Rod. 'We've got a long day tomorrow so we're all having an early night.'

There were no complaints. The team did exactly as they were told. The thirteen men undressed and carefully hung their uniforms on a row of hangers. Two men were posted on watch. The other eleven men climbed into their campbeds and the lights were extinguished. By midnight, all that could be heard in the warehouse was the sound of snoring.

Skellen lay awake for some time, wondering how

he could reach a telephone and decided that it was going to be impossible. For one thing Rod had devised a rota so that two members of the team were always on watch. Skellen wasn't included on the rota. The taciturn, lanky, young man was a good planner.

Apart from the danger that Jenny and Samantha were in, it was Rod's organizational ability that was worrying Skellen. It was organization, or the lack of it, that was a major weakness in more terrorist operations.

66

Clegg and Dowsett moved on tiptoe as they carefully shifted Alan Martin's furniture away from the wall and set it down without making an unnecessary sound. They left the television blaring in the corner. Grant helped them spread dust sheets on the floor. Alan Martin watched the proceedings in disbelief as Clegg silently worked an icepick into the wall a metre above the floor and prised a section of plaster away. Dowsett seized hold of the plaster and eased it back and forth until it came away in his hands. Small crumbs of plaster were hanging from the main piece by coarse hairs.

Dowsett gave Grant a triumphant grin. 'Look at that. Fibrous plaster. We're laughing.'

Grant examined the lump of plaster with some satisfaction. 19th Century builders mixed horsehair into their plaster to help it bind together as a mass. Also, fibrous plaster had a degree of flexibility; it had none of the brittleness of modern plasters and therefore was not prone to cracking.

'Providing it's the same on the other side of the wall,' Grant remarked cautiously.

'I'm sure it will be,' said Alan Martin. 'This used to be my mother's house. I've lived here all my life and I don't think there's been that much rebuilding.'

'How about war damage rebuilding?' asked Grant.

'This street was lucky,' Alan Martin answered. 'It escaped the worst of the blitz.'

Clegg worked some more plaster away from the wall and exposed some thin horizontal wooden strips. 'Better and better,' the soldier observed. 'Lath and plaster. We're quids in, although I'll need some help getting the rest of the plaster off.'

Grant used Alan Martin's phone. Two technicians entered the room at five-minute intervals from an army truck parked in a neighbouring street. They silently unpacked their tools and helped Clegg gently prise the plaster away from a square metre of wall. Clegg brushed the loose plaster away from the exposed horizontal laths with a stiff brush, taking care to prevent the larger pieces from falling to the floor by catching them in a plastic dustpan. He and Grant tested the strength of the laths. Over 150 years old and they were still sound.

'What next?' asked Clegg. 'An endoscope?'

Grant nodded. 'Yes. We ought to see what they're

up to first. You'll need the electrospark machine equipment.'

Samantha woke up and started crying. Trisha's expression hardened. 'Shut her up.'

Jenny cuddled Samantha and made soothing noises. Eventually she quietened down.

'She ought to be in bed,' said Jenny.

'I'll take her up,' offered Mac, standing up.

'No!' said Jenny vehemently, holding Samantha tightly to her. 'You're not going to touch her.'

Mac shrugged and sat down again.

Alan Martin watched with bewilderment as the two technicians carried the heavy electrospark erosion machine into his front room and set it down on the floor. They tapped its heavy supply leads directly into the mains because ordinary domestic electrical sockets could not handle the machine's loads.

'What on earth is that thing?' he asked.

'It's an industrial device that uses an ultra-high temperature spark to machine ceramics,' Grant explained. 'It melts the ceramic and it works just as well on masonry.'

The tool Clegg was holding resembled an oxy-acetylene cutting torch, but was connected to the electrospark erosion machine by an electricity supply cable instead of hoses. He pulled on a welder's helmet and operated the triggr experimentally. A blinding white light appeared at the tip of the torch. He applied the torch to the wooden laths and swiftly cut them away, filling the room momentarily with acrid fumes. Then he applied the torch to the centre of the exposed area of brickwork and began burning a hole.

'May I take a closer look?' asked Alan Martin.

Grant gave him a pair of welder's goggles. 'You'd better wear these.'

Alan Martin put the goggles on and became totally absorbed in the spectacle of masonry turning to glowing lava that ran down the wall in tiny rivulets and solidified as the tip of the burning torch sank silently into the brickwork.

Clegg carefully enlarged the hole. He quickly discovered that following the lines of mortar with the torch enabled some bricks to be lifted out intact – all without making a sound. The smell of burning wood filled the room again. Clegg switched off the torch and pushed the visor up on his welder's helmet.

'I'm through to the laths on the far side,' he announced.

Dowsett used the microphones and amplifier. He listened on the headphones for a moment and said that he could distinguish four voices.

Grant inspected the blind hold that Clegg had cut. He inserted a broaching tool in the hole and carefully twisted it back and forth. He withdrew the tool and examined the fibres clinging to its tip.

'You're through to the plaster,' he warned Clegg. 'For God's sake be careful.'

With painstaking care, Clegg eased the torch into the hole and switched the torch on for a burn that lasted less than five seconds.

'Tweezers,' he said.

Grant passed him a pair of tweezers which Clegg used to pick out tiny pieces of plaster. He worked for five minutes, pausing occasionally to wipe the sweat from his forehead with his sleeve.

'Probe.'

The unreal dialogue reminded Alan Martin of a movie operating theatre scene. Then he realised that four lives were at stake during this operation not just one.

Clegg eased the probe into the hole and moved it from side to side with extreme caution. He withdrew it, grinned at Grant and said simply: 'Wallpaper.'

'Have you punctured it?'

'No.'

The SAS officer was pleased. Clegg had done the seemingly impossible: he had bored through the wall with such precision that he had ended up with a tiny hole covered only by the wallpaper on the wall in the adjoining house.

'Right,' said Grant. 'Let's take a look at them.'

67

Colonel Hadley arrived at New Scotland Yard at 11:30 pm and was taken up to the command centre, where he was welcomed by Commander Powell and the Commissioner of Police of the Metropolis. The open plan room was busy. All the telephone lines were in use, manned by plainclothes men who were sifting through every scrap of incoming information which might shed some light on the impending terrorist operation. Wall maps of the Greater London area and principal cities throughout the United Kingdom bore flags marking possible targets. There were also maps of rural areas covering British and American military bases. Harry Renshaw, the Home Secretary, arrived five minutes later, still wearing his evening engagement dinner jacket.

'Someone brief me please, gentlemen,' said Renshaw briskly.

Colonel Hadley outlined the developments that were taking place at the Skellens' house in Tooting. He concluded: 'So if we can take the two alive, some fairly direct questioning will tell us what's going to happen and where and when.'

'*If* they're taken alive,' said the Home Secretary quietly. 'Which is unlikely, isn't it?'

Colonel Hadley nodded. 'Under the circumstances – yes, sir.'

68

Clegg inserted the sharpened steel knitting needle into the hole and gingerly punctured the wallpaper covering the living-room wall in the adjoining house. He withdrew the needle and signalled to Grant. The

SAS major examined the point of light shining from the adjoining room and nodded. At least they hadn't come out behind a picture. Clegg picked up the industrial endoscope and, with infinite care, guided the slender wide-angled viewing head into the hole while Dowsett connected the endoscope's image collector to a miniature TV camera. The endoscope employed the remarkable light-conducting properties of optical fibres to view the interior of machinery. It worked on the same principle as a broncoscope – used to examine the inside of the human body. It consisted of a slender tube, rather like a rifle, that tapered to a viewing head that was not much larger than a pinhead.

The image on the gadget's television monitor screen swam while Clegg moved the head around, trying to locate the pinprick hole in the wallpaper. The picture steadied. Although the image was distorted by the fisheye lens effect of the system it was possible to distinguish Jenny, with Trisha and Mac further away. Grant made a video recording of the scene, while Dowsett experimented with various microphones and confirmed that no one in the room was talking. Altering the angle of the endoscope slightly and adjusting its controls showed that Mac and Trisha were holding weapons of some sort although the definition was not good enough to establish exactly what their firearms were.

'Mr Martin,' said Grant. 'I'll have to ask you to leave the house now.'

'Can't I stay and see the . . . See what happens?'

'It would be too dangerous, sir, I'm sorry.'

A plainclothes policeman escorted Alan Martin from the room.

'Send Dr Hackett in,' Grant told the plainclothes policeman as he left the house.

The doctor was in the uniform of an SAS Territorial. In civilian life he was a GP. He studied the screen while Grant outlined the situation.

'How old's the kid?' asked Hackett.

'Eighteen months.'

'Bloody hell.'

Grant nodded. 'That's what I thought you'd say. Let's discuss it outside.'

Grant passed Clegg a mass of softened plasticine which the SAS man used to hold the endoscope in place. All the SAS men moved into the hallway for a conference, leaving the door open so that they could see the monitor screen.

'You'd have to lob the stun grenade into the middle of the room – right?' Hackett queried.

Grant nodded.

'A toddler,' said Hackett. 'Slow reactions at that age. Co-ordination. Motor responses not fully developed. At that range – in that confined space – there'd be damage to her sight and hearing.'

'Permanent?' asked Clegg.

'It's a safe bet.'

Grant thought for a moment. 'Okay. No flashbangs. And there's another problem. If possible, we've got to take one of those jokers alive for questioning.'

Clegg looked dismayed. 'How?'

'The orders are "if possible"', said Grant carefully.

'Well it's not possible, is it?'

Grant stared at the shadowy figures on the television screen 'No,' he said at length. 'It's not possible.'

'Then how if we don't use flash-bangs?' asked Clegg.

'Two will have to go in together,' Grant answered. 'Side by side.'

Clegg considered while staring at the wall. 'It'll mean making a fucking great hole.'

Samantha woke up and was fretful.

'Please,' Jenny pleaded. 'You must let me put her to bed.'

'You're both staying in this room,' said Trisha. 'Either that or you let Mac take her up.'

Clegg's face creased in concentration as the burning tip of his torch sliced through the mortar. He worked methodically, working upwards, removing diminishing quantities of bricks from each course so the top of the eventual hole in the wall would be in the shape of an arch, reducing the risk of masonry collapsing when the hole had been opened out to its full size. Dowsett removed the bricks one by one and passed them to one of the technicians, who in turn added them to the growing pile in the hallway.

The hole Clegg was making was nearly four feet wide – wide enough for two men to charge through side by side during the assault. He took particular care not to disturb the increasing area of lath and plaster lining the adjoining room that his work was exposing. The hole had six courses of header and stretcher brickwork left above the floor when the SAS men held another conference in the hall way.

'We'll take the brick work away right down to floor level,' Grant decided. 'It'll reduce the risk of any one tripping when they go in.'

Clegg and Dowsett went back to work to remove the final courses of headers and stretchers.

Samantha got bored. She started crying with renewed vigour. The noise grated on Trisha's nerves. Her eyes hardened. She stood and took a threatening step towards the child. 'Shut that brat up!' she snarled.

Jenny snatched Samantha up and wrapped her arms protectively around her daughter. Samantha disliked the abrupt handling and let her feelings be forcibly known.

'If I have to do it, I will!' Trisha shouted.

And Jenny knew she meant it.

With light flourishes of the cutting torch, Clegg deftly and silently removed the laths from the thin skin of plaster that separated the two rooms. The strips of wood, their ends smoldering where the torch had burned them through were passed into the hallway. The floor of the Martins' room was uncluttered – all the debris had been cleared away.

The latest arrivals were two of the heaviest troopers in Major Grant's London-based squadron. They were dressed in black and wore Balaclava helmets. They had finished checking their machine pistols and were studying a video recording of the adjoining room while listening to Major Grants' briefing. Both men were thickset and powerfully built: they looked capable of bursting through the wall even with the bricks in place.

Clegg removed the last lath with infinite care. The whole area of exposed plaster was like a delicate diaphragm; it even moved slightly as some of the plaster clung to the lath before coming free with a soft tearing sound. Samantha's screaming was clearly audible through the thin partition.

'Right!' shouted Trisha. 'Give her to me!'

'No!' screamed Jenny.

Trisha pressed the muzzle of her gun against Samantha's head. 'You give her to me or I'll blow her brains all over you!'

Clegg had finished. He moved away from the wall and dragged his equipment clear. The two SAS troopers took up their positions side by side opposite the hole and braced themselves for their charge. Trisha jammed her gun in her belt and dragged Samantha, kicking and howling from her mother's arms. She threw the child on the floor, snatched up a poker and swung it aloft.

'No!' screamed Jenny. She dived forward at Trisha's legs. Mac fired at Jenny and the bullet chewed into the chair where Jenny had been sitting. Trisha toppled over and managed to claw her automatic from her belt. Mac swung his gun towards Jenny. Then the impossible happened with appalling suddenness.

The entire wall of the living room burst inwards and two figures in black launched themselves through the hole. The first one fired several rounds at Mac. The force of the impact destroyed his face and hurled him backwards.

'Jenny! Down! Down!' yelled the second figure.

Not really knowing what she was doing Jenny snatched up Samantha and stood, blocking the second SAS trooper's line of fire. Suddenly, she was knocked off her feet just as Trisha raised her gun to fire at Samantha.

At the exact moment that Trisha's finger tightened on the trigger, four bullets slammed into her body. Two hit her in the chest, one passed through her neck and the fourth hit her in the temple. The exit wound from the nine-millimetre slug was such that fragments of her skull smashed the room's front window and shattered a wall mirror. Her lifeless body keeled over.

The rounds that killed her were the same calibre as she had used to kill Wilcox outside the Houses of Parliament.

69

The 2:00 am raid on the offices of the People's Lobby and the Christian Youth Travel Association was led by Detective Sergeant Clover of the Special Branch armed with two search warrants to cover both premises. Among the plainclothes men in his team was a man from the dead: a man whose body was supposed to have been recovered from the Thames. Detective Sergeant Pope.

The police team worked quickly and thoroughly. Every document, every scrap of paper, every receipt and invoice, went into labelled plastic sacks. The filing cabinets were moved away from walls in the search for stray documents and the drawers themselves were removed and loaded into the two waiting Transit vans. Even yellowing business cards Blu-tacked to the wall were removed and the floor coverings ripped up. The refuse bags were systematically emptied, and posters taken down, including those of Bishop Crick.

After thirty minutes intensive work, there was not as much as a bus ticket left in the offices of the Peoples' Lobby and the Christian Youth Travel Association. The policemen even took Trisha's moped that they found padlocked to a drainpipe at the back of the premises.

At 2:35 am, after a final look round by Clover and Pope, the two laden Transits pulled out of the narrow Soho street and headed back towards New Scotland Yard.

70

Somebody had once said, jocularly, about Verna: 'I wouldn't like to run up against her in a dark alley.'

She was tough, no doubt about it. Well built, buxom, even muscular. And she had been well-trained in the terrorist camps of Yemen and the Lebanon, taught how to garotte with a piece of wire, kill outright with one stab of a dagger (not as easy as it sounds), hurl a grenade, to assassinate and murder and booby trap.

She was a crack shot, could handle a rocket-launcher, knew how to make a time bomb, and how to kill with her bare hands. There was no method of ending lives that she didn't know about. Her instructors were proud of her, and she had since passed on her skills to many young men and women. She was a good teacher too.

To those who liked their women big and powerful, she was even attractive. Verna herself had little time for such frivolities. Those who disliked her said that she got sexual satisfaction only from using a rifle muzzle as a dildo, others that she was merely asexual.

CIA records showed that her closest friends had been women like Gudrun Enslin, and Ulrike Meinhof, Elizabeth Van Dyck, and other heroines of world revolution, most of whom had died as Verna herself would wish to go – on active service.

But she also had a ferocious temper, and once smashed the jaw of a girl in Hamburg who had, she thought, made a remark about her companions, two Palestinians who were posing as Turks in Hamburg, on their way to blow up a Jewish café in Berlin.

Verna's links with people like Frankie Leith and Rod Walker were tenuous. She wasn't a member of any political group in the United Kingdom. She fitted into the organization as a technician, part of the pool of experts on call worldwide to revolutionary movements. She trained activists at establishments available to them in Libya, Aden and the Lebanon. She taught them what she knew best, how to murder.

Perhaps it was foolish of her to come to England, but Verna wasn't going to miss out on the action. Nor did she lack courage, although some would call it recklessness.

She had done so much to train the young militants of the People's Lobby, and she wanted to be there when they proved themselves.

Verna flew into Gatwick: she had deliberately avoided landing at Heathrow because security and immigration were much tighter there, she had been told.

She walked into Gatwick's arrival hall, carelessly dressed as usual, and no makeup. Verna spent little money on clothes and cosmetics.

She produced a West German passport at the immigration desk.

'Fraulein Hildegard Westhof?' said the immigration officer, comparing the passport photograph with its bearer.

'Ja,' nodded Verna, unsmiling. She could never bring herself to be pleasant to the lackeys of the capitalist regime, whichever country they represented.

The passport was genuine: only the photograph had been cunningly substituted. The girl whose travel document it was had lost it in a department store, so she thought. Neither she nor the police had realised that it had been intentionally stolen from her handbag.

'How long will you be in Britain?' enquired the immigration oficer. That should have warned Verna. Belonging to the EC meant the West Germans had free entry into the UK. It was unusual to ask them such a question.

'Just a few days,' replied Verna. She forced herself to smile 'A small vacation. To see some plays. Visit some friends . . .'

The immigration officer nodded and waved her on. He didn't even stamp the passport.

Verna went through and made her way to the train station. She left behind an immigration officer who happened to have an excellent photographic memory which had been carefully cultivated. It seemed to him that Verna's face was vaguely familiar. He checked the Stop List. No Hildegard Westhof was on it.

He tried to think where he had seen that face before. It didn't occur to him that she was one of

thirty terrorists listed on a Europe-wide circular to be
stopped at any frontier post.

71

Saturday promised to be a fine day. Sunlight
streamed through the warehouse's high windows
and the fumes from bacon and eggs sizzling on
camping cookers defined the sun's early rays. Frankie
was more vivacious than usual during the communal
breakfast. She chatted away non-stop to Skellen
about the need for one Western country to set a lead
for the others to follow. Skellen guessed that she was
talking to cover her nervousness about the impending operation.

As soon as the meal was cleared away, Frankie
addressed the team. She spoke with quiet dedication.
She was grave, and she make them aware of the
seriousness of that which they were about to under-
take. She stressed that it was only because they were
all convinced that the end justified the means that
they would take such a dramatic step. People would
be hurt during the next twenty-four hours, it was
inevitable, but for every life lost, a million would be
saved in the future. Also, those who might be dying
would be those who had ordained that the world
should live in such fear.

'We have to be strong to make others stronger. We

have to fulfil the hopes and prayers of millions by our deeds. All over the world people are asking that something be done to avert a holocaust. It falls to us to see to it that we do it.'

The team clung on her every word and would have applauded her when she finished speaking but for Rod's admonition about not making unnecessary noise.

Rod unrolled an architect's plan of a country mansion on one of the tables and weighted the corners with ashtrays.

'You've seen this drawing before, it's the target,' he announced.

Skellen looked for an address on the drawing but there was nothing. 'I've not seen it before, Rod.'

'The side entrance where we'll be going in,' said Rod, ignoring Skellen and pointing to the drawing. 'The servants' quarters . . . The master switch for the security system, not that that will concern us . . . And this is the dining room.' His long finger came to rest on a large room at the rear of the house. 'As you know from your training, it's more the size of a banqueting hall. All the hostages will be on the second course of their dinner when we take the house over this evening.'

'Where is the house?' asked Joe Belchamber.

'You'll find out this evening, Joe,' said Frankie.

'And the hostages?'

Frankie shook her head. 'I'm sorry, Joe. Only Rod and I know the venue, who the hostages will be, and what our demands will be. It's better that way.'

'And I just twiddle my thumbs?' asked Skellen.

Frankie stared thoughtfully at Skellen for a moment.

'Your job, soldier boy, is to keep us briefed on SAS procedure and to help set up the cameras,' Rod intervened. 'Nothing else.'

Skellen began to get angry. 'Listen, Walker, I'm as committed to this as anyone. By tomorrow we'll all be either dead villains or live heroes. Whatever happens, I want to be part of this because I've got more cause than any of you.'

The two men squared up to each other in mutual dislike. It was Frankie who broke the tension:

'Can you drive a coach, Peter?' she asked.

72

Verna's face kept bothering the immigration officer. Long after the hefty woman, whose passport said she was Hildegard Westhof, had passed through the Gatwick arrivals hall, it kept nagging him.

He knew he had seen that face before.

The name check had proved blank. So did a Home Office check. And the German Embassy security department didn't have anything on the name. But the immigration officer was a persistent man. Instead of going to the airport canteen for his coffee break, he spent the time leafing through the picture files in passport control.

And there, at last, he found her. She wasn't listed by the name under which she had travelled. But she had several others. Liselotte Hahn. Trude Weisskopf. Gisela Fuchs. She had five different passports. And she was wanted in the West.

Verna had links with anarchists and terrorism going back to 1970. She had helped to rob a bank in Basle. She had become involved with the Spanish Basques in ETA, the Red Brigade in Verona, and Dutch Red Help. She was suspected of having been in a shoot-out with police in Rotterdam, which ended with two detectives dead and the assailant at large. She then linked up with Arab revolutionaries, and had been reported helping to train terrorists in the Habash-Haddad Camp at Khayat in the Middle East. One of the last sightings was in Libya. For the last twelve months, there had been no trace of her. She was wanted, on sight, for the bank robbery and murder.

'Approach with caution,' added the citation. 'This woman is dangerous and always armed.'

Well, mused the immigration officer, as he reached for the phone, at least she wasn't armed when she landed. The metal detectors would have picked up a gun.

By the time he called Scotland Yard, and an all-areas warning went out on the police network, Verna was already in London. She felt secure. Gatwick had gone very smoothly, and the immigration pig, surly bastard that he was, seemed satisfied.

She had several addresses of sympathizers who would provide safe houses. There was also a squat-

211

ters' commune where she could disappear. Verna was well-trained in security, and planned to be careful about being seen at the People's Lobby premises. She looked forward to a reunion with Frankie and, especially with Trisha. The pert little brunette had always been a favourite. But prudence stopped her calling them right away. Their phones were probably tapped, and it would never do to tip off the Special Branch. First she had to sniff out things.

It was Verna's bad luck that the Yard teleprinter chattered out her description, and the fact that she had arrived in London, just as Detective Sergeant Irene Conway was leaving Kensington Police Station. Sergeant Conway, a tall, slim, dark haired young woman, looked an unlikely detective. And an even more unlikely Special Branch officer.

She glanced at the teleprinter and registered Verna's description. Hefty, buxom, blonde. Well-built. She went over to the bulletin board where the poster with the pictures of certain wanted terrorists had been stuck for months. Verna under her various aliases, was amongst them. She was second from the left third row.

It was even more Verna's bad luck that she should be walking past Redcliffe Gardens just as Sergeant Conway came along.

The woman Special Branch officer glanced twice at her without betraying any recognition. Instead she slowed down so that she fell behind Verna, and started following her. She considered, momentarily, making for a phone but she'd probably lose Verna in the meantime. Best to trail her.

Verna sauntered along, unaware that she was being shadowed. She came to the Syrian cafè, but it was closed.

'*Verfluchtt*,' cursed Verna. The rucksack she was carrying was getting heavier. She could do with a rest. She looked round, spotting Luigi's bistro and went inside.

So did Sergeant Conway.

Verna sat at a table by the counter. She ordered an espresso and a plate of spaghetti bolognaise. She never worried about her figure.

At the table across from her, Sergeant Conway also sipped a coffee. And made up her mind. It would take Verna at least ten minutes to eat her pasta. There was a phone kiosk on the other side of the road.

The woman detective paid and left without even glancing at Verna. In the kiosk she dialled her office. What she told her senior officer set wheels in motion.

Sergeant Conway left the phone booth and bought a newspaper before returning to the bistro and ordering another coffee. Verna was shovelling spaghetti into her mouth, suspecting nothing.

In the street outside, a Hillman Minx with three men in it pulled up by the pavement. So did a green Ford a little further away. Two men got out.

Verna ordered another coffee. She felt better now. She decided that she might try phoning Frankie. Great caution would be needed. From Frankie's reaction, Verna was confident that she could judge if it was safe to talk and arrange where to meet.

The three men who had arrived in the Minx entered the bistro. Verna glanced up, her eyes nar-

213

rowing. A decade of war against the state had given her the instinct of a wild animal in the jungle. The men could have been anything they were roughly dressed. But something about them . . .

Sergeant Conway was suddenly at her side, twisting her arm behind her back. At the same time the three men were round the table, grabbing her.

'All right, *fraulein*,' said Sergeant Conway, quite politely. 'Don't make any trouble.'

'You're under arrest,' added one of the men unnecessarily. The second man was standing, feet apart arms extended in approved style, a .38 clasped in his hands pointing straight at Verna's head. The third man kicked her rucksack to one side.

'What is this?' demanded Verna. 'I'm a tourist.'

She tried to get to her feet. As one of the men produced handcuffs she lashed out with her right foot and caught him in the stomach. Sergeant Conway who was holding her arm, lost her balance. Verna's head butted her savagely. The Special Branch woman staggered and Verna kicked out again teeth bared. She was a formidable fighter and much of her bulk was sheer, hard muscle.

'Stop!' yelled the detective with a gun. Verna launched herself at him, and almost as a reflex action he fired. The bullet at point-blank range ploughed into her throat. Verna croaked briefly, blood gushing. Then her body crashed to the floor, half-chewed spaghetti spilling from her mouth. The indignity of her ignominious end was a fitting reward for the death and misery she had inflicted on the world.

'Christ,' whispered the detective with the gun. He was white-faced.

For weeks afterwards, various publications would have a field day elaborating on the incident in which armed police had shot down an unarmed German tourist. They would make much of the fact that Verna did not even have a gun on her.

There would be little mention of the two detectives she had killed in Rotterdam. Nor would she be linked with the People's Lobby.

73

By 11:30 am most of the detectives who had worked all night urgently sifting through the documents removed from the offices of the People's Lobby were red-eyed and yawning from lack of sleep.

The long trestle tables that had been set-up specially for the operation were piled high with folders and loose documents.

'Nothing, sir,' a detective inspector reported to Commander Powell. 'A few leaflets that border on incitement, but nothing that points to any form of terrorist activity.'

Powell picked up a revolutionary magazine from a heap on one of the tables and idly leafed through it for a moment. Bishop Crick's smiling cherubic face was the subject of the journal's centre page spread.

Powell tossed the magazine contemptuously back on the table.

'It's what I expected,' sighed Powell. 'The People's Lobby are a bit more with it than your usual run-of-the-mill Trot shop merchants. Okay – send everyone home with my thanks and get the second team started on the bumpf from that phoney travel association.'

74

It was beginning to get dark when Rod ran back to his car and tossed his binoculars on the back seat beside Skellen.

'They're coming,' he said shortly, sliding his lanky frame behind the wheel and starting the engine, 'About a mile down the road.'

Frankie turned in her seat and peered past Skellen through the rear windscreen as Rod accelerated along the slip road and joined the light traffic heading north towards London on the A3 Portsmouth Road. They were on a fast stretch where the six-lane highway skirted the Royal Horticultural Society Gardens at Wisley.

'What were they doing in Portsmouth?' asked Skellen.

'A charity fete,' said Frankie.

'And an engagement this evening. They work hard.'

'I suppose they're well-paid,' said Frankie. 'I don't really care.'

Rod stayed in the nearside lane and kept his speed down, forcing even slow-moving heavy vehicles into the middle lane in order to overtake. He made a minor adjustment to the position of his driving mirror. A small 20-seater coach was five hundred metres behind in the same lane, rapidly closing the gap. Its offside turn indicators started flashing and the driver began easing his vehicle into the centre lane.

'Here she is. Get ready.' said Rod.

Skellen and Frankie wound down their respective windows. The coach bore the markings and insignia of the United States Air Force. It overtook the car and returned to the nearside lane. The vehicle's passengers were about a dozen men in USAF uniforms. They were laughing and talking. One of the passengers was an attractive WAAF, a brunette. She was standing up having an animated conversation with a sergeant. Rod accelerated to maintain a constant gap behind the coach.

'Okay – now!' Rod shouted. He pressed the accelerator pedal to the floor and held the horn button down, working the headlight flasher at the same time.

The car swerved into the middle lane and drew alongside the coach. Frankie and Skellen leaned out of their windows and gestured frantically at the coach's offside rear wheel. Fresh-complexioned faces stared down at them.

'STOP! STOP! STOP!' screamed Frankie above the

roar of the car's slipstream. To the USAF bandsmen in the coach, Frankie's desperately yelled words were unheard but they understood what she was saying. Some of them shouted at the driver, but Rod's blaring horn and flashing lights had already attracted his attention. The coach lost speed and its nearside turn indicator began flashing. Rod pulled in front of the coach and slowed down. The coach driver steered onto the hard shoulder and braked to a standstill. Rod, Frankie and Skellen leapt from their car and ran back to the coach. The passengers boarding door hissed open. 'What's wrong then?' demanded the puzzled driver, who had half-risen from his seat.

'Nothing's wrong,' said Frankie who was first up the coach's steps. She pulled her pistol out of her anorak and pointed it at the driver. 'Provided you do exactly as you're told.'

'That goes for all of you!' Rod barked at the bandsmen, levelling his pistol at them. 'You're all to lie on the floor. Anyone who sticks their head up gets it blown off!'

The young bandsmen and the WAAF stared uncomprehendingly at the lanky man who was threatening them with a pistol.

'Shift that junk onto the seats and lie on the floor!' ordered Rod.

The airmen obediently started moving the bulkier musical instrument cases from the coach's centre aisle and stacking them on the seats. Frankie ordered the driver to help them. Skellen slipped into the seat vacated by the driver and started the engine.

One by one the airmen and the driver went down

onto the floor of the coach with the exception of the girl who continued to stare at Rod in terror.

A black musician took hold of her wrist and drew her down. 'I think the gentleman means what he says, honey,' he said gently. He grinned at Rod from where he was lying between the seats. 'This a hijacking, man?'

'You're amazingly perceptive,' Rod observed.

'Why don't you all shut up,' said Frankie impatiently.

Skellen gauged the passing traffic and swung the coach northwards. He drove fast, winding the vehicle up through the gears.

75

Mrs Crick was a bosomy lady with enough beads around her neck to have purchased Manhattan had she been around four hundred years earlier. She carefully examined Pope's and Clover's warrant cards, and showed them into her husband's study where he was working on the final draft of his speech at the next People's Lobby rally.

Clover noticed that the subject matter of the books on the shelves was such that the bishop's study could have been an annex to the bookshop in Charing Cross Road. There were framed photographs on the wall. One showed the bishop sitting at a microphone in a Radio Moscow studio. Another showed him when he was younger being forcibly removed by police from a sit-in protest at the entrance to the American Embassy. All this was no surprise to the policeman; the wily Bishop of Camden Town was well-known to the Special Branch. They were followers of the bishop but not supporters. They attended his meetings, took down his speeches and read the outpourings of his typewriter with great interest.

They told him what they wanted and the bishop gave a very dangerous smile.

'You realise, of course, what an outrage this is,' he announced. 'I would expect this to happen in South Africa or Chile, but I didn't think we had yet become the complete police state. On whose orders are you here?'

'On the instructions of my superiors,' replied Clover.

'Well, naturally, I fully appreciate you are only carrying out your job but I must warn you there will be serious consequences. I'm sure the matter will be raised in other places and I hope your superiors have a very good explanation ready. Obviously I will assist you in every way I can but I want you to note my protest. What is this all about?'

Clover handed him a photograph of Trisha. 'I believe you know this young lady, bishop?'

'Ah – Trisha. She's the manager of the Christian Youth Travel Association of which I am chairman.'

'Not any more, bishop,' said Clover shortly. 'She's dead.'

Bishop Crick's florid face paled as the policeman

outlined the events that had taken place the previous night. Pope made notes and left Clover to do all the talking.

'You must understand that I am a non-executive chairman of the association,' pointed out Bishop Crick, skillfully recovering his composure. 'I chair the quarterly meetings and have nothing to do with its day-to-day running. It's important that you understand that.'

'We understand, bishop.'

Bishop Crick smiled blandly. 'No court in the country would hold me responsible for what my followers get up to if I don't know about it. He frowned. 'Who exactly was responsible for the death of the poor girl in this incident? You? The police?'

'The authorities,' replied Clover vaguely. 'I'm afraid she was killed resisting arrest.'

'The very phrase the Nazis used,' commented the bishop coldly.

'We have reason to believe that the gun found in the girl's possession was used in the murder of two other people during the past month.'

Bishop Crick looked horrified. 'Not Trisha. There must be some mistake, officer. I'm sure she would never . . . She abhorred violence. You people really have the most curious ideas about our followers. Protest does not equate with violence, you know. We wouldn't be doing the things we are if we didn't hate and detest all forms of violence . . .'

Clover interrupted with some more searching questions about Trisha's association with Rod Walker and Frankie Leith.

'Yes,' said the bishop nodding his head emphatically. 'They run the People's Lobby.'

'Of which you are also the chairman?'

Bishop Crick smiled smugly. 'It's no secret.'

'Do you know where Leith and Walker are now?'

'Engaged on the work of the organization I should imagine. Both are completely dedicated.'

'I asked where they are, bishop. Not what are they doing.'

Bishop Crick spread his hands and gave Clover a sly smile. 'I'm not their keeper. What they do in their spare time is their affair. Why? Where do *you* think they are?'

Clover regarded the cleric steadily. He produced a card from his pocket, wrote down a telephone number and handed it to Bishop Crick. 'If you hear from them, bishop, would you please call that number immediately.'

Bishop Crick studied the card. 'Of course, I needn't bother if they phone me, need I? Your people have – what is your polite word for a tap on a telephone? An intercept on my line? Yes?'

'Call the number if they get in touch,' said Clover evenly. He stood up. 'We're sorry to have taken up your time, bishop. We'll let you get back to your speech.'

'I'll send you a copy,' the bishop promised, a smile creasing his face. 'It'll save you having to make a tape recording at the next rally.'

As soon as the detectives had left, the bishop got busy. He pulled the phone towards him and started calling the *Guardian*, and some other newspapers to get his version in of the outrageous police raid on his residence. He made himself available to television news and said it would be perfectly all right for them to come to his home to film and interview.

And then he called seven Members of Parliament. Very friendly MPs. Within half an hour four of them had promised to raise embarrassing questions about this latest Gestapo-like atrocity. Two said that they would raise the matter during the next Prime Minister's Question Time in the House of Commons. Bishop Crick was well-pleased. They were prominent MPs, certain to catch the Speaker's eye.

76

Skellen was approaching Esher when a driver of an overtaking car misjudged the road and pulled in front of the coach, forcing Skellen to brake sharply. Frankie and Rod were off balance momentarily. The black airman saw his opportunity. He drew his legs under him and sprang at Rod, managing to grab at his wrist holding the gun. He was stronger and heavier than Rod.

Frankie was momentarily unsighted, unable to use her gun because Rod was between her and the black airman he was grappling with.

'Come on, you guys!' the airman yelled at his colleagues who were lying motionless on the floor.

They looked up uncertainly. The airman swung Rod's hand against the back of a seat and knocked the gun to the floor. The WAAF snatched it up and was about to throw it to the nearest airman when Frankie jumped onto a seat, pointed her gun down at the girl and fired three times. The girl gave a little cry and fell back dying, blood gushing from her terrible head wounds. Without pausing to see what effect her shots had had, Frankie turned the gun on the black airman and shot him twice in the head at a range of less than a metre.

Rod recovered his gun and pointed it at the stunned airmen. 'Anyone else want to find out if we mean business?' he invited.

'Sonofabitch,' spat an Airman First Class. But nobody moved. They maintained a horrified silence.

Skellen had observed the entire incident in one of the driving mirrors. The killings sickened him but he maintained a stoic expression. He thought wryly about the times he had deliberately needled Frankie about action and not words.

The rest of the journey passed without incident. While Frankie kept the airmen covered, Rod searched through the driver's papers and found the document he was looking for. He mentioned his find to Frankie who nodded. Despite the recent upset, everything was going according to plan.

It was dark by the time Skellen reversed the coach up to the warehouse's loading bay. Frankie went inside while Rod kept the silent airmen covered. Two members of the team opened the loading bay's sliding doors enabling Skellen to reverse the coach inside.

'Okay,' said Rod to the airmen once the doors were closed again. 'All of you out. And bring those bodies with you.'

'Trouble, Frankie?' asked Belchamber unnecessarily, as the subdued hostages carried the dead girl and airman out of the coach.

'Sort of,' said Frankie cryptically. 'Okay. Tie them up.'

The tying-up of the airmen and the coach driver was done professionally under Skellen's supervision. Each man was trussed to a separate iron pillar with nylon cord so that there was no question of one man being able to help another. Also the bindings were tightly secured in such a way that it would not be possible to fray them against the rusty iron work. As a final precaution each man had a large piece of adhesive plaster taped over his mouth.

'Very good, Peter,' complimented Frankie when she inspected Skellen's handiwork.

'What's next?'

'We load the coach.'

The team worked quickly. The musical instruments were removed from their cases and substituted for various weapons. The double bass player's case provided a home for all the Sterling submachine-guns; the machine pistols and ammunition went into the wind instrument cases, and the hand grenades fitted neatly into two clarinet cases.

The television cameras and the monitor sets went straight into the coach's stowage bay. The last item to be loaded aboard the coach was the Honda generator.

As each item was accounted for, Rod ticked it off against his check list which he later burned when he was satisfied that everything was correct.

Frankie looked at her watch. They were two minutes behind schedule. 'Okay,' she said. 'Everyone into their uniforms.'

Ten minutes later, Rod and Frankie inspected their team, now resplendent in their USAF uniforms, their faces pink and well-scrubbed, and their hair neatly combed.

'You look good, Peter,' said Frankie when she came to Skellen. 'Reagan would be proud of you.'

'Okay,' said Rod. 'Everyone aboard. Mike and Joe – open the doors.'

The team carried their instrument cases aboard the coach and sat quietly in their seats, their backs straight.

'Do you want me to drive?' offered Skellen when Rod sat in the driver's seat.

Rod looked hard at the SAS man. 'How? You don't know where we're going.'

'True,' Skellen admitted, 'but you could tell me.'

'Just sit down at the back there,' ordered Rod.

Skellen took a seat in the third row. He was tense. And yet he felt curiously exhilarated. It was the same feeling he always got when he found himself in danger and knew that it would depend on him and him alone whether he'd get out alive.

Rod started the engine and drove the coach out of

the warehouse. He paused, waiting for the two men to close the loading bay doors and lock-up.

They made sure the doors were secure and climbed aboard the coach. The passenger door hissed shut. Rod gunned the engine and let out the clutch.

It was 7:30 pm.

77

The lights were burning in the US Ambassador's residence: a blaze of welcome for the chauffeur-driven limousines, Rolls Royces, Cadillacs and Bentleys, that made their way at intervals up the sweeping gravel drive to the mansion's front entrance.

Walton House was a millionaire's folly which the tycoon who had originally built it bequeathed to the United States Government on his death bed. In his will he had suggested that it might make a pleasant holiday home for US presidents, without appreciating that no American president had ever spent his vacation in the United Kingdom. Washington was, however, grateful for the bequest and it was decided to utilize Walton House as the second official residence of American ambassadors to the Court of St James.

Thanks to the eccentricity of the tycoon it had been designed as a Spanish style mansion, set amid two hectares of Philishaved lawns fringed with a dense screen of bamboo and fast-growing eucalyptus trees. The entire property was surrounded by an eight foot high wall.

It had good security. The grounds were watched by closed-circuit television, there were infrared intruder alarms, and British police guarded the entrance and checked all arrivals. Once anyone stepped beyond the wall they stood in American territory where security was the responsibility of the marines. Walton House had the same diplomatic status as the US Embassy in Grosvenor Square but for tonight's bash, with British ministers present, the Americans had agreed to the presence of British police.

The Foreign Secretary's official Rover was the last car to arrive. It was stopped at the front gates by the uniformed police for a brief but careful check before being waved along the drive towards the lights.

There were more police patrolling the perimeter of the magnificent house armed with .38s and two-way radios. It was to be a long evening for them: the ambassador's 'at homes' had a reputation for going on until 3:00 am.

78

'What do you make of this, sir?' asked the detective inspector, handing Commander Powell the typewritten list.

The senior policeman studied the document. It was a list of ten married couples who had booked holidays with the Christian Youth Travel Associations.

'What do *you* make of it?' Powell countered.

'It's odd, sir. I mean married couples. Ninety-nine per cent of the booking forms we've checked are for single people – mostly students.'

'See if you can find the original booking forms that match these names,' Powell ordered.

'Going back how many years, guv'nor?'

'Check the whole damn lot,' Powell growled.

79

Rod drove the coach round Kingston's huge one-way circulatory system and picked up the New Malden road instead of taking the more direct route to London over Kingston Hill.

'So we're not going to London?' Skellen observed.

'No,' said Frankie.

'Then do you mind telling me where the hell we are going?'

'Wimbledon.'

'It's another two months until tennis fortnight,' Skellen pointed out.'

'We're going to a dinner party given by the United States Ambassador at his official residence.'

'I take it we're not invited to this dinner party?'

'Oh, but we are. We're supposed to be providing the after-dinner entertainment.'

'And the guests are those people we saw on the news the other night?'

'That's right,' said Frankie. 'Lord Staunton, the Foreign Secretary; Arthur Curry, Secretary of State. There's the head of Strategic Air Command, General Ira Potter; and three senators and a congressman. Quite a gathering.'

Skellen was silent for a moment while he digested this. 'And their wives?'

'And some wives,' Frankie confirmed.

'Where did you get your information from?'

'That's none of your business.'

'Let me guess . . .'

'I said that it's none of your business.'

They lapsed into silence. Skellen's thoughts were with Jenny and his daughter.

Twenty minutes later the coach was skirting Wimbledon Common along Parkside. Rod followed a signpost to Lady Jane's Wood and turned onto an unmade road. Entrances among the trees on each side of the lane marked the approaches of unseen mansions. The coach's headlights picked out a discreet signboard marked 'Lady Jane's Wood'. It was the ambassador's house. Rod stopped at the barrier manned by three uniformed policemen. One of them was carrying a clipboard. He came aboard the coach. Rod switched the interior lights on. The policeman took in at a glance the smartly-turned out bandsmen and the instrument cases piled in the aisle.

'You're late,' commented the policeman, examining the pass that Rod gave him.

'A flat,' drawled Rod.

'Musical or mechanical?' The policeman laughed at his own joke. 'Okay. Drive past the parked cars and turn left round to the back of the house. There's a courtyard with plenty of room to park.'

The policeman jumped down and gestured to his colleagues to open the barrier. The wave of relief from the coach's passengers was very nearly audible. Frankie gave Skellen's hand a squeeze. Rod drove past the rows of parked limousines and turned down the side of the mansion and into a courtyard that was surrounded by single-storey outbuildings and garages. Rod parked beside two vans emblazoned with the name of an upmarket specialist catering concern. A man dressed in a dinner jacket that failed to conceal the bulge of his shoulder holster emerged from the tradesmen's entrance and hurried across to Rod's window. He spoke with an English accent:

'If two of you follow me, I'll show you where to take your instruments.'

Rod and Joe followed the man through a large kitchen that was alive with noisy but organized activity as maids rushed in and out laden with tureens and fine pieces belonging to a Minton dinnerware table service set. A room off the kitchen was crammed with chauffeurs eating at a standup buffet.

'They're on the fish,' explained the armed man. 'So you've plenty of time to sort yourselves out.'

He showed Rod and Joe into a spacious library that had been cleared of furniture with the exception of a few easy chairs. The carpet had been rolled back to form a dance floor.

'I'll leave you to it then,' said the armed man, and withdrew.

It took five minutes for the team to transfer the musical instrument cases from the coach to the library. Skellen was posted on the door while the team unfastened the cases and quickly assembled and loaded the Sterling submachine-guns and machine pistols. There was a knock on the door. On a signal from Frankie, all the weapons disappeared behind the easy chairs and into the double bass case.

Skellen opened the door. A maid entered pushing a trolley that was piled high with cold food and paper plates. There were also two large coffee flasks and some plastic cups.

'I was told to ask you not to get it all over the floor,' said the maid, smiling at everyone in their dress uniforms as she trundled the trolley into the middle of the room. One of the protruding castors caught on the upright double bass case. It toppled sideways. The door burst open and a miscellany of weapons cascaded onto the floor. The maid's eyes widened in astonishment. She was about to scream when Joe, without waiting for orders from Rod or Frankie, clapped a hand over her mouth from behind and drove a knife upwards into her left side just as Verna had taught him. Joe caught her under the armpits as she fell and another member of the team grabbed hold of her ankles. Together they heaved the girl's lifeless body hebind a settee.

232

'You bloody fool!' cried Rod. 'Have you gone crazy or something?'

Joe was taken aback by his fury. 'She was about to bring the place down,' he explained. 'Somebody had to do something.'

'Save it for the right people, not the bloody peons,' growled Rod. 'You didn't have to kill her.'

It fitted Skellen's image of Rod. The man was a fanatic, a terrorist killer, but the frightening thing was that he had his own strict code of morality. Killing servants was a breach of the code. He wanted a classless world, but his thinking was totally class conscious.

The weapons were hidden away and everyone helped themselves to food. The armed man put his head round the door five minutes later.

'Everything okay, gentlemen?'

'No,' said Rod, finishing his salad.

The armed man entered the library. Skellen closed the door.

'What's the matter?' asked the armed man.

The process with the maid was repeated. The armed man's body was unceremoniously dumped behind the same settee.

Rod had no qualms this time. The armed man was a Special Branch officer. A pig. Killing him was what it was all about.

'Okay,' said Rod. 'Let's get started.'

The Foreign Secretary's private detective was talking to the girl who operatd the switchboard, when the door of the tiny room opened. The bandsman in

USAF uniform pointed his machine pistol at them both.

'The house has been taken over by the People's Lobby,' announced the bandsman. He disarmed the detective, waved the couple into the corridor and marched them into the glass-roofed indoor swimming pool room where two more of the armed bandsmen were already posted.

'Into the pool,' ordered the bandsman.

'What?'

'I said into the pool!'

The detective helped the girl down the Roman steps at the pool's shallow end. They stood fully dressed with the water around their waist, feeling very foolish and bewildered.

'Into the middle,' ordered the bandsman, keeping his pistol pointing down at them.

They did as they were told. The private detective realised just how vulnerable one was when standing in a swimming pool; any sudden effective move was impossible, and the aggressor had the strategic advantage of being able to look down on his captors. Frankie slipped into the vacated switchboard room and closed all the telephone lines with the exception of the extension in the library. She welded each switch in the closed position by the simple expedient of squirting some superglue around all the controls. The adhesive melted the plastic. It took less than a minute for it to harden. When it had done so, the only telephone in the house that could be operated was the one in the library.

*

Beatrice Franklin, the ambassador's wife, listened politely to General Ira Potter, but she was more concerned about the non-appearance of the game course rather than General Potter's views on the strategic value of cruise missiles based in Eastern England.

'One of our real on-going problems,' General Potter was saying, 'is our corporate image. The British have come to see us as a twentieth century bogeyman instead of guarantors of their peace and freedom.'

'Of course,' Mrs Franklin murmured politely. She glanced up and down the long table. Everyone had finished. She tried to catch her husband's eye but he was deep in conversation with the Foreign Secretary's wife.'

'I've lost count of the committees I've told this to,' General Potter continued. 'But SAC ought to have a proper overseas corporate advertising budget to let people know what we're doing and what we stand for. I'm a great believer in keeping people informed.'

'It sounds like a good idea,' said Mrs Franklin absently. Where the devil were the stupid girls? It was spoiling what was promising to be one of her more successful 'at homes'. The ambassador's wife loved her social gatherings: she enjoyed seeing top people at their best and enjoying themselves. She loved the glitter of jewels and the glamour of fine evening gowns; immaculate dinner jackets and sparkling conversation (General Potter's conversation excluded), and the heady feeling that she was at the centre of events.

235

'Would you excuse me a moment, please, general,' she said, taking advantage of a break in General Potter's diatribe when he paused to sip his wine.

She had half-risen from her seat when the double doors at the far end of the dining room burst open and two bandsmen led by a girl with long blonde hair also dressed in uniform, rushed into the room. All three were holding submachine-guns. For an impossible moment Mrs Franklin thought that it was some sort of bizarre entertainment laid on by the USAF band.

'No one is to move!' cried Frankie, very controlled. 'This house has been captured by the people and you are our prisoners! Anyone who moves will be shot immediately!'

Mrs Franklin sat down abruptly, more from shock rather than any inclination to obey the uniformed girl's orders. She swivelled her eyes round to her husband. Everyone was staring at the three intruders. Harrison Franklin was the first to break the silence:

'Just what in hell is all this?'

Frankie smiled in triumph and pointed her weapon at the ambassador. She was Jeanne d'Arc, Boadica, Ulrike Meinhof. The name Leith would become a new clarion call in the English language. A word that would become associated with liberation and a new freedom from the tyranny of fear brought about by living in the shadow of nuclear weapons.

'This is a new beginning, Mr Franklin,' she declared. 'Together we're all going to make history this weekend. I want everyone to put their hands flat on the table.'

The twenty diners did as they were told while a member of the team checked them for arms. He relieved Congressman Alonzo Kraft of a Smith and Wesson .38 – the only weapon he found.

'All stand,' said Frankie.

They all stood with the exception of General Potter. He removed a cigar from its tube and lit it.

'On your feet, please,' said Frankie levelly.

'Ira,' said Secretary of State Arthur Curry. 'Do as the kid says.'

General Potter exhaled a thin stream of cigar smoke. 'You know this place is surrounded by police?'

'We know,' said Frankie pleasantly. 'Now would you please stand up, general, before I shoot you and kill the lady on your left. And I wouldn't give a damn.'

'That figures,' muttered the general, and stood.

'Turn and face the door.' Frankie's voice was calm and her hands were steady. 'Fine. Now walk slowly into the hall. Slowly, mind. Try not to make any sudden move that might upset my nerves.'

One by one the diners filed out into the hall where they were waved towards the back of the house. Rod was waiting for them in the indoor pool room. He jerked his Sterling at the pool for the benefit of the first arrivals.

Arthur Curry's eyes goggled when he saw the group of terrified caterers and chauffeurs who were already clustered in the centre of the swiming pool, standing up to their waists in the clear tepid water.

'In you get,' said Rod.

The Secretary for Defence turned to Rod. 'Are you serious about this? I mean – '

'It's not cold!' Rod snarled. 'Now get in!'

Arthur Curry did as he was told.

Mrs Franklin began to cry. The ambassador put a comforting arm around her. 'Surely my wife does not have to . . .' He asked.

'You all do. Now stop wasting time.'

The diners went down the steps. The women's evening gowns ballooned around their waists and they had to be steadied by the men. They waded into the centre of the pool and joined the group already in the middle. All of them were too concerned about their safety and each other's safety to be aware of the incongruity of the situation: men and women in evening attire standing up to their waists in the middle of an indoor swimming pool. General Potter still had a cigar clenched angrily between his teeth.

Rod motioned to two of the team. They sat themselves down at either end of the pool with their submachine-guns across their laps.

Skellen was genuinely impressed when he saw the forlorn group. 'Clever,' he remarked to Frankie. 'There's not much they can do in there.'

'You can put it down to Rod's planning.' Frankie replied. 'Okay, Peter, get the cameras rigged.'

The phone rang in the library. Joe answered it. 'Yes?'

'Main gate,' said a voice. 'Me and the lads are a bit

famished. Any chance of some of that grub being sent down?'

'I think it's all been eaten,' Joe replied, signalling to Frankie who crossed the library and listened in.

'It can't be,' complained the voice. 'One of the birds from the catering company said there's bound to be a ton of grub left over.'

Frankie took the phone. 'There may be some sandwiches,' she said.

There was a pause. Then the voice asked suspiciously: 'Is that all?'

''Fraid so. That's all that's left.'

'Okay, miss. Sounds fine. Can you send down enough for three of us, please?'

'I'll get one of the bandsmen to bring you down a trayful,' Frankie promised and replaced the handset.

'Why?' asked Joe.

'Because I don't want them coming to the house,' said Frankie. 'We've got too many hostages to cope with as it is. We didn't know about the catering firm.'

A bandsman held the Russian vine clear while Skellen carefully positioned the TV camera on the mounting clamp that he had attached to an upstairs bedroom window frame.

The garden was in total darkness, as was the bedroom where they were working yet the image on the portable television monitor that was connected to the camera was bright although blurred.

Skellen set the focus of the heat-sensitive infrared lens to infinity and trained the camera down at a slight angle, checking the monitor as he did so. The group of shrubs at the far end of the garden that the cameras covered were invisible and yet they showed up on the monitor screen as though it was daylight outside.

'Isn't this all a bloody waste of time?' asked Frankie. 'This place has a perfectly good closed-circuit TV system, hasn't it? What the hell did we have to rig up this stuff for?'

Rod looked at her pityingly. 'You never worked it out, did you? Their monitors are all in the gate lodge at the entrance to the grounds. If we're holed up in here, surrounded by the law we won't have access to the lodge therefore we won't be able to watch the monitors, will we? So we've got to have our own circuit so we can cover everything from in here. Savvy?'

'Good thinking,' admitted Frankie, a little grudgingly.

'Isn't it just?' Skellen said sarcastically, to cover his own surprise at the efficiency of the TV cameras. He slid off the window sill and stared at the portable monitor in some disquiet. He was familiar with infrared TV cameras, the SAS used them and he had set them up on several occasions, but these were cameras that had been bought off-the-shelf in High Street retail shops and yet their performance was very nearly the equal of the professional equipment that the SAS used. The effectiveness of the domestic cameras was all the more frightening because it was unexpected.

'Okay,' said Skellen.

The bandsman carefully lowered the fronds of Russian vine and draped them around the camera so that only the lens was protruding from the foliage. Skellen closed the window and drew the curtains. There had been no sign of anyone in the grounds and no opportunity had arisen for him to flash a morse signal with the bedroom's lights.

'Hurry up and get the other cameras working, soldier boy. We want to make our announcement before ten, otherwise we'll miss the TV bulletins,' ordered Rod.

'I can manage alone,' said Skellen, nodding to the bandsman.

'Not allowed,' said Rod, going towards the door. 'Two of you together at all times.'

Skellen uncoiled a camera extension lead and picked up the portable monitor. 'Okay,' he said to the bandsman. 'Let's get them all rigged.'

80

'Now look,' said Mrs Belchamber to Detective Sergeant Pope. 'My Joe's a law to 'imself. 'E comes and goes as 'e pleases without a by your leave. 'Is room's 'ere when 'e wants it and 'e pays me a fair whack to keep it for 'im.'

Pope spotted the postcards Blu-tacked to the grimy kitchen wall. The colour scenes were of North Africa. 'Are these from Joe, Mrs Belchamber?'

'Yes. What of it?'

'May we look at them, please?'

The peppery grey lady shrugged indifferently. Pope took the cards down and gave some to Clover. The two men read through them quickly. Gossip about the weather; the swimming; the beach; girls. In short – nothing.

'These cover a period of four months,' Pope commented.

'What of it?'

'It's a long time for someone who's unemployed to spend abroad.'

''E draws 'is dole and sitting all day on a beach don't cost much once you're there, now do it? And the prices out there are half what they are here – that's what 'e reckons.'

'When he came home, did he give any idea where he was going?' asked Clover.

'No, because I didn't ask 'im.'

'You mentioned his room, Mrs Belchamber,' said Pope. 'We haven't got a search warrant, but we'd be grateful if you'd kindly let us look at it. It's in Joe's own interests, so that we can eliminate him from our inquiries.'

The woman considered for a moment and then relented. 'Or right. Only don't mess it up or nothing.'

Pope and Clover found no clue in the bedroom as to Joe Belchamber's likely whereabouts.

'One thing Mrs Belchamber,' said Clover before they left. 'Could you loan us a recent photograph of Joe please? We'll return it on Monday without fail.'

Mrs Belchamber was about to refuse but changed

her mind. She produced a colour portrait of her son and gave it to Clover.

'Of course,' she said. ''E don't look so much like that now.'

'Why not?'

'Because 'e's brown, 'e is – really sunburnt. Looks like a Hovis on legs.'

81

By 9:55 pm there were ten television monitors stacked on a table in the library. All the labelled screens were showing pinsharp pictures of the surroundings of the house fed from TV cameras concealed in the foliage on the walls of the house. They covered every vantage point – the gardens in all directions, the courtyard, and even the curving front drive. Cables connecting the monitors with their cameras snaked across the floor and out of the library door. There was even a heavy power supply cable that lead to the standby Honda generator.

'Hey! Look at that!' laughed one of the bandsmen, pointing at one of the screens. A scavenging hedge-hog was scuttling across the lawn in its search for choice earthworms. The cameras were so arranged that as the creature appeared briefly on one screen, it disappeared off another.

'Evans,' said Rod.

'Rod?' said one of the bandsmen.

'I want you to take a breath of fresh air . . . A wander right round the house with a drink in your hand. Casual. Stay about twenty metres away all the time.'

'What for, Rod?'

'To test for blindspots, you idiot!'

The bandsman went outside and walked slowly round the house pausing occasionally to take a pull at a can of lager. At no time during his circumnavigation of the building did he disappear simultaneously from all the television monitors.

'That's pretty good, Skellen.' said Rod grudgingly. 'Okay – now if you were in your old mob and you had to carry out an assault on the house, where would you do it from?'

Skellen studied the screens for a moment before answering 'I'd carry out a two-pronged assault. Eight men tackling the left rear and eight men tackling the right rear.'

'From the golf course?'

'Yes.'

'Why?'

'Because that's where it's darkest.'

Rod nodded. He had come to the same conclusion. He decided that maybe Skellen could be trusted after all. To a degree. Certainly, the former SAS captain had done a good job rigging the cameras.

'What would you do, soldier boy?' pursued Rod. 'Come through the downstairs windows?'

'Not if all the curtains were kept drawn as they are now and there was no sign of a lookout. I'd send men onto the roof and get them all into the house either through the upstairs windows – or the more stealthy way by removing tiles and a section of roof lining and getting them all into the loft. We'd use microphones to determine which rooms were empty before cutting through the ceiling. We've got gear that can pick up the sound of a gnat's fart at a hundred metres.'

'We've?' Rod queried.

'They've,' Skellen amended. He added. 'Of course, the powers-that-be might not authorise the use of the SAS. It all depends on your demands and whether or not you start killing hostages or threatening to kill them.'

Rod laughed. 'It's a pretty safe bet that your mob will be used against us, Peter. I'm looking forward to it – sixteen men coming across that lawn – thinking we can't see them. It'll be like lambs to the slaughter.'

Skellen shook his head. 'I don't think I would ever describe a squadron of SAS as lambs.'

Rod looked sharply at Skellen and slapped his Sterling affectionately. 'Even so, that's what its's going to be like. Right?'

Skellen looked at the seemingly daylight scenes of the approaches to the house on the monitor screens. He nodded. 'Right,' he said.

The conviction in his voice was genuine. An SAS assault on the house was a certainty and so was the failure of that assault. There was the distinct possibility that some of his former comrades would be killed . . . Unless he could find a way of getting a message out.

And then he thought of Jenny and Samantha . . .
And Trisha.

82

David Evans was an insurance broker. Middle-aged.
A local councillor. A pillar of Swiss Cottage society.
Anxious to help the police and desperately worried
about his son.

'He always was a difficult boy,' he confessed as
Pope and Clover searched his son's room. 'We tried
to understand him and yet for some reason he turned
against all our standards. He was arrested at the
Reading pop festival two years ago for possessing
cannabis, and then he got involved with this crazy
lot. I mean – they're all anarchists aren't they?'

'No, sir, they're not,' said Clover emphatically.
'Most of them, the overwhelming majority in fact,
are ordinary decent law-abiding citizens who find the
whole concept of nuclear weapons repugnant.
What's happened is that their organizations have
picked up a few nutters who get all the publicity.'

'I'm afraid Charles is one of those nutters,' said
David Evans sadly.

Clover stopped searching through a drawer and
looked sharply at the insurance broker. 'Why's that,
sir?'

'When he got back from this long trip to Libya, he

told me and his mother that if it was necessary to kill people in order to bring about world peace, then that's what he was prepared to do.'

There was a brief silence. Pope picked up a framed photograph. 'Is this a recent picture of your son, sir?'

'Yes.'

'May we borrow it?'

'Yes, of course. Bear in mind that he doesn't look quite like that at the moment. He's extremely suntanned.'

83

Frankie and Skellen were in the darkened library watching Rod on the television monitors. The lanky young man knelt down on the lawn at the back of the house. He quickly dug the gardening trowel into the ground and prised up a clod of the finely mown turf. The trowel's curved blade was exactly the right size and made a hollow that the hand grenade fitted into perfectly. Rod pressed the bomb firmly home into the soil with the detonator pull-ring uppermost. He tied some tough black twine to the ring before replacing the piece of turf on top of the grenade and pressing it flat. He inspected his handiwork with the aid of a penlight torch that he kept on for no longer than two seconds. The turf was flush with the rest of the lawn, there was nothing to indicate that it had been disturbed.

Paying out the twine as he ran, Rod raced back to the library window. The bottom louvre was open a few inches. He passed the end of the twine through to Frankie in exchange for another hand grenade.

Skellen watched in silence as Rod repeated the performance with ten more hand grenades. When they had finished, there was a semi-circle of booby traps planted in the lawns around the rear of the house and close to the house, the direction which Skellen had said would most likely be used for an assault. The grenades had a standard eight second fuse, which was about the time it would take an assault team to cover the 75 metres across the lawn from the cover of the shrubbery. As soon as the men were spotted on the monitor screens, all that was needed was for someone on watch in the library to yank on the appropriate lengths of twine and . . .

Frankie turned on the lights in the library. 'What do you think, Peter?' she asked.

Skellen helped her set the lengths of twine out in a neat row on the floor. 'Bloody glad I'm no longer in the mob,' he replied with some feeling. 'Taking a crack at us isn't going to be another Iranian embassy job.'

'They were a bunch of amateurs,' Frankie remarked contemptuously. 'No planning. No way of seeing through their objectives.' She knotted labelled clothes pegs to the lengths of twine that passed under the curtains and out through the window.

'I still don't know what our objectives are supposed to be.' Skellen reminded her.

Rod entered the library. His once-smart USAF uniform was crumpled and stained from his after-dark activities. 'Just got the final checks now, Frankie,' he said, looking at his watch. 'It'll take about twenty minutes.'

Frankie looked at her own watch. 'Bang on schedule.' She glanced at Skellen curiously. 'You'll know in twenty minutes, Peter. Think you can wait that long?'

84

There were thirteen photographs spread out on the desk in the operations room. The thirteen faces, which included those of Frankie Leith, Rod Walker and Peter Skellen, stared back at Commander Powell. The senior police officer swore softly to himself under his breath.

'All right,' he grumbled to Clover. 'We now know who they are, fine. But what concerns me is *where* they are.'

'Pope came up with a possibility on the last search,' said Clover, pointing at one of the faces. 'A four-digit number scrawled in his diary on last Thursday's date. It could be the last group of a telephone number. British Telecom are sending us names and addresses of all their telephone subscribers who've been assigned that group. They'll be routed through on our Prestel pages as their computer throws them up.'

The first of the teletext data pages started coming through three minutes later. Commander Powell watched with some impatience as columns of names and addresses appeared on the Prestel receiver's screen in telephone area sequence: a newsagent's in Ripley; a public library in Woking; a jeweller in Farnborough.

'The London area,' he fumed.

'Still coming through,' said a detective operating the receiver's keypad.

The London area telephone numbers appeared. Private names and addresses: the Abbots of Cricklewood: the Bryants of Wembley. Dozens of them. Powell wasn't as concerned with the private telephone users as he was with the commercial subscribers; the minicab firms; the pubs and cafès; pool rooms; backstreet warehouses and garages – places whose very names and location caused his sixth sense to twitch.

'That's a possible,' he said, jabbing a finger at the screen. 'And that one.'

The detective noted down the names and addresses. At the end of ten minutes he had four names and addresses of premises that had triggered his chief's instincts: a club in Soho: a pub in Lambeth; a warehouse in Kingston; and a garage in Bethnal Green.

The telephone calls went out.

85

Frankie sauntered to the edge of the swimming pool and sat on a lounger. She rested her Sterling across her knees and regarded the group of men and women standing in the water. They stared back at her in silence, some showing obvious fear, some showing stoic defiance. General Potter still had a dead cigar clenched aggressively between his teeth.

Skellen sat on a springboard.

Rod leaned against the wall and returned Senator Robert Peck's hard stare of loathing.

'Okay,' said Frankie, speaking slowly to hide her excitement. 'I won't keep you people in suspense any longer.' She pulled a piece of paper out of her uniform's top pocket. 'These demands will be communicated to the Home Secretary on his private line in fifteen minutes. You're all going to hear a preview.'

86

The constable from Kingston-upon-Thames police station did as his colleague suggested: he stood gingerly on the wing of their panda car and shone his torch through one of the warehouse's high windows. The spot of light traversed the stained concrete floor and passed over a body of a girl. The constable swung the beam back and gaped through the grimy glass in disbelief.

'Bloody hell!' he breathed.

'What's up, laddie?' inquired his colleague.

And then the constable's torch picked out one of the USAF bandsmen lashed to a pillar; and then another bandsman; and yet another.

87

Powell's telephone rang. It was the Home Secretary. He sounded agitated.

'I was about to call you, sir,' said Powell.

'I know the target,' the minister cut in brusquely.

'That makes two of us.'

But the Home Secretary wasn't listening. 'I've just had a call from the People's Lobby. They're holed up in the American Ambassador's house. Do you have any idea of the people who are at that dinner he's giving tonight? The entire bloody Presidential Strategic Analysis Committee and Staunton.'

Powell's stomach muscles tightened. He had no idea that the Foreign Secretary was among the US Ambassador's guests. 'What are the PL demanding, sir?' he asked.

'I'll be with you in fifteen minutes,' said the Home Secretary. He hung up.

That was when Commander Powell called Hadley and Grant.

It was time to alert the SAS.

88

The replay of Frankie's voice came over reedy on the tape recorder but her words were clear enough to the listening men. She first read a list of all the VIP's that the People's Lobby were holding hostage in the US Ambassador's house before moving onto her demands:

'At noon tomorrow you are going to fire a cruise missile with a nuclear warhead into the Holy Loch submarine base. You have twelve hours to evacuate the area. If you don't that's your problem, but the missile must be fired, and it must be shown on television. Once we have seen the impact, we will release the hostages. This is the only way we know to bring home to the public the full extent of the nuclear horror that these missiles can unleash. When people see what just one missile can do and the full extent of the destruction, they will recognise the madness and futility of basing these obscenities on this island. If you do not fire the missile at noon tomorrow, we will start killing the hostages one by one in alphabetic order at ten-minute intervals until you do. If you doubt our sincerity then go to Symes' Warehouse in Kingston where you will find positive evidence that we mean business. We have an expert advisor, so please don't waste your time or ours with siege psychologists because we won't listen to them. Nor are we prepared to negotiate the time-scales that we have laid down. We have wired the house with explosives. The lives of the hostages are in your hands. This is the People's Lobby.' The recording ended.

'My God,' muttered Powell, breaking the silence that followed.

'How expert is Skellen?' asked the Home Secretary.

'The best,' Colonel Hadley replied.

'I see,' said the Home Secretary bitterly. 'So what we've done, in fact, is hand them a loaded pistol for them to point at our heads.'

'Shall we take a close look at the place before passing judgement?' suggested Hadley. He looked sharply at the Minister.

'That is if you want us in just yet, sir?'

'The PM says you must be involved from right now,' said the Home Secretary. 'We're to pull together.' The politician turned to Powell. 'I'm sure you understand, commander.

'Let's get over there,' said Powell, rising to his feet.

89

Like all good journalists, Yuri Vopov, the special correspondent of *Pravda*, hated headlines. Although he had been a newspaper man for years, they still rushed up on him like unstoppable express trains.

And now, once again, he was fighting the clock. The feature he was typing had to be on the telex to Moscow first thing in the morning. If messed-up there would be hell to pay at head office. He was supposed to have delivered the piece 48 hours previously.

Vopov, a studious man with horn-rimmed glasses, was one of his paper's top reporters, a skilled writer who was sent round the world to do 'specials' – assignments which needed the expert touch. He was an excellent journalist, a man of high intelligence, who spoke English and German fluently.

He had flown into London for a story on the peace wave. The growing pacifist tide. The disarmament movements. The anti-nuclear upsurge. He had already been in Britain three weeks, and had seen plenty of evidence of it. On the face of it, the material should have flowed from his typewriter.

But somehow, he wasn't finding it easy. Moscow wanted the anti-NATO slant. Much reference to 'peace-loving workers' and 'righteous indignation of the proletariat'. Vituperation about 'Yankee war-bases', and 'capitalist scaremongering'.

He had found plenty of material, the right quotes, all the rest of it. But he had gradually become aware that none of it could happen in his own country. At least, not yet. Perhaps it was the huge demonstration he had watched at Speaker's Corner that had started him thinking. It could not have taken place in Red Square. Not like that. Not today.

Vopov had no illusions; he was cynical about the West. But this was heady stuff. The fringe circus and the hangers on didn't impress him. They were the slogan-shouting trendies, the nuts like the People's Lobby. But the real people, the young parents with their children in pushchairs and prams, the old folk, the ex-servicemen, the middle-class couples. They demonstrated from the heart.

It was infectious. They really did want peace. But he had to concentrate on the slogans, and the banners, and the organized fringe hangers-on who shouted what *Pravda* wanted to read. Vopov could make his editors happy, but he wanted to write something else.

He sighed and stubbed out his cigarette. There wasn't much room for anti-government pacifists in his country. Short shrift for trouble makers. Anti-nuclear protests against the Soviet Union's own H-bombs and missiles were prohibited. Strict regime labour camps for conscientious objectors. Dissent was a criminal offence.

Maybe that was why the copy wasn't coming easily. He was being bothered by deviationist thoughts.

Vopov smiled to himself, a little bitterly. In his mind, he was even using the right phrasing. But he thought how wrong the apparatchiks could be. Like the press attaché at the embassy who had sneered the previous day:

'Just look at the British marching on their ritualistic Sunday demos, shrieking anti-war mottos. I tell you, comrade you're watching a people who've lost their backbone. You know what they are? They're *scared*. Three million unemployed have demoralised them.'

Vopov, a student of history, had kept quiet. But he thought that mistake had been made before. Didn't the students of Oxford affirm in 1939 that they would never fight for King and country? And weren't those same students piloting the Spitfires two years later, blowing the Hitlerites out of the sky? And who were the real enemies of his country? Not the dissidents but Party itself and those privileged members who were using their position to raid his country's wealth.

He got up from his desk and walked over to the window, looking down on Fleet Street from the third-floor office. The city was spread before him, the hub of capitalism, the heart of imperialism. And below him the street of ink, churning out every type of opinion, arguing every point of view, across the spectrum. That too wasn't possible in Mother Russia.

He lit another cigarette, he was smoking sixty a day now, and his voice had a distinct rasp. He cleared his throat, and yet again looked at his watch.

'Get on with it, Yuri, you stupid son of a goat,' he muttered to himself. 'It's got to be done.'

He returned to his typewriter just as the Press Association teleprinter in the corner rang its bell urgently. Vopov went across to the machine. He still experienced a thrill when a teleprinter had a news flash. It was a feeling he had never lost since the days he was a copy boy.

The teleprinter was spouting out a brief bulletin:

SNAP. BRITISH FOREIGN SECRETARY AND UNITED STATES ENVOYS BEING HELD HOSTAGE BY ARMED GUNMEN.

Vopov stared in disbelief.

The teleprinter was chattering again.

SCOTLAND YARD CONFIRM THAT FOREIGN SECRETARY, UNITED STATES AMBASSADOR AND UNITED STATES SECRETARY OF STATE IN HANDS OF TERRORIST GANG. MORE.

Vopov was not a religious man but he still referred to the deity in moments of stress. That's why he gasped: 'Holy Mother.'

The way he said it in Russian it was a good expletive.

And again the teleprinter gushed forth. The message now had a slug line: HOSTAGES.

UNDERSTOOD THAT GROUP OF ARMED TERRORISTS HAVE SEIZED RESIDENCE OF AMERICAN AMBASSADOR AND ARE HOLDING OCCUPANTS HOSTAGE. MORE.

But Vopov had already grabbed his telephone. All his philosophising was swept to one side. He was the professional again. The *Pravda* professional. And the first thing a *Pravda* man did when a sensation like this broke was to obtain guidance.

Guidance from his embassy.

90

Malek was not impressed by English television. One of the things he enjoyed when his affairs took him to the United States, where he invariably stayed at the best hotels, was to order room service in his suite, and the switch around the TV channels. Channel hopping the Americans called it. Very apt. Fourteen channels in New York, plus cable, provided plenty of choice. His preferences might have surprised some people. He had a soft spot, for example, for *Hill Street Blues*.

Here in London, on this trip, he had been disappointed. Malek liked his own company and enjoyed a pleasant evening on his own. But the television this evening was rotten. An hour-long documentary on a steel works that had gone bankrupt, an unintelligible variety show in which people flung paint over each other, and two pot-bellied men throwing darts between drinking pints of beer.

Arnold had saved the evening by providing a first-rate meal. As a butler he had no faults and if Malek wasn't the sort of man who, between popping up all over the map disappeared in a void, he would seriously have considered hiring Arnold as his permanent servant. He conjured up excellent meals; Malek had no idea if he prepared them himself, or hired a chef, or had the food brought in from a restaurant, but the final result that was served up would have done a king proud.

Now Malek was sitting in the big, winged armchair watching the 24-inch television set. It didn't hold his attention. He would have liked some company, feminine company, which could be made available in half an hour. Charming, discreet company. But he had imposed on himself a strict discipline. The little gamble the other night, well, that was a momentary lapse. He did not want to pile up his sins.

Bored with the television and the incomprehensible scoring rules of the darts match, Malek turned to the stack of publications on the round table next to the armchair. He had already read the air copy of the *New York Times*, and the *Guardian*. He picked up the *Economist* and leafed through it. Malek was a great student of the ups and downs of capitalism.

He had begun reading an article about OPEC, when he heard a pulse-quickening announcement:

'We are now taking you over to the newsroom for an urgent newsflash.'

Malek looked at the television in anticipation. A grave-expressioned newsreader appeared on the screen. 'News is coming in that an armed group has taken over Walton House the residence of the American Ambassador and is holding several people hostage. According to so-far unconfirmed reports they include Lord Staunton, the Foreign Secretary, and the American Secretary of State, Mr Arthur Curry. As soon as we get any more details there will be a further bulletin.'

Then the programme came on again, the two beer-swilling men resumed throwing their darts.

Malek sat very still. He rang for Arnold. 'More coffee,' he commanded. 'And keep it coming.'

'Certainly, sir.' said Arnold.

Malek settled back, and actually started watching the darts match.

It might, he reflected, turn into a very interesting evening.

91

Rod stared hard at each of the monitors in turn. There was no sign of any activity. Nearly an hour had passed since Frankie had put through the phone call to the Home Secretary. Everything seemed strangely quiet. It was as if the phone call had never been made – that no one outside really cared.

Skellen noted Rod's unease. The SAS man was stretched out in one of the library's chairs, deliberately allowing as many muscles as possible to relax because it was the next best thing to sleep. The drink he sipped occasionally was orange juice because even a light lager could add a few milliseconds to what might be a crucial reaction time. That much Skellen had learned in Northern Ireland. Whatever the outcome of the evening he was determined, even though he was unarmed, that he was going to survive.

Frankie came in and whispered worriedly to Rod.

'You're playing into their hands,' said Skellen lazily.

Frankie looked across at him. 'How do you mean?'

'You're getting tense, worked up. Your initial feeling of euphoria has passed. You're no longer as confident as you were an hour ago because you've had an extra hour in which to think. And now you're beginning to worry about the silence. Okay – so you've done as I suggested and told them that you wouldn't talk to seige psychologists. That's good. What they're gambling on now is that after another hour you'll be willing that phone to ring because you'll be desperate to talk to anyone, just to reassure yourselves that you've got them worried.'

Frankie nodded to the monitor screen. 'But why is everything so quiet?'

Skellen gazed at the screen for a moment. 'It's a pity we can't see the main gate from here but my guess is that there will now be a cordon of about three hundred wooden tops around the outside wall to make sure it stays quiet. It's an easy house to isolate.'

Rod grinned. 'But a bastard to launch an assault against.'

'Yes,' Skellen agreed. 'It's going to be a bastard.'

He turned to Frankie and said in a low voice: 'Listen, can we talk somewhere?'

She glanced uncertainly at Rod.

'It's important,' added Skellen.

Frankie hesitated. 'All right. This way.'

Rod made no secret of his hostility, but he said nothing as Skellen and Frankie went into the hall.

'Well,' demanded Frankie, 'what's so important?'

Skellen faced her boldly. 'It's this crazy ultimatum of yours. Demanding that they destroy Holy Loch with one of our own warheads. It's insane. They can't do it. No way can they give in. No government could.'

'Of course not,' agreed Frankie. She was smiling coldly. 'No government ever could.'

Skellen stared at her. 'You mean you *know* you're asking the impossible?'

'Of course,' she said coolly.

'But, then why . . . ?'

His bewilderment seemed to amuse her.

'For Christ's sake, you are naive, Peter. You don't understand what it's all about, do you? It's the publicity that matters. We're going to get the biggest media coverage the world's ever seen. That's the object, isn't it? People's minds. Getting talked about. Becoming a force to be reckoned with. Of course, the demands don't matter. The more impossible the demands the better . . . The bigger the headlines.'

Skellen took a deep breath. 'It's you who's being naive. You won't get out of this alive.'

The way she shrugged her shoulders was almost studied. 'You poor sap. You've got so much to learn.

Do you think I care? Do you think any of us care? Give us credit for being dedicated. We're not afraid of death. If we get killed, we'll be martyrs whose fate will inspire thousands. How does the saying go – "what greater love hath a man than that his friend should give his life for him?" Something like that.'

Skellen shivered. She meant every word. Her sincerity was more than appalling, it was terrifying. For the first time he was scared although he was careful not to show it.

'Any other questions?' asked Frankie.

He shook his head. 'I guess not,' he said slowly. 'No more questions.'

92

'It'll be tricky,' said Major Grant thoughtfully.

He and Colonel Hadley were sitting in *Mobile One* studying the plans of the house and its grounds. Understatement was one of his traits. Two uniformed policemen had called on Aubrey Fenwick, the senior partner in the firm of architects who had refurbished the ambassador's mansion, and had dragged him away from his television to provide them with half a dozen dyeline prints of the property and copies of the building specification. The architect had been asked to stay and was sitting outside in a police car.

The unmade approach road to the ambassador's

residence was jammed with police vehicles ranging from Transits to dog handlers' vans. The SAS's *Mobile One* command centre was the largest vehicle of them all. Also parked nearby was *Mobile Two*, the logistic support vehicle. Police were standing about in small groups, some talking into their personal radios, some chatting to occupants of the other palatial houses in the road who had ventured out to see what all the excitement was about.

The police had set up two cordons. The inner cordon consisted of men and women posted at ten-metre intervals around the outside of the house's perimeter wall. Some were even out on the golf course. The men whose duty it was to patrol the grounds of the house had been withdrawn on Major Grant's advice. The second cordon were road blocks to control the numbers of people entering the Lady Jane's Wood area. A corps of fretting newsmen had been held back and were awaiting a press conference. Two army technicians and a team of British Telecom engineers were connecting an umbilical communication cable to *Mobile One*.

Despite the sporadic activity, there was an air of unreal calmness pervading, especially around the main gate.

Grant ran his finger around the gardens of the house as shown on one of the plans. 'These damned trees are a problem. We can't see a thing at the moment and there's none close enough to the house to give us cover.'

An army technician entered the mobile centre and

proceeded to test the telephones and extension speakers.

'We'll need cherry pickers,' said Hadley. 'We've got to watch that house all the time from every angle. If Skellen's with them, he may try to signal us.'

'Do you think he is in there?'

'All the USAF bandsmen identified Skellen from his mug-shot,' Hadley reminded.

'Would he signal if he believes his wife and daughter are in danger?'

'Yes,' said Hadley without hesitation. 'I'm certain of it.'

Grant nodded. 'I agree with you. We'll need at least four pickers, one to cover each side.' Grant paused and checked a clipboard. He frowned. 'There's something else that's worrying me. Why did it take them seventy minutes from the time they arrived before they contacted the Home Secretary?'

'They claim to have rigged up some charges,' Hadley pointed out.

'Even so, sir, but seventy minutes . . .'

Hadley met Grant's eye. 'I agree with you. So let's assume they've rigged a lot of charges.'

'The phones are working,' announced the technician.

As if to demonstrate the truth of the statement, one of them rang. Hadley answered it. It was the Home Secretary.

'How secure are these lines, Colonel?'

'They're secure, sir.'

'The PM has been in personal contact with the President. The President's view is that he will support whatever action is deemed necessary, and if we decide to go in, then the President will back us all the way.'

'And what about their demands?' asked Hadley, guessing what the answer would be.

'An emphatic "no",' said the Home Secretary curtly. 'Also there's to be no waiting on this one, as from now it's an SAS baby. I'm on my way to you now with the chief commissioner.'

Hadley replaced the handset and looked up at Grant. 'We've got the green light.'

Grant made no reply but moved to a small console and operated the controls.

93

Rod stiffened and pointed to one of the monitor screens. 'What the hell's that thing!' he rasped.

Skellen stopped wrestling with the problem of how to get a message out of the house and looked at the screen. He chuckled. A vertical, rod-like mast with an indistinct blob on the top was rising above the trees. 'That's the action you're craving, Rod. The tiptoe mob are here. It's a camera with an image intensifier. The makers claim that it can spot black cats in dark alleys on moonless nights. It's got a twenty-to-one zoom that can count a gnat's freckles at a hundred metres. A surprising number of rooftop gunmen in Ulster have come to grief at night with the aid of gadgets like that. Get some men at one or two windows.'

Rod looked stunned. 'What!'

'Do as I say! They're not going to start anything yet, they're just looking. But they are going to get puzzled and suspicious very quickly if they see that we're not maintaining some sort of watch.'

'You'd better do it, Rod,' said Frankie.

Rod saw the logic in Skellen's reasoning. He gave a sly grin and rose to his feet. 'But we don't put anyone at the back, eh?'

'Why?' asked Skellen, puzzled.

'Let's give them a weakness for them to work on.'

Skellen's face was impassive. He nodded. 'You're learning fast, Rod.'

'Sure,' said Rod. He went out into the hallway and shouted orders.

'We've got too many hostages, Frankie.' Skellen commented. 'The staff and all those catering girls. They're not bargaining chips and they're a liability.'

'Okay. So we release them.'

'Not yet. We let them negotiate for their release. That way we let them think that they're getting round us.' Skellen smiled. 'We use psychology on them, not the other way round.'

Frankie laughed. 'Thank God we found each other, Peter.'

94

The TV news teams arrived in force at Lady Jane's Wood. Their mass of equipment included a large trailer-mounted dish antenna because the most efficient way of getting hi-band pictures the few kilometres to London was via a satellite poised 35,000 kilometres out in space above the equator; such are the paradoxes of modern electronic news-gathering techniques. ITN were particularly proud of their foresight in renting a cherry picker for the spectacular that they were certain was about to be staged in Wimbledon. The hydraulically operated elbow-shaped arm with truck on one end and a platform on the other was designed for maintenance work on overhead cameras where there were trees and other obstructions to contend with. They made ideal camera platforms which was why they were a common sight at televised golf tournaments.

'Sorry, lads,' said the SAS sergeant to the ITN crew. 'But we're commandeering your cherry picker.'

The ITN crew were aghast. 'Why?' they wanted to know.

'Because our need is greater than yours,' said the sergeant.

On whose authority? the ITN crew wanted to know.

'Well,' said the sergeant. 'Look at it this way; we're armed and you're not.'

Five minutes later, BBC Television News arrived in force. They were particularly proud of their foresight in bringing along a cherry picker. The SAS sergeant's brief discussion with them that touched on the subject of the SAS's armament, ended with the BBC being deprived of their cherished cherry picker; a deed that bolstered the morale of the ITN crew.

Two more cherry pickers arrived onto the scene, courtesy of the London Electricity Board. All four vehicles were dispersed at strategic points around the house: one on Wimbledon Common, one on the golf course, one in the grounds of a nearby house and one in the road. Each platform was provided with a telephone link to *Mobile One* plus two SAS troopers equipped with nightsight binoculars and SG Brown headsets so that they could provide *Mobile One* with a running commentary if the need arose.

One by one the platforms extended upwards until they were just clear of the trees.

The ambassador's house was staked out.

It was 11:30 pm. Exactly 12 hours and 30 minutes before the deadline given by the People's Lobby expired.

95

The picture on the television screen in *Mobile One* was a close-up of the house's vine-covered facade. Major Grant was operating the camera's remote controls while firing questions at the architect. The Home Secretary, Powell, and the Chief Commissioner looked on. An SAS sergeant took notes of the questioning. Three other SAS men were busy at the row of telephones, talking in low tones, giving instructions, recording messages.

'Could that ivy support a man's weight, Mr Fenwick?'

The architect looked shocked. 'Good heavens, no. It's not ivy, it's Russian vine. It grows so quickly that it can't even support it's own weight.'

The picture moved and came to rest on an upstairs window. A shadowy figure was standing behind the glass holding a Sterling submachine-gun across his chest.

'Is that one of them, Major?' asked the architect, fascinated.

Grant nodded. 'Tell me about the windows – '

'You could pick him off, couldn't you?'

'We could. Unfortunately they would start picking off the thirty-five hostages they're holding. What sort of windows are they?'

'Dynamite-Nobel.'

Grant looked surprised. 'Who?'

'A Swedish firm. They also make aluminium casements that look like wood. Expensive.'

'How thick's the glass?'

'Six millimetre float.'

'Toughened?'

'Yes. Very tough. Double-skinned with a fifty mill sound insulation gap. They'll take some getting through.'

'I'm sure we'll manage,' said Grant, poker-faced. He moved the camera up to cover the eaves. 'What are those gutters made of?'

'Plastic,' said Fenwick, adding hurriedly. 'But very high-grade stuff, you understand.'

'Needless to say, they wouldn't take a man's weight if a grappling iron was used on them?'

Fenwick considered. 'The soffits and facias would hold, but I think the fittings would tear out. In fact I'm certain they would. Look, I'm sorry to be so negative but private houses aren't designed these days to stand up to men swarming all over them.' He thought of something and brightened. 'But there are window cleaners' D-rings set into the walls.'

Grant roamed the camera over the dense foliage. 'Where exactly?'

Fenwick remained silent. Grant focussed the camera on one of the house's chimney stacks.

'That stack could take the weight of several men,' said Fenwick helpfully.

'Thank goodness for that,' Grant murmured. 'It's . . . fifteen metres high would you say?' He glanced at the front elevation plan. 'Seventeen metres. How would you suggest we get ropes round it?'

Fenwick was stumped for a reply for a moment. 'Ah – you could lasso it.'

'Could we? Let's discuss the roof, Mr Fenwick. Those tiles look beautiful. Rare in this country. Spanish style. What are they?'

'Roman tiles,' said Fenwick. 'Semi-circular. Huge things.'

'How are they fixed? Could we remove some without making a noise?'

The architect looked uncomfortable. 'I'm sorry,' he confessed, 'but I know nothing about that sort of roofing. The man who built the house was rather eccentric. He came from California. The Spanish influence in architecture is very strong in the southern states. It originates from Mexico of course.'

Grant looked at the plans for a moment. 'What sort of lining is immediately under the tiles, Mr Fenwick? Plywood? Felt? How close together are the battens? It is very important that I know these things before I send my men up there.'

Fenwick looked even more uncomfortable. 'I'm sorry, Major. But I can't help you.'

Hadley took the white handset from one of the troopers. It was the direct line to Chelsea Barracks. He quietly asked for Captain Hagen to get to the scene as fast as possible.

'Mr Fenwick. You've been most helpful. We may need some more advice, so would you please remain in one of the police cars.'

The architect left the mobile command centre clearly relieved that the ordeal was over.

'Hagen will be here in a few minutes,' said Hadley.

'Who's he?' the Home Secretary demanded.

Hadley explained about the US Ranger, adding, 'He's a Texan, sir. Also the US Rangers train very thoroughly in siege-breaking. It's a long shot, but he might know something about that sort of roofing.'

'For God's sake, get on with it, gentlemen,' said the Home Secretary.

The needle on Hagen's speedometer hit 90 miles per hour but he stayed right on the tail of the police Jaguar whose continually howling siren and flashing blue lights were clearing a path for him through the late Saturday night traffic. Both cars took the big Tibbets Corner roundabout at eighty before scorching south down Wimbledon Park Side, occasionally driving on the right to pass other vehicles.

96

The secretary fainted. Her legs buckled and her head would have slipped under the water had not the Foreign Secretary and a detective grabbed her. The sudden movement in the swimming pool brought the bandsman to his feet, his finger nervously on the trigger of his Sterling.

'What's the matter?' he demanded.

'Use your eyes,' Staunton snapped. 'This girl has fainted.'

He and the other detective started moving the girl to the side of the pool.

The bandsman levelled his submachine-gun. 'Get back,' he warned.

'Don't be so bloody juvenile,' snapped Staunton. 'We've got to get her out of the water.'

The bandsman glanced across at his colleague on the far side of the pool and moved to the edge where the two men were supporting the unconscious girl. 'Give me her wrist,' he ordered.

Staunton lifted the girl's limp arm. The bandsman grabbed hold of her, dragging her unceremoniously out of the water and rolled her body with his foot onto the pool's marble surround. The detective made a move to climb out of the pool to attend to the girl, but the bandsman put a foot on his face and thrust the detective back into the water.

'You can't leave her like that,' said the detective.

'Watch me. Now get back into the middle!'

'For pity's sake, man,' Staunton protested. 'She's soaked through!'

'And we're all freezing,' Ambassador Harrison Franklin called out. 'The heating went off some time ago. At least let the women out.'

'Get back into the middle!' yelled the bandsman, levelling his submachine-gun at the detective.

'Do as he says, David,' ordered Staunton.

The detective hesitated and returned to the group huddled together at the centre of the pool.

Harrison Franklin waded a few steps nearer the bandsman and stared at him with cold loathing. 'You've got to see to that girl and you've got to let the women out before there's more passing out!'

The bandsman was uncertain what to do. He glanced at the unconscious secretary. She was unnaturally pale.

'You'd better get Frankie,' one of the guards called out to the bandsman. 'I'm watching them all.'

The bandsman left the swimming pool room, leaving the other bandsmen to redouble their vigilance.

The incident had been watched in silence by all the hostages, but none with the same degree of interest as shown by General Ira Potter. He began to formulate a plan.

97

Both the Home Secretary and the chief commissioner had left for the operations room by the time Hagen arrived. The US Ranger was shown in to *Mobile One* where he studied the close-ups of the roof of the ambassador's house.

'No problem, Major. Just like home. I've busted through similar roofs on siege exercises.'

'Can you do it without making a sound?'

'Hope so. What are you cooking up?'

Colonel Hadley spoke. 'We've got two options. A

blitz through the windows or we put a tiptoe squadron into the house first and then blitz once they know where the hostages are.'

'What's your first option, Colonel?'

'Through the windows,' Hadley replied.

Hagen stared at the colonel. 'What about the house's TV surveillance system?'

'It's under our control. The monitors are in the guardhouse – not in the house.'

Hagen thought for a moment. 'Colonel.'

'Yes?'

'Put me in command of your second option mob.'

'That's out of the question,' said Hadley curtly.

'Why?'

'It would be unprecedented.'

Hagen sat down and lifted his boots onto a chair. 'The way I see it, Colonel, the killing of the President's Strategic Analysis Committee would be about as unprecedented as you can get. And if your mob fail and my mob fail then at least you politicians will be able to say that it was a joint operation that screwed up. That ought to stop a lot of flak heading your way from a lot of angry Americans. And there's something else . . .'

'Which is?' Hadley prompted.

Hagen gave a lazy smile. 'Think back a few days, Colonel. You owe me a big favour.'

Hadley caught Grant's eye and turned to the US Ranger. 'Are you threatening me, Captain Hagen?'

Hagen looked mildly shocked and then his smile broadened. 'Hell no, Colonel. I'm blackmailing you.'

98

As soon as the unconscious secretary had been carried out of the swimming pool room, General Ira Potter gave Lord Staunton a barely perceptible nod. The Foreign Secretary didn't acknowledge the nod, but he did call out to Frankie as she was about to leave.

'Miss Leith!'

Frankie turned round. Staunton waded towards her but Frankie warned him to stop by raising her Sterling. 'That's near enough.'

'I take it you've heard of COBRA, the Cabinet Office Briefing Room Committee?'

Frankie smiled. 'A nice melodramatic title, Staunton. Who dreamed it up? You?'

'The Head of COBRA is the Prime Minister and it includes a number of my cabinet colleagues. They'll be in session at this moment. And I promise you they will never sanction the firing of that missile.'

Frankie waved her Sterling at the group. 'Don't under-estimate the importance of your guests in this country, Mr Staunton.'

'Nuts,' said General Potter, taking a tiny, shuffling step forwards that edged him towards Frankie. 'We don't matter a damn. You're on a hiding to nothing, kid.'

'Some years ago,' Staunton continued. 'We had a prime minister who caved in to terrorist demands and released a PLO terrorist. Successive governments have resolved that never again would we ever yield to terrorist demands. You're fifteen years too late, Miss Leith.'

'That's your opinion,' Frankie replied coolly. 'Let's hope, for all your sakes, that the next twelve hours proves you wrong.'

General Potter took another shuffling step forwards. The pool's continuously broken surface hid his movements.

'Miss Leith,' said Staunton. 'I can't talk for others here, but I don't give a damn for myself. If I was with the COBRA committee right now I would be refusing to gve in to you, even if you were holding half the royal family.'

Frankie stared down at the politician contemptuously. 'It's the morality of you and leaders like you who've forced us to do what we are doing now, Mr Staunton.'

'You're a fine one to talk about morality, Miss Leith,' broke in Senator Robert Peck. 'Mr Foreign Secretary is right, our lives don't matter when you weigh then against what you are proposing should be done to the people of Scotland.'

General Potter eased himself forward another step.

'There's time to evacuate the area,' said Frankie. 'Our actions today will help people understand the full horror of nuclear weapons. Future generations will come to thank us for taking a positive stand against you people.'

'You will go down in history as a murdering lunatic,' said the Secretary of State bitingly. 'How do you equate killing innocent people with a moral stand against nuclear weapons?'

Frankie sat down on the edge of the pool with her heels resting on the swimmer's handrail. General Potter sized up her new position and decided it would work to his advantage – it brought her Sterling within grabbing distance that much sooner. He took two more imperceptible steps nearer the blonde girl.

'Don't teach me history,' said Frankie. 'If the allies had stood up to Hitler when he occupied the Rhineland in 1936, people would've been killed – but not that many. There would have been no Second World War. We're standing up to you now in order to avert a Third World War. It's better that a few should die now in order to save the many in the future.'

General Potter shuffled again. The careful movements took him within three metres of Frankie. He felt with the soles of his shoes for an unevenness in the tiles on the bottom of the pool that would prevent him slipping at the fateful moment.

'Do you include yourself among those few?' Harrison Franklin inquired.

'We're all prepared to die,' said Frankie simply.

Slowly and silently, General Potter sucked in a deep breath of air. 'Down!' he suddenly yelled and launched himself at Frankie. As one, everyone in the pool plunged underwater. With superhuman bursts of energy, the detective and the plainclothes marines arrowed under the surface to where the bandsmen were standing – the detective headed towards Joe

Belchamber at the deep end. General Potter's fingers closed round the barrel of Frankie's submachine-gun and he tried to wrestle it from her. She fought back with savage strength.

Joe jumped clear of the edge as the detective surfaced and began hauling himself out of the water by the grab rail. The weight of water in the detective's sodden clothing slowed his movements down. Joe was offbalance for a crucial second as he fired. The roar from his Sterling was deafening. The weapon sent rounds stitching across the surface of the water. Then the bullets found their mark. Joe steadied his aim and pumped a sustained burst into the detective's head. The exiting bullets sprayed blood, brains and bone into the water and the detective's virtually decapitated body fell back into the pool.

General Potter seized hold of a handful of Frankie's hair and yanked. She screamed, but clung grimly to her Sterling. A marine surfaced beside General Potter and proceeded to try to break Frankie's hold by banging her fingers on the pool's marble edge. The nearest bandsman aimed his muzzle at the melee but the tangle of fighting bodies and the screaming of the girls prevented coherent thought. He ran along the edge of the pool, jumping over a hand that reached out to trip him and pulled Frankie clear. General Potter had hold of her Sterling. He turned it on the bandsman but the bandsman opened fire first. The rounds hit General Potter in the chest then moved up to dissolve his face. His hand groped blindly around the Sterling's frame as he fell back. His finger tightened in death spasm on the weapon's trigger and the spray of fire chewed into the pool's marble surround. Ricochets and marble chippings screamed in all directions – one punched a hole in the glass roof. Another hit the bandsman in the eye and killed him immediately. He fell into the pool with blood pumping from his eye socket. Deafened by the firing and the screaming, Frankie jumped into the pool and tore her submachine-gun from General Potter's lifeless fingers before his body slipped under water.

Rod burst through a door with two bandsmen and Skellen close behind and saw a marine running along the edge of the pool, coming up behind Belchamber.

'Joe!'

Belchamber wheeled round and loosed off a burst into the marine who was within two feet of him. The marine gave a little cry and teetered on his feet for a moment before toppling into the pool.

Suddenly the carnage was over except for the hysterical screaming of the terrified women in the reddening pool.

'To hell with the psychologists,' Colonel Hadley growled. 'I want to know what's going on.' He reached for the white telephone and stabbed the handset's memory key that would cause the telephone to automatically call the Ambassador's house.

'Into the middle! All of you!' Rod yelled, his face contorted in fury. 'Move! Move!'

Skellen had seen much during his career in the

army but nothing that came near to equalling the grotesque nightmare of the carnage of the swimming pool.

The frightened hostages gathered into a confused group in the centre of the pool. Their fearful movements blended blood and the swimming pool's water to a delicate shade of pink. The Ambassador held his wife close to him. Her shoulders were trembling uncontrollably as she sobbed. A secretary cried out in terror as the detective's near headless body, trailing strands of bright scarlet from the remains of his mangled skull, drifted into her. Frankie snarled at the girl to be quiet.

From Frankie's drawn expression and her trembling hands clutching her Sterling, Skellen guessed that she was badly unnerved by the scene that confronted her. Rod was obviously shaken but Joe Belchamber was grinning. It was as if he had found the massacre a welcome diversion.

Skellen could hear a telephone ringing. No one else seemed to have noticed it. He edged towards the door.

'For mercy's sake,' pleaded the ambassador, his voice cracking with desperation. 'You can't make us stay in here!'

'You stay right there, Ambassador, and you don't move!' Rod shouted. 'Maybe you realise now that we mean business!'

'You're finished,' croaked the Secretary of State. 'You're all dead.'

'Then we've got nothing to lose, have we, Mr Secretary?' was Rod's harsh reply. He saw a movement out of the corner of his eye and spun round. 'Where the hell do you think you're going, Skellen?'

'The telephone,' explained Skellen.

'Frankie will answer it.'

'It'll be them,' said Frankie, moving to the entrance. 'You'd better come with me, Peter.'

They went into the library. The two bandsmen who were on duty watching the television monitors looked up as they entered. One was standing uncertainly by the ringing telephone. 'You said that only you or Rod were to answer it if it rang, Frankie,' he explained.

Frankie nodded and motioned Skellen to a chair by the telephone. She picked up the handset and recited the ambassador's telephone number in a matter of fact voice. She held the earpiece away from her ear so that Skellen could hear the caller. Frankie had regained her composure and self-control.

'Who is that?'

Skellen recognised Colonel Hadley's gruff voice that was virtually shouted from the earpiece.

'The People's Lobby. If you're a siege psychologist or whatever, then I'm not interested in talking to you,' said Frankie curtly.

'I'm a security officer,' Hadley replied. 'I want to know what the shooting was about.'

Skellen attracted Frankie's attention and drew letters S-A-S in the air with his forefinger.

'Welcome to the SAS bogeymen,' said Frankie. 'What's been keeping you?'

'I want to know what the shooting was about.'

Frankie laughed. 'We wanted to test your curiosity.

We're psychologists as well, and we're winning, it seems.'

Skellen could visualise the colonel's reaction.

'Your demands are under discussion,' said Hadley in a reasonable tone. 'I can't say yet whether or not they will be met, but it will be seen as a gesture of good faith on your part if you release all the women, the catering staff, the chauffeurs and members of the ambassador's household.'

Skellen nodded to Frankie and mouthed a 'yes'.

'Are you including the marines in the ambassador's staff?' Frankie inquired.

'Yes,' said Hadley.

'Hold on a minute,' said Frankie and replaced the handset. She looked at her watch. 'I'll give him exactly sixty seconds.'

Skellen was disappointed. Frankie knew more about telephones than he had supposed. The library instrument was a Trimphone. He had hoped that he could have had a conversation with Frankie while she kept her hand cupped over the mouthpiece. Such an action was useless with a trimphone's handset because the microphone in the slender instrument was located by the earpiece. To muffle a trimphone effectively it was necessary to cup one hand over the earpiece and one hand over the mouthpiece. Frankie also knew what few people knew – that hanging up on an incoming call did not disconnect the line. There was little chance now of him being able to talk to Frankie while the line was open so that Colonel Hadley would recognise his voice. It was a risk he dare not take. Not with the lives of Jenny and Samantha at stake.

Frankie picked up the handset. 'Are you there, SAS?'

'I'm listening,' said Hadley.

'We're going to release everyone who isn't a member of the presidential committee, with the exception of the ambassador. We will send them down the drive in twos. No one is to meet them before they are out of sight of the house, or we will open fire on them. Is that understood?'

'Understood,' said Hadley brusquely.

'Another thing, SAS. We may want to use this phone so don't block any outgoing calls.'

'Who will you want to call?'

'Well,' said Frankie lightly. 'Around midday tomorrow, we'll be interested in finding out the right time.'

Hadley cut the line without answering.

'Who was he?' asked Frankie, replacing the handset.

'Colonel fucking Hadley,' said Skellen savagely. 'By Christ, I hope that smug bastard's shitting bricks right now over this.'

Frankie gazed thoughtfully at Skellen and said, 'I'm glad you didn't try to speak to him, Peter.'

99

Twenty of the surviving hostages were not members of the presidential committee. With the exception of the ambassador, they were ushered out of the pool's pink water and herded towards the entrance. The girls and chauffeurs were exhausted and walked unsteadily. The marines and other security men were in better physical condition. They glared their defiance at the bandsmen pointing submachine-guns at them but offered no resistance. Two secretaries helped the ambassador's wife up the pool's steps. At first she had courageously refused to leave her husband's side in the pool, but he and Rod had insisted that she go with the other hostages.

Skellen stopped one of the dripping marines in the hallway. In Frankie's hearing he said: 'They're going to question you about us, soldier boy. You tell them that the hostages won't be in the pool any more, they'll be dispersed around the house. We'll be watching them all the time, soldier boy. We've got tiger's eyes and claws. At the first sign of trouble, they'll be torn apart. You understand?'

The young marine nodded dumbly and joined the other hostages shuffling through the kitchen and out of the tradesmen's entrance.

'What an odd thing to say,' commented Frankie. 'Tiger's eyes and claws.'

Skellen grinned. 'Maybe. But I reckon he got the message.'

'You're right, of course. We'll have to move them.' She frowned. 'But why did you have to tell him about them being dispersed?'

'Because they won't be,' said Skellen. 'It'll be crazy to do so because it'll disperse our men. But it won't hurt to give those bastards out there the wrong idea.'

Frankie nodded. 'Good tactics.'

'So they used to tell me.'

One of the television screens in the library showed the released hostages moving in stumbling pairs down the gravel drive to freedom.

The chief commissioner and Powell were careful to conceal their anger when they heard about the swimming pool massacre from the released hostages.

Colonel Hadley was less of a political animal than the two police officers and expressed his feelings more forcibly: 'We're going to nail those bastards before daylight.'

'You've got four hours,' Powell reminded him.

'Plenty of time.'

A policeman poked his head round the door of *Mobile One*. 'The marines are in good shape, sir. One wants to debrief right now.'

'Chuck him in,' growled Hadley.

The American marine who entered was a black sergeant. Sergeant Leroy W. Jackson had two rows of service ribbons and a sharp-shooting badge. He belonged to the elite group from which embassy and diplomatic guards were picked. And he was a very good witness. He came sharply to attention and saluted. Nothing about his manner betrayed the ordeal he had just been through. He provided Hadley, Grant and Powell with an accurate report of the conditions in the house and, most important, the mental state of the terrorists.

'Which one was killed?' asked Grant, setting out the copies of the photographs.

The marine pointed. 'That one, sir.'

'You're sure? It's very important.'

'Positive, sir.'

'Number Six,' said Grant over his shoulder to the SAS sergeant who was taking notes. His comrade called Chelsea Barracks and told them to: 'Scrub Number Six'.

'One of them said something sort of strange to me just before I left.' The marine repeated Skellen's parting words. At the mention of 'tiger's eyes', both Grant and Hadley looked sharply at the young man.

'Which one said that?' fired Grant.

The marine pointed to the photograph of Skellen. 'That one, sir.'

Powell raised a questioning eyebrow at Hadley. The SAS colonel nodded.

'I think he might be the leader,' said the marine. 'But I'm not sure.'

'Why' asked Grant.

'Well, sir, he was the only one who wasn't armed. And whenever he said anything, the others took notice.'

'Did you notice anything else?' asked Powell. 'Anything unusual – it doesn't matter how minor?'

The marine thought for a moment. 'There were cables going everywhere?'

'Cables?'

'Electricity cables. Trailing up the stairs – through the hall – everywhere.'

'What size?'

'Just ordinary PVC electric cable by the look of it.' The marine suddenly remembered something else. 'Some of them went to a mobile generator by the tradesmen's door. It was a Honda and it looked new. I think they must have rigged up some emergency lighting in case the main supply was cut off.'

Grant nodded. The marine's deduction made sense. 'How many terrorists were all together at any one time?'

'Five. Maybe six. I think there were seven during the shooting.' The marine's eyes went to the photographs. 'That's another odd thing, sir. You'd think that with such large grounds to watch that they'd have more men. And yet there couldn't have been more than six keeping watch at any one time.'

Sergeant Jackson answered questions for another five minutes but was unable to add much to what he had already said. Major Grant thanked him.

'One other thing, sir,' said Jackson.

'Go on.'

The marine looked at them straight. 'I hope you get the bastards,' he said very quietly.

There was a silence for a moment after the marine had left.

'So Skellen's definitely with them,' Hadley remarked.

'But unarmed,' Powell pointed out.

'Not by choice,' said Grant. 'You can be sure of that.'

'The chances are that he knows about those two who were put onto his wife and kid and therefore we've got to find a way of letting him know they're okay.'

'There are the cherry pickers,' said Grant. 'Skellen may be one of those keeping watch. It's worth a try. Especially if he can signal us as to where the hostages are now being held.'

'It's certain that Skellen said that the hostages would be dispersed so that we'd know he meant the opposite,' said Powell. 'With six men on watch, they haven't got the numbers to risk dispersing them.'

'Six men on watch,' Hadley mused. 'That bears out what we're getting on the CCTV system. It sounds like over-confidence on their part and yet from what we can gather about them, I would've thought that they were much too shrewd to allow themselves to fall into the trap of being over-confident.'

'Unless it's a trap for *us* to fall into?' Powell ventured.

'That,' murmured Hadley, 'is precisely what I'm afraid of.'

100

By 1:00 am the four ex-servicemen who ran a small target-making and signboard business from a workshop and print room in Hammersmith had finished work on their urgent commission, and the results of their intensive activity were being loaded into the back of an SAS Range Rover. The four men had a service contract with the Ministry of Defence Procurement Executive therefore placing the order had been a simple matter of issuing them with a local purchase order warrant.

Each target they had made was their standard full-size human figure in thin plywood. The feet of each target had been provided with a simple wooden block so that they could stand upright. But there was a difference: the face of each target consisted of an enlarged portrait copied from a set of photographs that had accompanied the warrant. Ten of the portrait pictures had been subjected to some expert retouching on the skin tones.

One of the unretouched faces was familiar to the four men from numerous pictures that had appeared of him in newspapers and on television: Arthur Curry, the United States Secretary of State. Another photograph that had been provided to the partners was that of a USAF uniform. Under the supervision of an SAS officer and a plainclothes policeman, the partners had enlarged the uniform to lifesize on their copying camera and pasted thirteen prints onto thirteen of the targets. The SAS officer had gone to considerable pains to ensure that the correct faces were matched to those targets that bore the USAF uniforms. One of the faces was that of a particularly beautiful blonde.

Altogether the four men made six sets of targets.

The senior partner approached the Range Rover's driver's window as the vehicle was about to move off.

'I won't ask what it's all about because we've seen the news on the box,' said the senior partner. 'But we would like to offer you our best wishes.'

'Thanks, John,' said the SAS officer, and let in the Range Rover's clutch.

The senior partner watched the vehicle's tail lights disappear down the deserted street and reflected that there was going to be a lot of killing carried out that night.

101

Rod looked in on the hostages who had been shepherded into the dining room. They were languishing in chairs and lying on the floor under the watchful eyes of four bandsmen. All the hostages were wearing an assortment of clothes belonging to the ambassador and his male staff. A pile of ruined dinner jackets and trousers had been pushed into a corner. The ambassador's massive dining room table had been dismantled and the heavy sections of polished rosewood were standing upright at the window, leaning against the floor to ceiling curtains. Chairs and furniture had, in turn, been piled in a formidable barricade against the table sections.

Harrison Franklin, Congressman Alonzo Kraft and Senator Albert Mancini were playing Scrabble with a game that had been rescued from a sideboard that was now standing on end as part of the window barricade.

The hostages stared back at Rod with tired, lustreless eyes. There was no fight in them.

'Everything okay, Joe?'

'Fine, Rod.'

'Your turn to sleep in an hour.'

Rod closed the door and returned to the library. Skellen had unbuttoned his tunic and was asleep in a deep chair. Frankie was watching the battery of monitor screens. It was quiet and yet the humped shapes on the platforms of the distant cherry pickers indicated that the house was still under close observation.

Frankie was edgy. She was twisting and untwisting her handkerchief.

'All okay,' said Rod, dropping into a chair.

Frankie gestured to Skellen. 'How can he sleep?'

'He's being sensible,' said Rod. 'You ought to do the same.'

'It's this waiting for something to happen that I can't stand.'

'So go and make some coffee. I'll keep watch.'

Frankie rose from her chair. Rod suddenly stiffened. 'Screen Four,' he said tersely.

Skellen parted an eyelid a fraction. A light was flashing from one of the cherry picker platforms. Morse. He didn't move. His arms remained draped limply over the arms of his chair.

'Morse code,' said Rod.

'Who are they signalling to?' asked Frankie.

'Christ knows. Each other maybe.'

'Perhaps they're worried in case we've got radio receivers?'

Frankie suggested. 'Do you know Morse?'

'No. None of us does.'

The message started again. Skellen didn't move. He prayed that Rod and Frankie stayed where they were and didn't block his view of the screen.

'T-I-G-E-R' flashed on the monitor.

'It should have been included in the training schedule,' said Frankie.

'We had more important things to learn,' Rod replied.

'C-U-B'

'Peter's bound to know,' Frankie suggested.

'A-N-D'

Rod shrugged. 'What does it matter?'

'M-A-T-E'

'Peter!'

Skellen feigned sleep. He stirred as though half comatose.

'S-A-F-E'

'Peter!' Frankie called out again.

Skellen pretended to wake up. His expression gave no indication of the great surge of elation and relief he was experiencing. 'Whassermatter?'

'Can you read Morse, Peter?'

'Yes,' said Skellen.

'So what are they signalling?' asked Rod.

Skellen looked at the monitor screen. The first message was repeated. There was a pause and then: 'Q-T-H'

'Well?' pressed Rod.

It was the code for 'where hostages?'

'I don't know what they're saying,' said Skellen. 'They've adopted a code in case we've got radio scanners. Standard procedure.'

The logic behind Skellen's explanation seemed to satisfy Rod.

Skellen decided that it was time for action. The messages that Jenny and Samantha were safe had changed everything. The time for him to take positive action had arrived.

102

Clegg kicked the door open. He and Dowsett went in low, doing a neat roll through the doorway and swinging their Browning pistols to the firing position at the same time.

'Arthur!' yelled Clegg. 'Get down!'

At the same time Dowsett shouted at Robert Peck: 'Ralf! Get down! Down!'

Both men opened fire simultaneously, each providing a pre-arranged radius of fire so that the entire area beyond the door was covered. Four bandsmen were shot in the head and chest; Frankie was hit in the neck and, much to Clegg's regret, the American ambassador was shot twice through the heart. The simple plywood targets rocked but didn't topple.

The close-quarters battle instructor was a sergeant. He switched on the extractor fans to rid the room of fumes and compared the damaged targets with his clipboard.

'Have you got a grudge against Americans?' the instructor asked Clegg. 'That's the second time you've killed the ambassador.'

'My apologies to the ambassador,' said Clegg.

'Keep it up, lad, and you will have wiped out the entire US Diplomatic Corps.' He turned to Dowsett. 'Who was Ralf?'

Dowsett pointed at one of the targets he had hit. 'Ralf Kohoskie – one of the senators.'

The answer saddened the instructor. He shook his head. 'That one's a senator right enough. Senator Robert Peck. Diminutive?'

'Bob,' Dowsett answered promptly.

The instructor cheered up. Getting the first names of hostages right was vital; operational research had shown they tended to react more quickly to their first names than when orders were shouted to them using their surnames.

'Okay,' said the instructor. 'We'll try again with you two in five minutes. Remember that your prime targets are USAF uniforms.'

He consulted his clipboard and yelled out: 'Hagen and Fox!'

All of Hagen's thirteen rounds found a target, including Benjamin Stringer. The instructor sighed and looked at his watch. He had an hour in which to drill both teams to perfection. It had to be perfection or nothing.

103

The two downstairs toilets were assigned for use by the hostages. The doors had been removed. Skellen decided to try the upstairs toilet. He was mounting the stairs when Rod came out of the library.

'Where are you going, Skellen?'

'Where do you think?'

'We use the kitchen staff lavatories. You know that.'

A flashing light would not be seen from the kitchen staff toilets and Skellen had no intention of using them. 'I heard that the ambassador had quite a bathroom. I'd like to see it.'

'You'll use the staff lavatories!' Rod snapped.

104

It was quiet in the road outside the entrance to the ambassador's house. The number of police vehicles had dwindled as the night wore on. Less than six policemen were standing around talking to soldiers, two ambulances were parked nearby. The nurses and drivers were inside one of them, playing cards with a doctor to ease the boredom. There had been a flurry of activity earlier when the Prime Minister had arrived for a brief inspection, the frustrated newsmen and women were being held at the road block – disconsolately sitting in a large caravan, sending their equally frustrated night editors reams of zero copy. The architect was sound asleep in the back of a police car. Nearby residents had finally gone back to bed. At first the chief commissioner had toyed with the idea of evacuating them, but the distances between the houses was such that no residents were in danger and nor were they being a nuisance.

Major Grant sat on the steps of *Mobile One* to escape the dehydrating effect of its air-conditioning system for a few minutes. He looked at his watch. 2:00 am and still no word from Skellen. He stood up and entered the mobile command centre. It was time to use other measures.

*

Trooper George Reed used the levers on the cherry picker's platform to make fine adjustments to his position. He was peering through the sights of an infrared laser surveillance aid that was aimed at the centre of one of the downstairs windows of the ambassador's house two hundred metres away. The fine adjustments were necessary until the beam of invisible infrared being fired at the window was bounded back into the aid's collector. The light emitting diodes visible at the bottom of the sight suddenly glowed. Reed tightened up the knurled screws of the aid's clamps and said into his headset microphone: 'Charlie-Papa One-locked onto Window One.'

In *Mobile One* Grant drew a line on a map that depicted the sight-line that Trooper Reed had on his target window.

'Okay,' said Hadley to the technician manning the high-gain amplifier.

'Charlie-Papa Three,' said another voice from a wall speaker. 'I'm locked onto Window Six.'

Hadley fingered down a talk-back key. 'Charlie-Papa Three,' he acknowledged into a microphone. 'Wait.'

The technician switched the amplifier into Trooper Reed's channel and increased the volume. All that could be heard was the continuous hiss of white noise.

'NR's in, sir,' said the technician.

Everyone in the command centre listened intently. The laser surveillance aids work on the principle that voices in a room induce infinitesimal vibrations in

300

the window glass of that room. Those vibrations could, in turn, cause a laser beam bounced off the window to vibrate and the resulting modulations could be fed through an amplifier and thence to a speaker to reproduce the voices or sounds generated in the room. It was a technique used with devastating effectiveness by the Royal Ulster Constabulary who had perfected the art of infrared laser surveillance to the point where any suitable object in a room, a wall mirror or a flower vase, could be used as a reflector. Much useful evidence had been collected in similar manner by eavesdropping on conversations in cars, sometimes using the interior driving mirror as a reflector.

'No one in the ambassador's study,' said Grant, writing on a pad.

Hadley fingered the talk-back key. 'Negative. Charlie-Papa One. Realign on Window Two. On you, Charlie-Papa Three.'

The technician switched the amplifier to a new channel. Muffled dialogue could be heard. Everyone listened intently. The technician did his best to sharpen the sound but it remained muffled and indistinct.

'Sorry, sir. But that's the best I can do. They must be very heavy curtains to have such a damping effect.'

'It sounds like two people,' Hadley commented.

Grant checked his plans and maps and made a note. 'So that's the library occupied. Hostages possibly.'

'Charlie-Papa-Three,' said Hadley. 'You're positive. Stay aligned. On you Charlie-Papa Four.'

'Charlie-Papa Four,' said a voice from the speaker. 'I'm aligned on Window Seven.'

Again the muffled dialogue from the speaker. It was impossible to distinguish individuals or hear what they were saying.

'That's the dining room occupied,' said Grant, making notes.

The surveillance continued for fifteen minutes. At the end of the period it was established that it was unlikely that any of the upstairs rooms were occupied. There was significant occupation of the library and the dining room. What the laser surveillance could not tell the SAS men was which room or rooms wee occupied by the hostages, and whether they were in rooms where they were remaining silent.

'It must be those curtains,' one of the technicians commented. 'They must be as heavy as fire blankets.'

Hadley called up the cherry pickers that had supplied positive responses and told them to remain aligned on their respective windows and to monitor on headphones. If they heard anything unusual, they were to switch their channels straight through to *Mobile One*.

'Is Skellen familiar with LSA devices?' Hadley asked Grant.

'Yes, sir.'

Hadley looked faintly annoyed. 'Then he must know the problems we're up against.'

'He does,' Grant confirmed. The SAS major looked up at the television screen. It was hardly surprising that the upstairs rooms were unoccupied. It was a chilly evening and the bottom louvres of every window were open. Odd.

Hadley looked at his watch. It was 2:30 am. The assault was timed for 2:50 am. He felt uneasy. He sensed that something was wrong. Something that he could not put his finger on. Then he realized that his feeling of unease was something more fundamental.

It was fear.

Frankie made certain that the bedroom's heavy curtains were properly drawn before she switched on the lights. The ambassador's clothes were strewn everywhere after the raid on his considerable wardrobe in the search for a change of clothes for the hostages.

Without putting her Sterling down, Frankie picked up a pair of trousers from a hanger and tossed them to Skellen. 'Try these.'

Skellen pulled the trouses on and zipped them up.

'We'd better get back,' said Frankie. She stepped back through the doorway and kept well clear of Skellen as he followed her out of the bedroom. He was disappointed. All he needed was a few seconds with a light switch. It was getting dangerously late. He estimated that the assault would take place within the hour. Unless he could warn them, there was a very real danger of it turning into a disaster. He felt about as effective as a blind man trying to solve a Rubik's cube.

They returned to the library. Rod looked up from

the monitor screens he was watching. He was about to say something when the telephone rang. Frankie answered it.

'Hallo?'

'Miss Leith?' said Hadley.

'Hall, SAS.'

'A progress report, Miss Leith. The cabinet are considering your demands. I cannot give any more information at the moment.'

The line went dead.

'The telephone rang in the library,' Grant reported.

Hadley was beginning to feel better. They now knew which room the terrorists were using as a base.

There were four bandsmen guarding the hostages when Skellen sauntered casually into the dining room, his hands thrust into his pockets. He looked bored.

'Everything okay?' he asked one of the guards.

'No trouble. What happened to your uniform?'

'Too bloody tight. Would've ruined me for life.'

Skellen strolled across to the ambassador. 'I've borrowed a pair of your pants, Mr Ambassador. They fit just fine.'

Harrison Franklin gave Skellen a withering look and returned his attention to the game of Scrabble he was playing on the floor with Congressman Kraft and Senator Mancini.

Skellen watched the Scrabble game for a few seconds. 'I've got a good word for you, sir.'

'Really? I can think of several for you.'

The nearest guard chuckled.

Skellen knelt down, obstructing the nearest guard's sight line. He rearranged some of the letter tiles on the board to read:

IM A FRIEND

SING

Harrison Franklin read the message and looked sharply at Skellen.

'You see?' said Skellen. 'The word's "America". I'm surprised you didn't get it. Not a bad score either, and the second letter picks up points on a triple letter score square. Do you understand the score. Your Excellency?'

The ambassador stared hard at Skellen for a moment. 'Yes,' he said slowly. 'I understand perfectly.'

Skellen rose to his feet and sauntered from the room.

His bored expression belied his inner feelings. The problem of the hand grenades that Rod had buried in the rear lawn was taking on ever-increasingly monstrous proportions with each minute that ticked by.

105

The two counter revolutionary warfare teams picked from the London-based SAS squadrons for the assault on the ambassador's house arrived at Lady Jane's Wood in four Range Rovers. 'A' team, under the command of Lieutenant Michael (Charlie) Chaplin, were in the lead vehicles and 'B' team, under Captain Robert Hagen, brought up the rear.

All the men piled out of the vehicles. They were dressed in black combat dress. Weapons were checked. Balaclava helmets pulled on, the CS gas-masks made ready.

'"A" team final briefing,' Grant called out, holding the door of *Mobile One* open.

Lieutenant Chaplin led his twelve men into the command centre. At that moment, Trooper Scott, who was manning cherry picker Charlie-Papa Four with his laser surveillance aid trained on Window Seven, picked up several male voices singing in his headphones. Loud but not clear. Not clear enough to distinguish the words but the tune was unmistakable.

It was *America*.

Rod's face was white with rage when he burst into the dining room.

'Stop them!' he bellowed at the nearest bandsman.

'I've tried to, Rod,' said the shaken guard. 'But they don't take no notice.'

Clutching a Browning pistol in one hand, Rod stormed across the room to where Ambassador Franklin was conducting all the hostages in their lusty singing. Only Lord Staunton, as the only non-US citizen present, appeared to be having difficulty with the words.

'Stop!' Rod yelled.

The ambassador carried on conducting, and the hostages although watching Rod in considerable anxiety, continued with their singing.

Rod held his pistol with two hands, knuckles white; his arms outstretched, the muzzle pointing at the ambassador's head. 'If you don't stop, he's dead! One . . .' Rod's face was contorted with fury that could not be achieved by bluffing.

Harrison Franklin ignored the pistol aimed at his head from a distance of two metres and continued beating time with his hands. Two members of his impromptu choir lost heart when they realised the danger he was in and stopped singing.

'Keep it up!' urged the ambassador.

'Two!'

The singing died away to an electric silence.

'Aw, come on, fellers,' complained the ambassador.

All the hostages were watching Rod. Gradually his knuckles slackened their grip on the Browning and the rage faded from his face. He slowly lowered the pistol.

'Whose idea was that?' he demanded.

'Mine,' said Harrison Franklin. 'What are you going to do about it?'

'If it happens again, I'll kill you, Mr Ambassador,' warned Rod. He turned and moved to the doorway from where Skellen had witnessed the entire incident.

The technicians played the recording of the singing again. The mobile command centre was crowded with Lieutenant Chaplin and the members of his 'A' team. As they listened, they were staring fixedly at the photographs of the occupants of the house that were pinned to the wall – a last-minute opportunity to make doubly certain that every appropriate face and its owner's first name was imprinted on their minds.

'It could be as many as ten men,' said the technician, as the singing ended with Rod's muffled shouting.

Hadley nodded and pointed at the plans of the house. 'We work on the basis that all the hostages are in the library and there's a good chance that they'll be lying down or sitting and the guards will be standing – let's hope so.'

Hadley paused. He had the full attention of everyone present. 'One final point,' he continued. 'A released hostage said that there were cables going everywhere. We don't know if they're for an emergency lighting system that the terrorists have rigged in case we decided to turn off the mains supply, or whether or not they were speaking the truth when they said that they had wired the house with HE. If they have we don't know how the charges are detonated. It could be by a switch concealed in a particular spot under a carpet – it could be by a hundred and one different methods that just one terrorist could easily activate, even after a surrender. It's "Nimrod" all over again.'

Hadley's expression hardened. 'It's up to you to ensure that those bastards in there are unable to continue fighting even if they've surrendered. They don't recognise any rules of war. If they can fight in any way even after they've surrendered they'll do so. Purists might argue about the legality of what is necessary, but I'm no purist and nor are the people we're up against.'

Hadley noticed that a number of eyes went to the picture of Frankie. 'If any man has even the slightest doubt about doing what will be necessary, then he should say so now and I give my word that it will not reflect in any way on his service in the regiment. The only people that matter are the hostages. Do you understand what I'm saying?'

They did. There was a silence. No one stirred.

'Okay,' said Hadley, saluting Lieutenant Chaplin. 'Break a leg.'

'A' team were dismissed. They filed out of *Mobile One*. There was a final check of stun grenades, gas grenades, gasmasks, Browning pistols and HK MP 5 submachine-guns. Three of the soldiers were carrying frame charges to blow the library and dining room windows. Jokes were made. Laughter and some backchat. It helped ease tension, but not much.

One by one the men nodded to Lieutenant Chaplin, who in turn inspected each man to ensure that what little of their faces was visible was properly blackened. Satisfied that everyone was ready, he gave the word and the twelve men melted into the night.

Their departure was watched by Captain Robert Hagen and the nine men of his 'B' company.

*

Skellen's third attempt to reach an upstairs light switch looked like succeeding. He was on the landing when there was a sudden shout from Frankie. Two bandsmen ran out of the library holding their Sterlings and headed up the stairs.

'What's up?' asked Skellen.

'Something at the back,' shouted one of the men as they raced into a rear bedroom without switching on the lights. Skellen realised then that he was too late. He toyed with the idea of rushing the two men but knew that the consequences of such a move would be fatal. All the bandsmen had been too well-trained.

Hadley was not a man given to swearing but he did so roundly when the television screen showed that two armed men had appeared at an upstairs rear window. That they had appeared so early was a certain harbinger of the assault's impending failure.

Joe Belchamber was ready. The attack wasn't coming from the courtyard side of the house. He opened an upper louvre on one of the kitchen windows, ready to fire a yachtsman's distress flare as soon as the shooting started.

Skellen returned to the library in time to see two groups of soldiers break cover at the rear of the garden and sprint towards the house. Rod already had in his hands the toggles attached to the detonator lines that ran out to the grenades buried under the lawn. He was staring at the screens with the feverish concentration of a marionette operator awaiting his cue. He jerked one line then another and seized a third.

The two groups of soldiers began fanning out as their dash brought them near the house. A group appeared to be racing straight towards one of the concealed television cameras. The monitor screen suddenly turned white. The explosion shook the library windows. In the kitchen, Joe broke the seal on the flare and pointed it at the sky out of the window. He yanked the ignitor and closed his eyes to preserve his night vision. The rocket gave an explosive hiss and streaked into the sky. At the top of its climb, the magnesium flare erupted like a fireball and hovered in the sky on a small parachute, turning night into day in the grounds.

The fogged monitor screen in the library cleared to reveal several dead and wounded men lying near two small craters in the lawn. The picture was grossly over-exposed – caused by the burning flare.

'We've done it!' Rod yelled in exultation.

One of the men struggled to his feet. There was the sound of submachine-guns firing from upstairs. Clods of earth spat into the air all around the staggering soldier and he fell. The flying clods hammered towards a second soldier who seemed to be crawling instinctively towards his submachine-gun that had been torn from his grasp by the force of the explosion. The murderous fire reached the soldier and he stopped crawling. Another soldier courageously tried to return the fire but the blinding flashes of the exploding grenades had destroyed his night vision.

He too was cut down by the savage fire from the bedroom.

There was another explosion that shattered the dining room window and rocked the furniture barricade. The terrified hostages threw themselves flat. There was a bright flash around the edges of the barricade and the curtains began to burn. The gas-masked SAS soldier jumped through the flames caused by the flash-bang and discovered that his way was barred by sections of dining room table. The CS grenade he had fired immediately after the flash-bang was fizzing at his feet – building up a dense cloud of gas that obscured his vision and which was of such a concentration that his gasmask's chemical absorbent could not filter it effectively.

'Now!' screamed a voice.

There was a burst of firing from several sub-machine-guns. Bullets ripped into the table – splintering and tearing a path through the rosewood for other bullets to follow. The SAS soldier was slammed back against the window casement. He gave a loud cry of pain. He vaguely heard a voice yell, 'Got the bastard!' More rounds punched through the table and ploughed deep into his body. He slumped over the windowsill, his head and arms hanging out of the shattered window, blood gushing from his open mouth and spattering onto the trampled spring flowers that Beatrice Franklin had sown the previous year.

Suddenly it was all over except for the burning flare drifting down through the trees like a setting sun. The mind-numbing carnage and uproar had lasted for less than thirty seconds.

Hagen virtually kicked down the door of *Mobile One*.

'What the fuck's going . . .' he began, but the sentence died on his lips when he saw the tragedy being played out on the television screen. He stood rooted. Like the others in the mobile command centre he was a man of action – paralysed by the awesome realization that there was nothing he could do to save the men who were being mown down by sub-machine-gun fire. The scene was a hideously stark re-enactment of the nightmare that has haunted all soldiers since the invention of firearms – to be pinned down in the open by enemy fire coming from a protected position; to be blinded by explosions; with no hope of reaching cover in time. It was as brutal as it was quick.

When the shooting stopped, the camera revealed two wounded men crawling with painful slowness towards the meagre cover afforded by a sparse clump of young bamboo.

Hagen swore again and dived out of the command centre.

106

The fate of Congressman Alonzo Kraft was decided because he happened to be nearest the door and Rod saw him first.

'Him!' snapped the lanky young man, pointing with a finger that was trembling. 'Into the library!'

Two of the bandsmen grabbed the congressman by the arms and started dragging him to the door. Harrison Franklin stepped forward to protest but Rod swung his Sterling and hit the ambassador hard in the stomach.

'Just you keep out of my fucking way, you stinking Yankee piss artist!' Rod snarled at the diplomat as he doubled up and sank to the floor clutching his stomach and groaning with pain.

The two bandsmen did as Rod directed and hauled the struggling politician through the hall and across the library floor to near the telephone where they pinned him down with their knees on his arms.

'Hold his legs down, Skellen,' Rod commanded.

Skellen guessed what was coming next and hesitated.

'Hold his legs!' Rod screamed, swinging his Browning at the SAS man. 'Or, by Christ, you'll get it too!'

There was no doubt in his present state of mind

that the crazed young man meant what he said. Skellen seized hold of Kraft's flailing legs by the ankles and pinned them to the floor.

'Apart!' barked Rod.

Skellen forced the American's legs apart.

Rod nodded to the telephone. 'Okay, Frankie.'

Frankie was about to pick up the handset when the telephone rang. 'Why, SAS,' said Frankie. 'We were about to call you. I wanted to tell you about how we intend to honour our pledges but I think actions speak louder than words. Listen . . .'

Frankie held the handset in the direction of Kraft. Rod aimed his Browning at the American's groin and fired. Kraft gave a terrible scream and arched his body off the floor with such force that he nearly dislodged the two bandsmen who were kneeling on his biceps. One of his ankles broke free of Skellen's grip and lashed out in blind agony. He continued to scream.

'Hallo, SAS!' Frankie shouted into the mouthpiece. 'That's the sound of a hostage who's just had his balls shot off! And now for the *coup de grace!*'

She held the handset out again. Rod motioned to Skellen and the two bandsmen to move clear. Kraft was released. He thrashed about on the floor, still screaming. Rod put him out of his misery with two shots at point blank range through the head.

The silence that followed the uproar was almost obscene in its intensity.

'You heard that, SAS?' said Frankie. 'We've just killed the gentleman. All the others will die in the same way if that missile isn't fired by noon.' She

315

replaced the handset and looked at Rod and Skellen. At first her face was drawn, and then it broke into a smile. 'We're going to do it,' she said in wonder. And then in delight: 'We're going to do it!' She grabbed Rod and kept repeating: 'We're going to do it . . . ! We're going to do it . . . ! Don't you think it's all been worthwhile, Peter?'

Skellen had seen plenty of violence during his career but there had only been one occasion when he had experienced the raw, gut-churning that he was experiencing now.

'Yeah,' he said expressionlessly. 'Great.'

Hagen and Clegg dropped silently from the wall followed by six other men in his team. The last two remained on top of the wall. The American darted forward with Clegg following. The big man moved like a ghost, weaving from shrub to shrub. Clegg began to appreciate why Hagen had been such a bastard to catch on the exercise in Wales. They both threw themselves flat behind a clump of bamboo that was on the edge of the lawn. They were less than ten metres from the two wounded men. One was moaning softly. To reach them meant exposure. Hagen was convinced that the terrorists must have rigged up some form of infrared surveillance system.

'You ready, Clegg?'

'Ready!'

'You get that one,' ordered Hagen. 'I'll get the one on the right. Think you can manage?'

'Christ, no. I think that's Rogers. All one-twenty kilos of him.'

'Go,' said Hagen.

The two men sprinted across the grass.

'More visitors!' said Frankie, pointing at the monitor screen. 'It looks like they've come for their wounded!'

'Let them,' said Rod calmly. 'Maybe they'll learn from them that we mean real business.'

Skellen watched in silence as the two shadowy figures scooped up the forms lying on the lawn, slung them over their shoulders and merged back into the undergrowth at the far end of the garden.

He was certain that the larger of the two figures had been Hagen.

The two wounded men were lifted to the top of the wall by a human pyramid which the SAS men formed by standing on each others' shoulders. They all then scrambled to the top of the wall and reversed the process on the far side, passing the two unconscious men carefully to the ground. Five minutes later Rogers and his comrade were being tended in one of the ambulances by the doctor and nurses. Both men were in a bad way and would have died had they not been rescued. Rogers had lost a foot and a good deal of blood, and his comrade had stopped a grenade splinter in the neck. Neither man was in any condition to talk about the abortive assault which, as far as Hagen was concerned, had not been the purpose of pulling them out.

'I'd like to thank you, Captain Hagen,' said Hadley as he entered *Mobile One* after a visit to the ambulance, before it went charging off.

'That's another big favour you owe me,' said Hagen amiably.

Hadley turned to the Home Secretary who had just arrived with the chief commissioner. 'What's been decided, sir?'

The Home Secretary's expression was haggard. He turned to face the SAS officer and said quietly: 'Colonel Hadley, what guarantee of success can you offer if you launch another assault? Better than a fifty-fifty chance?'

It was the question that Hadley had been dreading. The events of the past hour had aged him but not affected his honesty. He raised his eyes to the politician and said slowly: 'I'm sorry, sir. But in view of what's happened I can't offer odds even approaching that.'

The Home Secretary stared hard at the soldier. 'How many men?'

'Ten.'

'Ten!'

Hadley nodded.

'Bad,' the Home Secretary muttered.

'Yes, sir.'

'Very bad publicity,' he added as an afterthought.

'Sir,' Hagen tried to interject.

'So what are COBRA's orders?' asked Hadley stiffly.

The Home Secretary rarely smoked but he picked up someone's packet of cigarettes and a box of matches and lit one. 'There's no question of accepting any demands from these people. You will already have realised also that we will never launch that missile. We don't negotiate with these people.'

'You appreciate that there is no question that the terrorists are not bluffing about their threat?' said Hadley tightly. 'They've already murdered one hostage in cold blood in my hearing over the phone.'

'Yes,' said the Minister, angrily stubbing out the cigarette after only two drags. 'Major Grant just told me.'

'Sir,' said Hagen again.

'Two Chieftains are on their way,' the Home Secretary continued, ignoring the interruption. 'As soon as the terrorists start killing the hostages, the tanks start shelling. And they'll keep on shelling until the place is razed. It's as simple and as ghastly as that.'

There was a total silence in the command centre apart from the hum of its air-conditioning.

'Permission to speak,' interrupted Hagen in his best West Point parade voice.

Everyone looked at the US Ranger.

'There's nine men waiting outside,' said Hagen bluntly. 'You give me what I need within the hour and they'll get those hostages out of that house alive and we'll kill everyone of those fucking creatures in there at the same time.'

Hadley started to protest but the Home Secretary cut him short with an upraised hand. The politician turned to face the US Ranger and said mildly: 'What exactly do you need, Captain Hagen?'

Hagen told him.

107

The Royal Navy Sea King helicopter dropped through the low cloud base. It spotted the two pairs of flashing Range Rover headlights and swung towards them, eventually settling on Wimbledon Common's grass between the two widely-spaced vehicles and cutting its turbine. Three naval crewmen in flying suits jumped out of the machine's open bay and introduced themselves to Hagen and his team.

'Bloody navy helping out,' moaned Clegg to Dowsett. 'I'll never be able to hold up my head in a Chelsea pub again.'

'No one will ever notice as you're always under a table,' was Dowsett's unkind reply.

'Come on, you guys,' barked Hagen. 'Help get the rope out.'

The huge coil of rope that completely filled the Sea King's freight bay required the efforts of all ten soldiers in order to ease it out onto the grass.

'Going to need a big kitten to play with this,' remarked one of the soldiers.

'How much is there here?' asked Clegg, fingering the black Dacron rope that was nearly as thick as a broomstick.

'Nine hundred fathoms,' said the pilot, a lieutenant.

'Five and a half thousand feet,' converted Hagen for his team. 'Now will you guys quit cackling and help get the net unloaded.'

It was a large cargo net complete with reinforced lifting shackles at each corner. The corners were gathered and attached to one end of the huge coil of rope. The other end of the rope was, in turn, shackled to the lifting winch projecting from above the Sea King's open bay. The fastenings were double-checked and checked again. The net shackle was equipped with a standard docker's quick-release lanyard that could only be operated once the cargo net had been lowered into the hold of a ship and there was no longer a load on the lifting rope.

The soldiers checked all their weapons and equipment in the Range Rovers' headlight beams while Hagen held a brief map conference with the helicopter's crew. The ambassador's house was less than four miles away. Its exact position was plotted and the lieutenant loaded the information into his inertial navigation computer.

'The error over the distance will be infinitesimal,' the pilot assured Hagen. 'We'll be able to drop you straight down the chimney. Swaying and fine altitude control before touch down is going to be the chief problem, but I'll do my damndest to give you a soft landing.'

'Just watch that the rope pays out evenly with no kinking,' was the helicopter winchman's final warning. 'Sing out if it does and we'll stop lifting until you've sorted it out. Let's go.'

'Okay, you guys,' called Hagen as the pitch of the

helicopter's turbine rose and the rotors began turn-ing. 'Let's have everyone sitting in the middle of the net! Come on! Move it!'

The nine SAS men and Hagen piled into the centre of the net. The helicopter lifted. The assault team stared at the mountain of steadily lessening rope as the coils snaked into the sky. The helicopter lifted steadily and evenly.

'Thank Christ there's no wind,' said Hagen. He was holding a two-way radio.

The sound of the helicopter faded. The coil of rope continued to diminish in bulk.

'She's doing fine, Meathook,' said Hagen into the radio.

The last coil of rope disappeared and the sides of the net began rising around the SAS soldiers.

There was a tiny jerk and they were airborne.

'We're off the deck, Meathook.'

'Bloody weird. You can hardly hear the chopper now.'

'You can't even see it,' observed one of the soldiers, peering up past the shackles at the rope that was soaring up into the night sky. 'It's above the cloud.'

The net, pulled into a pear-shape by the weight of its human cargo, stopped climbing in response to Hagen's command into the radio when it was well clear of the trees. It began moving westward. The change of motion was brought about very slowly by the helicopter pilot to prevent the net swinging.

Clegg was peering down at the tops of the trees that were drifting slowly past less than fifty feet

below the net. 'This is just like hot-air-ballooning,'
he observed. 'No noise. Weird.' A thought occurred
to him. 'Hey, where did you learn this?'

'A place called Vietnam,' Hagen replied.

'Did it work?'

'Nope.'

'Your candour is appreciated, Captain.'

'We didn't use a long enough rope.'

'Well I reckon we've got enough to hang ourselves
now,' said Clegg.

'Cleggy,' said a voice.

'Yes.'

'Shut your fucking mouth.'

Clegg lapsed into a crestfallen silence.

108

Rod suddenly noticed something.

'Why the hell aren't you wearing your uniform,
Skellen?'

'It was too tight.'

Rod was suspicious. 'It was okay at the fitting.'

Frankie looked annoyed. 'What does it matter?'
she asked irritably.

'It might matter a lot,' said Rod. He suddenly
snapped his fingers. 'That's it!'

'What?'

'The SAS will have been told to shoot at everyone

wearing USAF uniforms! Why the hell didn't I think of it before?'

'There won't be another assault,' said Frankie tiredly.

Rod's eyes mirrored his hatred as he stared at Skellen. 'You realised that, soldier boy, you bastard, and you kept quiet!' He raised his Browning. 'Christ, I'd like to kill you.'

'Oh, for God's sake, Rod!' cried Frankie. 'Look, if it makes you feel any better we'll make the hostages put on these uniforms and we'll wear their clothes.'

Rod lowered his pistol and looked admiringly at Frankie. 'That's smart thinking, Frankie.' He gave a cunning grin and turned to face Skellen. 'And lover boy here puts his uniform back on. I like that idea. I like it a lot.'

109

The journey was eerie, not only because the soldiers could hear the wind rustling in the dark shadows of the trees passing by beneath them, but because it was impossible to believe that the distant beat of the helicopter's rotors was anything to do with them. At times the cloud thickened and completely blanketed the faint whine of the machine's turbine, adding to the unreality.

Directly ahead the first delicate flush of dawn light

was seeping upwards like a stain from below a horizon that was picked out in the yellow glow of distant street lights. A screech owl swept past the net. Its sudden call caused several men to jump, evidence of strained, hair-trigger nerves that the banter had helped relieve.

Spokes from the rotating lights swept circles of blue in the midst of the trees about a mile ahead. They were the prearranged beacons provided by the police cars parked in the unmade road outside the ambassador's house.

'There's the house,' said Clegg softly, pointing down through the net's coarse mesh to the distinctive hips and valleys of a Roman tiled roof that was just visible above the trees in front of the lights.

Hagen spoke into the radio and the progress of the laden net slowed to a crawl.

The roof crept nearer.

'Up twenty, Meathook,' instructed Hagen.

The net lifted very gently. The control the unseen pilot in the inaudible machine had was superb.

'Forward one hundred, Meathook. You're looking good.'

The net eased slowly through the air towards the roof that was approximately sixty metres below the net.

'Start slowing, Meathook,' Hagen directed.

The roof drifted nearer with agonising slowness but the important thing was that the net was hanging straight and was not swinging.

'Forward twenty, Meathook.'

The net edged forward. The roof was gradually moving beneath the net.

'And ten, Meathook. That's great – you're doing just fine.'

The roof was directly beneath the net.

Hagen peered down through the mesh. This was the most dangerous part so far of the operation.

'Down twenty, Meathook . . . Easy . . . Easy . . .'

The net sank slowly towards the roof. The central ridge was thirty metres beneath the net. Hagen wanted the net to touch down in the tiled valley between two hips. Disembarking with the net draped over a ridge would be too tricky.

'East five, Meathook.'

Incredibly, the helicopter pilot managed the tiny change of direction.

'Beautiful,' confirmed Hagen, holding the key in the transmit position. 'Down five.'

The net sank into the valley. Clegg was the first to feel his trainer-shod feet touch the tiles. The net slackened.

'Down five, Meathook,' said Hagen calmly.

The laden net spread over the tiles. The soldiers began disentangling themselves and their weapons from the mesh and each other.

'The Eagle has landed,' advised Hagen cryptically into the radio. He jerked on the quick-release lanyard. The shackled opened and dropped the net around the soldiers.

'Okay, Meathook,' said Hagen speaking very softly. 'You can go home now with all our fondest love.'

326

A faint beat of rotors was heard briefly through a gap in a low cloud. The suspended shackle swung away from the roof and was swallowed into the night.

'Remind me to track the chopper pilot down and buy him a drink,' said Hagen quietly, picking his way out of the netting.

The assault team's ghostly airborne arrival on the roof of the ambassador's house had an almost magical quality about it that forced even the most cynical of the watchers in *Mobile One* onto the edges of their chairs.

'Good luck,' muttered the Home Secretary, watching in undisguised amazement as the black-clad figures moved cautiously about on the distant roof. Hopefully, it could still look good in the papers.

If it all worked out.

Hagen carefully levered out the copper nail from the last tile. He grasped the heavy tile and worked it away from its overlapping neighbours and passed it to Dowsett. Several rows of wooden tile battens were now exposed.

'Saw,' said Hagen.

A sharp, heavily-greased tenon-saw was passed to the US Ranger. He cut through all the battens in two places, pulling the centre sections away from an area of the bituminous felt roof-lining that was beneath the battens. Thankfully the gap between each rafter was wide enough for a man to pass through. Sawing through one of the rafters in two places would have cost valuable minutes and increased the risk of them being heard.

Hagen flashed his torch into the roof space for a few seconds. 'Okay – let's move.'

A rope was lashed to a rafter. The team lowered themselves one by one into the loft and stood carefully on the ceiling joists. A misplaced foot could easily punch through the ceiling plasterboard with disastrous consequences if there was anyone in the room below. Clegg found the loft inspection light-switch by the hatch exactly where it had been marked on the architect's plans. The joists were not designed to support the weight of ten men in one spot. They tended to creak, so Hagen ordered the men to gather round the cold-water storage tank – the strongest part of the ceiling – during the final checks before the assault.

Balaclava helmets were pulled on, gasmasks adjusted and weapons checked. There was even time for a final familiarization inspection of the house's plans, spread out on the water tank cover, before Hagen switched out the light and lifted the hatch open.

The ten soldiers lowered themselves through the hatch and dropped silently onto the thick pile carpet that covered the ambassador's upstairs landing. The door to one of the smaller bedrooms was ajar. There was the faint sound of deep breathing coming from the room. Hagen edged up to the door, pushed it open with the muzzle of his submachine-gun, and peered into the room. A man whose face matched a terrorist's face was sound asleep on the bed. Hagen nodded to Dowsett. The SAS soldier withdrew a dagger and entered the room on tiptoe. The man didn't even stir but his deep breathing stopped. Dowsett tiptoed out of the bedroom. The pillow the terrorist's head was resting on was rapidly changing colour from white to red.

Hagen held up his fingers to signify the number of terrorists left. The others all nodded. The team now outnumbered their foe. Those were odds Hagen liked.

They moved on tiptoe down the stairs, two abreast, with Hagen and Clegg in the lead.

Halfway down there was a sound. They froze. Frankie, the blonde in the photographs, emerged from the library and crossed the hall. She entered the dining room.

Once in the hall, the ten soldiers spread out in accordance with Hagen's carefully worked out plan of action: two men on each side of the library door; two men on each side of the dining room door; and one man, the heaviest in each case, in front of each door as the charger. Hagen was the library charger.

He gave the signal and hurled his bulk at the door. It burst inwards and he threw himself to one side so as to be out of his men's sight-line. As he rolled over, he had a fleeting glimpse of Skellen's surprised expression.

'Down, Peter!'

But Skellen was already flat on the floor as the CS grenade exploded into the room like a rocket-assisted flour bomb. Rod swung his gun round to fire at the intruders and was hit simultaneously by three bullets in the chest and head. He fell to the floor – dead.

Rod Walker had often wondered how he would die. He had imagined his end would come as a heroic martyrdom on the barricades, or shooting it out against a horde of imperialists. In a way, he was not disappointed in death, but it came too quickly for him to fully appreciate his dreams.

From the library there came loud yells of: 'Down, Harrison!' 'Down, Art!' 'Down, Bob!'

The uproar and explosions brought Joe Belchamber running from the kitchen. He threw down his gun and his arms went up in surrender when he saw the hooded men. It was his last living gesture, apart from his writhing and screaming from the agony of four slugs that ripped through his liver and kidneys.

In the library, Clegg's brain and Dowsett's brain locked onto five imprinted faces like an automaton that guided their hands so that their submachine-guns, spewing spent cases like crazed popcorn machines, hammered the five terrorists to death. A burst fired by Clegg whipped eddies of swirling CS gas as the slugs screamed between a bewildered Harrison Franklin and Arthur Curry. Both men were rooted in terror. There was a flash of blonde hair visible through the smoke but the two Americans were in the way.

'Harrison! Art!' Clegg bellowed. 'Down! Down! Down!'

The Americans dropped but the blonde hair had gone. There was a movement at the side. The restricted peripheral vision caused by the gasmask forced Clegg to snap his head round. An imprinted face. A burst of fire. Another terrorist dead.

'Hagen!' yelled Skellen from the floor. Hagen spun round. A bandsman was about to fire at him. The Texan's submachine-gun blazed at point blank range and lifted the dead terrorist off his feet.

The shooting stopped. People were coughing and retching. Skellen staggered to his feet, his eyes streaming and his head spinning from the effects of the gas.

Dowsett tried to open the front door but the deadlock had been turned. He shattered the lock with a burst from his submachine-gun and yanked the door open, spilling clouds of CS gas into the night. Clegg seized the Secretary of State by the arm and half-threw, half-pushed him through the dining room door and into the hall where another SAS soldier grabbed the American and launched him out of the hall into the open. Dazed, blinded, and coughing pitifully, the American tripped on the steps and would have fallen had not Dowsett caught him and pushed him flat on his face on the gravel.

'Stay there, mate. You'll be alright. Only don't move or you might get shot.'

The Secretary of State was vaguely aware of other groaning bodies being thrown down beside him but he was too sick and too disorientated to care who they were.

Skellen saw something on one of the television monitors before he too was seized and flung out of the front door.

In the dining room Clegg bellowed: 'Where the

fucking hell's the girl?' He leapt across the room, saw the gap between the table sections and the wall, and tore the barricade down. The dead soldier was still draped over the windowsill as Clegg had seen him on the television screen in the mobile command centre. The window had been blown, making escape for the girl easy. Clegg swore but didn't give chase – it would have been contrary to his orders.

Another body was hurled out of the front door for Dowsett to force to lie face down on the gravel. Skellen staggered to his feet.

'Stay down, Peter,' said Dowsett. 'You'll feel better in a minute.'

'Browning,' croaked Skellen.

'Lie down, sir!'

'Your Browning, Dowsett!' snapped Skellen. 'Now!'

Dowsett gave Skellen a pistol and watched him stagger round to the rear of the house.

Skellen stumbled across the lawn, moving in the direction he had seen Frankie take on the monitor screen. The cool night air helped clear his head and eyes and he realized that it was beginning to get light. He moved silently among shrubs, then heard a desperately smothered cough. He moved silently again, circling round towards the noise.

Frankie was huddled under a bush, holding a handkerchief to her face. She had her Sterling across her knees.

'Hi,' said Skellen casually, holding the Browning down at his side.

She looked up sharply. The fear in her eyes faded

when she saw who he was. 'Thank God you got away too. What are our chances of escaping from here?'

Skellen stared down at her. She really was an extraordinarily beautiful girl – but it was a terrible ugliness that Skellen saw. The ugliness of the soldiers who had been killed; the cold-blooded way she had murdered the WAAF girl on the coach; the telephone she had held out to a dying man.

He raised the Browning and fired.

For a long time afterwards he was going to remember the look on her face. An almost reproachful look, as if she couldn't quite believe that he would do this to her. A stricken look.

He had done her one final kindness. He had fired so that the bullet would kill instantly. Perhaps he felt he owed her that at least.

She lay sprawled at his feet but he felt no pride, no satisfaction in a job well done.

As he walked back to the house, it started to rain but he didn't feel it. He passed a dead SAS man lying on the lawn near one of the grenade craters, but he didn't see him.

The sickness in his stomach was not caused by the acrid burning aftertaste of the gas.

110

They had walked in silence for a long time among the tall elm trees at the edge of the park. The relief and the thankfulness of their reunion had ebbed and now there was time for reflection. All morning Jenny had been very thoughtful.

'You're going back?'

Her voice was flat. He wasn't sure whether she meant it as a question or a statement of fact.

'I never left,' said Skellen.

She nodded. 'Why didn't you tell me? Why the charade? Why pretend?'

'It was better that way. Believe me. Safer.'

Jenny avoided looking at him. 'Didn't you trust me?' She was trying to control herself. 'Don't you think I deserved to be told? For God's sake, Peter, what were you afraid of? That I'd blab my mouth off? Shout from the rooftops that my husband was on an undercover mission for the SAS? Is that what you think of me?'

He had never seen Jenny so bitter. She walked away from him and sat down on a bench by the path. He joined her, but it was almost like sitting next to a stranger. She was staring straight ahead at the Round Pond in the distance.

'I know it hasn't been easy for you,' he said gently.

'The shock of those maniacs . . . The things you went through.' He tried to pick his words carefully. 'But you've been through it before. You know the set up. You've been an SAS wife long enough . . .'

She turned on him, eyes blazing. 'I'm not a bloody SAS wife,' she flared up. 'I'm your wife. I married you, Peter, not a damn regiment. At least I kidded myself I had. Maybe it took all this to make me realise . . .' She stopped. More gently she went on. 'I'm sorry, Peter, you can't imagine the relief, the joy I felt when I thought you'd kissed it all goodbye. I know I'm not being fair, but I can't help it. Forgive me . . .' She bit her lip.

Skellen reached for her hand, it was icy cold. 'What do you want me to do, Jenny? Quit, really quit this time?'

She shook her head. 'I wouldn't love you if I made you do that. I know you. God knows why, but you live for this kind of thing.' She was very grave suddenly. 'I hope it doesn't kill you.'

They sat silent for a long time. Then Jenny spoke. 'They're bound to have a new mission for you soon. I think I'll take Samantha and go and stay with my parents for the time being.'

He started to react, but she went on: 'No, it's best. Let's see what happens. We've both got a lot to get over.'

He began to say something, then changed his mind. They got up and walked slowly towards the Serpentine, not speaking because what had to be said had been said, and what had not been said was best left unsaid.

111

Over the coffee the handsome man with the gently greying hair changed the subject. He was a well-known Member of Parliament, wealthy by birth, public school educated, a feared debater, and a charming host.

Malek enjoyed being his guest in the member's restaurant at the House of Commons; he savoured the ambience, the well-known faces, the murmur of informed chat as much as the excellent food.

'Well,' said the MP at last. 'How are you enjoying your visit?'

'It's been very pleasant,' acknowledged Malek. He stirred the four lumps of sugar in his coffee. He liked it very sweet.

The MP swallowed a pill and took a sip of water. His health had not been good lately. Then he asked: 'How long are you staying?'

'As a matter of fact, I'm leaving for Rome tomorrow. After that . . .' Malek shrugged.

'Ah, well, I hope to see more of you next time, my friend,' said the MP. 'We share so many mutual interests . . .' He glanced at his watch. 'I have to keep an eye on the time,' he apologised. 'The Home Secretary is due to make a statement on that terrible business over the weekend.'

'Yes, wasn't it shocking?' sighed Malek. 'So many people dead. Quite frightening, isn't it?'

The MP smoothed back his hair. 'The gutter press is having a field day, of course. You've seen the headlines I suppose? You'd think it was some sort of Roman carnival.' He lowered his voice. 'You notice that nobody was taken prisoner?'

Malek nodded.

'I may want to raise that in the House,' went on the MP, his voice still low. 'I find it remarkable. It does raise the question, doesn't it, whether these SAS men are really just hired killers.'

'That's not for me to say,' murmured Malek. 'I am, after all, just a visitor.'

The MP drank some coffee.

'You misunderstand me,' said the MP. 'I am against violence, of course. I have no time for people who pursue their ends with guns. However valid those ends are.'

Their eyes met across the table.

'I would certainly hate this country to become another Italy, for example. Kidnapping, assassination, bombings. Terrible. Except, regretfully, I suppose that to revolutionise society some hateful things have to be done.'

'Cruel to be kind, you mean?' suggested Malek softly.

'If you like. You see if it wasn't for the root grievances, the frustrations of the masses, this kind of thing wouldn't happen . . .'

'In my country, of course we have solved the problem,' pointed out Malek. 'We have the peoples' committee running everything . . . Some say it is inefficient, but it's a real democracy nevertheless, even though the West doesn't understand it.'

That seemed to remind the MP of something.

'Oh, incidentally, do tell the Colonel how grateful I am for his invitation to your country. As soon as my diary allows, I look forward to coming. I'll be fascinated to see how workers control the media, industry, society. As you say, that is real democracy.'

Malek smiled. 'You and your colleagues will be very welcome, I assure you. We will be delighted to roll out the red carpet . . .'

That amused the MP. Then he signalled to sign the bill. 'I am really most sorry that we have to cut this short, but the Home Secretary will speak at 2:30 and . . .'

Malek raised a well manicured hand. 'Please, not another word. Of course I understand. It was very good of you to find the time to renew our acquaintance.'

'And I haven't thanked you for my travel expenses,' added the MP.

Malek inclined his head deprecatingly.

They rose. The MP led his guest through the corridors of the Palace of Westminster into the great lobby. 'The rewarding aspect of our relationship,' he was saying, 'is that we both have the same interests and goals – the good of our peoples. Peace. Commerce. Purely altruistic, though. You and I gain nothing.'

'Indeed,' agreed Malek.

'I had meant to introduce you to some people.

Colleagues. Very sympathetic people. I'm sorry that there isn't time.'

Malek smiled gently. 'Please do not worry. There will be all the time in the world.'

The MP held out his hand. 'It's been a pleasure, Mr Malek,' he said. His grip was firm, positive.

'I know we'll meet again very soon,' said Malek. 'Perhaps in my country . . .'

'Who knows? Oh, by the way, if you get the chance, watch TV tonight. I'll be doing a little piece on Newsnight. Against this monstrous Anti-terrorism Act. Events have proved what a useless piece of legislation it is, haven't they? Just an excuse to get us used to an incipient police state . . . Well, goodbye. Have a good trip.'

The MP gave a little wave and turned into the Chamber.

Malek slowly strolled out of the House of Commons. He gave a polite nod to the policemen at the entrance.

All in all, his visit to England had been an outstanding success.

And there was still all the time in the world.

Also available in Mandarin Paperbacks

James Follett

SWIFT

There is a satellite through which, daily, pass all the interbank transactions between London and New York, currencies to the value of billions of pounds – moving not as bank notes, but as vulnerable streams of electrons. This, the most vital computer system in existence, is operated by SWIFT, guardians of the system on which depends the delicate stability of the world's currencies. And one man has a plan to destroy it.

That man is Charlie Rose, disaffected mobster boss with millions at his disposal. Assisted by a Soviet Tass correspondent with his own motives to pursue, and a brilliant but psychotic computer programmer, Rose has the audacity, the power and the driving will to dare the biggest, most sophisticated act of theft ever conceived.

James Follett

DOMINATOR

High above the earth's surface orbits one of NASA's latest space shuttles, Dominator. But the crew and cargo on board are beyond the control of the US space agency. Dominator has been hijacked and a nightmare is about to be unleashed.

How could it happen – and how will it end? James Follett's latest, heart-stopping novel spans three continents as it follows the fearfully possible outcome of a new deadlock between the Middle East factions and the United States. Standing innocently at the centre is Neil O'Hara, ex-astronaut, ex-drunk, whose rare skills and debatable loyalties may ultimately be the only barrier between us and the holocaust . . .

James Follett

CHURCHILL'S GOLD

1940 – Britain faces her darkest hour . . .

War has brought Britain to the verge of bankruptcy. Her debts to America are crippling. Her precious supplies of weapons and fuel are running desperately low.

Her last hope is gold – £42 millions worth of it, held in a bank vault in Pretoria, South Africa.

Only one man can bring that gold to Britain: Robert Garrard, captain of the 'Tulsar'. But lying in wait to intercept him is Germany's newest submarine U-330, captained by Kurt Milland, a pre-war colleague of Garrard's, handpicked to predict his every move. The duel to the death will be fought in the lonely wastes of the Atlantic . . .

James Follett

ICE

Beneath the desolate wastes of the South Atlantic lurks a malign force of unimaginable power

The top brass of Western Intelligence are badly rattled when transatlantic cables are inexplicably and provocatively cut, and Russian and American relations reach freezing-point when a luxury ocean liner and a Soviet supersub go down in a sea like honey.

Only Glyn Sherwood and Julia Hammond, two scientists working on the Antarctic can dare to guess the identity of an enemy well outside the diplomatic compass. It is a gargantuan slice of the glacial continent bearing millions of tons of rock in its grasp.

Swathed in its own fog, the frozen colossus triggers a series of disasters as it drifts inexorably north. On collision course with New York and impervious even to nuclear blast, it has the seismic force to cause Manhattan to shake like a dog.

With *Ice*, James Follett has conceived the teeth-chattering possibility of how Nature can punish those who foolishly believe they have mastered her.

'The most sensational thriller – and chiller – of the year.'
Edinburgh Evening News

A List of James Follett Titles Available from Mandarin

While every effort is made to keep prices low, it is sometimes necessary to increase prices at short notice. Mandarin Paperbacks reserves the right to show new retail prices on covers which may differ from those previously advertised in the text or elsewhere.

The prices shown below were correct at the time of going to press.

☐ 7493 0036 1	**Cage of Eagles**		£4.99
☐ 7493 0496 0	**Churchill's Gold**		£4.99
☐ 7493 0262 3	**Dominator**		£4.99
☐ 7493 0364 6	**Doomsday Ultimatum**		£3.99
☐ 7493 0110 4	**Ice**		£4.99
☐ 7493 0003 5	**Mirage**		£4.99
☐ 7493 1012 X	**Swift**		£4.99
☐ 7493 0492 8	**Torus**		£4.99
☐ 7493 0363 8	**Trojan**		£4.99
☐ 7493 0035 3	**U700**		£3.50

All these books are available at your bookshop or newsagent, or can be ordered direct from the address below. Just tick the titles you want and fill in the form below.

Cash Sales Department, PO Box 5, Rushden, Northants NN10 6YX.
Fax: 0933 410321 : Phone 0933 410511.

Please send cheque, payable to 'Reed Book Services Ltd.', or postal order for purchase price quoted and allow the following for postage and packing:

£1.00 for the first book, 50p for the second; **FREE POSTAGE AND PACKING FOR THREE BOOKS OR MORE PER ORDER.**

NAME (Block letters) ....

ADDRESS ....

....

☐ I enclose my remittance for ....

☐ I wish to pay by Access/Visa Card Number ⬚⬚⬚⬚⬚⬚⬚⬚⬚⬚⬚⬚⬚⬚⬚⬚

Expiry Date ⬚⬚⬚⬚

Signature ....

Please quote our reference: MAND